THE SIX-THIRTEEN FROM FAIRFIELD JUNCTION

AND OTHER CASES OF
SHERLOCK HOLMES

DENIS O. SMITH

First edition published in 2024
© Copyright 2024
Denis O Smith

The right of Denis O Smith to be identified as the author of this work has been asserted by him in accordance with the Copyright, Designs and Patents Act 1998.

All rights reserved. No reproduction, copy or transmission of this publication may be made without express prior written permission. No paragraph of this publication may be reproduced, copied or transmitted except with express prior written permission or in accordance with the provisions of the Copyright Act 1956 (as amended). Any person who commits any unauthorised act in relation to this publication may be liable to criminal prosecution and civil claims for damage.

All characters appearing in this work are fictitious. Any resemblance to real persons, living or dead, is purely coincidental. The opinions expressed herein are those of the author and not of MX Publishing.

ePub ISBN 978-1-80424-433-3
PDF ISBN 978-1-80424-434-0
Paperback ISBN 978-1-80424-432-6
Hardcover ISBN 978-1-80424-431-9

Published by MX Publishing
335 Princess Park Manor, Royal Drive,
London, N11 3GX
www.mxpublishing.co.uk

Cover by Awan.

CONTENTS

1 The Six-Thirteen from Fairfield Junction   1
2 The Hungarian Doctor   48
3 The Von Strauffhausen Papers   87
4 The Silver Buckle   146
5 The Broken Glass   171

THE SIX-THIRTEEN FROM FAIRFIELD JUNCTION

THERE CAN BE FEW among my readers who are entirely unfamiliar with the strange mystery connected with the *Marie Celeste*. It will readily be recalled, I am sure, that in 1873 the *Marie Celeste*, a handsome brigantine of some hundred foot length, was discovered drifting in the Atlantic Ocean, many miles from the nearest land. Her equipment was in good order, she was well provisioned, and her cargo was undisturbed. But, to the astonishment of those who found her, there was not a soul on board, and no clue as to what had become of the captain, the crew and the passengers. Nor, although a quarter of a century has now passed since her discovery, has any clue to the mystery ever been found.

What is not so generally known, however, is that another, strikingly similar, case occurred more recently, which also caused astonishment and mystification in those that first discovered it. Perhaps even more amazingly, this second case took place not on the high seas, hundreds of miles from the nearest human habitation, but on dry land, here in England, in the heart of the countryside. For this case concerned not a ship but a railway train. When the six-thirteen evening branch-line train from Fairfield Junction to Parlingham reached its destination, shortly after quarter to seven, all those known to have been aboard when it left Fairfield Junction had vanished without trace, despite the fact that the train had not stopped once on its journey.

News of this strange and sinister occurrence spread round the district like wildfire. What on earth could have happened, people wondered, to bring about such a weird and unprecedented state of affairs? It was too late in the evening for the following day's papers to carry anything but the barest of accounts of the matter, but, taking their lead from the local paper, they almost all described it as "The *Marie Celeste* of the railways".

It was certainly an interesting and surprising business, and I was fortunate that, sharing chambers as I did with the noted criminal investigator Sherlock Holmes, I was able to observe the matter at first hand, almost from the beginning.

Our introduction to the case was a dramatic one. It was a cold, wet and blustery period in early March, 1886, and neither Holmes nor I had ventured out of doors all day. As the evening wore on, the wind seemed to pick up yet more savage power and hurl sheets of rain against our window-panes. The clock on the mantelpiece was showing nearly ten to nine when, above the violent lashing of the wind and the rain, there came the sudden harsh jangling of the front door bell.

"Now, who can this be, out and about in this foul weather?" said Holmes, looking up from where he was pasting newspaper cuttings into a scrap-book.

"Perhaps it is some visitors for Mrs Hudson," I suggested, "no doubt hoping for a hot cup of tea."

My friend chuckled. "If so," said he, "their desire for tea must certainly be a desperate one, to lead them to brave the elements on such a night as this."

Moments later, however, there came the sound of rapid footsteps on the stair, followed by a sharp rat-a-tat-tat on our door. The visitor was evidently not for the landlady but for us, and, equally evidently, someone the maid knew well, as she had clearly not accompanied him up the stair. I sprang to my feet and pulled the door open. There stood our old friend Inspector Lestrade of Scotland Yard, his overcoat glistening wet.

"Come in, Lestrade, come in!" cried Holmes. "Dry yourself by the fire and tell us what we can do for you!"

Lestrade stepped to the fire, rubbing his hands together vigorously, but shook his head. "I've no time to get dry, Mr Holmes," said he. "I'm on an urgent errand, which will, I believe, be of great interest to you, and all I wish to know is if you will come with me or not."

"What is it, then?" asked Holmes, evidently struck, as I was, by the policeman's urgent tone.

"A very strange business, from the little I have heard," replied Lestrade. "I don't yet know all the details, but it sounds very much as if a violent crime has been committed."

"Where did this crime take place?"

"Gloucestershire."

"Gloucestershire!" I cried in surprise.

"Yes, I know it's a long way, Dr Watson. But they have asked for an experienced detective officer to be sent down there – someone reliable, and experienced in interviewing witnesses, they said – and I have been assigned to the case. The facts are simply these: that when the evening train from Fairfield Junction, in Gloucestershire, to somewhere or other, reached its destination, they found that there was no-one aboard!"

"Why, that is not so strange!" I cried, laughing. "These rural branch-lines are often very lightly used, Lestrade, especially in the evening. I have been on such a train a few times, and on at least one occasion I was the only passenger!"

"No, no, Dr Watson," Lestrade interrupted, shaking his head vigorously. "You don't understand. It is not simply that there were no passengers on the train – although that is true enough – there were no railway employees, either! The engine-driver had vanished without trace, as had the fireman, and as had the guard of the train! And yet the train had not stopped once on its run from Fairfield!"

"What!" I cried in astonishment. "How is that possible?"

"That is certainly a singular problem," said Holmes, springing to his feet. "When does your train for Gloucestershire leave?"

"Nine-fifteen, from Paddington," replied the policeman, with a glance at the clock. "It is the last train of the evening, and I must leave this minute if I am to catch it! I have a cab waiting downstairs. Will you come?"

"Certainly," said Holmes. "And Watson, too, I am sure. Yes? Then throw some clothes and your razor into a bag, old fellow, and be ready to leave in ninety seconds!" With that, my colleague dashed from the room.

A minute later, I returned from my bedroom and found Holmes and Lestrade waiting for me on the stairs. Holmes scribbled a note to the landlady, explaining our abrupt departure, which he left on the hall table, and a minute later we were in the cab and driving furiously for Paddington Station.

We boarded our train with scarcely a minute to spare, and soon we were slipping in the darkness through the dimly-lit western suburbs of London and into the dark and silent countryside beyond.

Our journey was a long and tedious one. Lestrade knew nothing more about the case than he had already told us, and, save the occasional brightly-lit station – through most of which we raced at great speed – the night was such a black one that there was nothing to be seen outside the confines of our small compartment. Having fairly rapidly exhausted our speculations about the mystery which was summoning us to the west of England, we all three lit our pipes and sat in silence for some time. Holmes and Lestrade then fell to discussing the current state of crime and detection in London, but I could not raise any interest in what seemed to me a very generalised discussion, and instead followed my own train of thought about the strange events in Gloucestershire.

How on earth, I wondered, could the locomotive and its train of carriages, several tons in weight, have proceeded from one end of the line to the other with no-one aboard to guide it, and no-one to stoke the fire in the boiler? What about the signals the train must have passed, and the intermediate stations, if there were any? And what happened at Parlingham, at the end of the line, with no-one aboard the train to apply the brakes? And, above all, how and why had everyone on the train vanished without trace? The driver and fireman would, presumably, have been on the footplate of the locomotive, at the front of the train, the guard probably in the last carriage of the train, with any passengers somewhere in between them. How could they all possibly have been affected in the same way? I asked myself many such questions, but could suggest plausible answers to none of them.

At length, after more than two hours of this monotonous journey, I felt the train begin to slow. Sherlock Holmes leaned forward, peering into the darkness outside. "I believe we are approaching Fairfield," said he, with a glance at his watch. "It is to be hoped there will be someone there to meet us."

"There should be," replied Lestrade. "Scotland Yard has sent a message that I am coming."

Even as he spoke, the train abruptly slowed with a jerk, as if a brake had been applied, and, moments later, we drew slowly into the brightly-lit platform at Fairfield Junction. The night air was very chilly. I glanced at the large station clock which was suspended over the platform, above our heads, and saw the time was about half past eleven.

As we made our way out into the carriage-yard, a fine rain was falling. A tall man in a braided uniform and cap stepped forward and introduced himself in a brisk and business-like manner as Superintendent Huggins of the Gloucestershire Constabulary. He and Lestrade shook hands.

"But who are these gentlemen?" the superintendent asked, indicating Holmes and myself.

"This is Mr Sherlock Holmes," replied Lestrade. "He is a consultant criminologist, who has often been of assistance to us in the past. And this is his colleague, Dr Watson, a medical man. They have a particular interest in unusual cases."

"Ah!" said Huggins. "If so, then they have come to the right place. I've been on the force nigh on thirty years, Mr Lestrade, and I don't ever recall a case as strange as this one! Well, I'm sure there is no objection to their accompanying us and observing our methods, if you vouch for them, although I don't think we shall have any need to 'consult' anyone about anything. But come, let us get aboard the van, and I'll describe it all to you as we go!"

"One moment," interrupted Holmes. "Where are we going?"

"To Parlingham," replied the superintendent in surprise. "That is where the chief police station for the district is situated. It is also where the train at the centre of this business is now standing."

"The situation of the police station is surely irrelevant to the case," responded Holmes. "I should prefer it if you would give us a brief account of the matter before we leave Fairfield. We may wish to question the staff here."

"But nothing of any consequence happened here."

"One cannot say that with any certainty," said Holmes. "The branch-line train departed from here on its singular journey. That is surely sufficient to make it of possible relevance to the case."

"Oh, very well," said Huggins, a trace of annoyance in his voice. He glanced at Lestrade. "But let us at least get out of this rain."

We followed him to the police van, which stood at the side of the carriage yard. "Now," said the policeman, as we clambered aboard. "Where shall I begin? I assume you have been given an outline of the matter," he added.

"Only the bare bones of the business," returned Lestrade. "We know that all those travelling on the train had disappeared by the time it reached the end of the line, but nothing more than that."

"Then you know almost as much as anyone does," said Huggins, with a short, bitter laugh.

"Any obvious clues?" interrupted Holmes. "Any doors on the train left open, for instance, or disorder in any of the compartments?"

Huggins shook his head. "No," said he, "there was no disorder anywhere – that is what is so mysterious about it. As for the doors, the only one which was open was that of the guard's compartment at the rear of the train, and that is not so surprising. As you are no doubt aware, unlike the doors of the passenger compartments, which all open outwards, the guard's door opens inwards and can be pegged back to keep it in that position. This is necessary, of course, as the guard sometimes has to hop on or off the train when it is moving very slowly – in a station, for instance. This open door was on the left side of the train – left, I mean, from the guard's point of view as he looks forward along the train."

"Is that the side that the station platforms are on?" asked Holmes.

"Yes, all the branch-line platforms are on that side. All the other doors on the train were closed. One of them – the door to one of the first-class compartments – was not closed very firmly, but I don't think that that is of any significance. You know what train doors are like: if you slam them they close soundly, but if you are a little too delicate with them they do still close, but in a loose, rattling sort of way. Anyhow, as the door in question was on the other side of the train, facing away from the platforms, I don't think it can have had anything to do with what happened tonight. It has probably been like that since the last time the carriage was cleaned, I imagine."

"I think we understand," remarked Lestrade. "What I should like to know now," he continued, "before you get into any details, is whether you have made any progress in the matter yet."

"Not exactly," replied Huggins after a moment's hesitation, "but I am hopeful of hearing something soon. I have men out all over the district, making enquiries. I also have men walking the line, one from the Parlingham end, and one from this end, but I have heard nothing back from them yet."

Lestrade nodded his head. "And what is your own opinion of the matter?" he asked.

"My opinion?" returned Huggins in surprise. "I don't really have one, Mr Lestrade. I've never been a great one for theories and opinions. One fact is worth a thousand theories, eh? In this case I don't mind admitting that I haven't the faintest idea what has become of the men who have disappeared."

"Does anyone else have an opinion?" persisted Lestrade.

Huggins snorted. "There are several opinions, most of them perfectly ridiculous. If I were to tell you what the opinion is that I have heard the most, you would not believe me!"

"Well?"

"Most folk are saying that it's all the work of the Old Man of the Woods."

"Who is this 'Old Man of the Woods'?" asked Holmes in surprise.

"You gentlemen are from London," returned Huggins after a moment, "and no doubt have a more refined view of things, so you might not understand. But I'd wager there isn't a country district in England that doesn't have its own particular myths and superstitions. In these parts, no doubt because of the dense woodlands round here, our local hobgoblin or bogey is known as 'The Old Man of the Woods'. He is generally supposed to be the fount of all evil and the cause of all troubles. He lives in the dark woods, and his only pleasure is to be wicked and to cause as much misery for everyone as possible. Of course, no-one has ever seen the Old Man of the Woods, but, despite that, everyone seems to know enough about him to terrify children with warnings about him, and he is the first explanation on everyone's lips when anything goes wrong."

"I see," said Holmes. "Well, I am sure we shall all give 'The Old Man of the Woods' the attention he deserves. Now, about the case itself, what can you tell us? You had best start at the beginning, and we can question you if anything is not clear to us. If you could tell us something about this branch-line, the stations on it and the train-service it offers, that would be a useful start, for we know nothing whatever about it."

"Very well," said the policeman after a moment. "The branch-line goes from Fairfield to Parlingham. It's very hilly country, up and down, so that sometimes the railway line is in a deep cutting and sometimes it is on a high embankment. There are also some very dense woodlands – as I've just mentioned – through which the line passes. It's no great distance from one end of the line to the other, so the train usually does it in about twenty minutes, even though it never goes very fast. Speed has never been much of a requirement in these parts. Much of the traffic is in goods – sheep and other livestock, farm produce, coal – that sort of thing. All in all, it's not a very busy line, especially on the passenger side. It varies from day to day, of course, and the earlier trains are generally busier than the later, but the six-thirteen, which is usually the last train of the day, often has only a handful of passengers – and, sometimes, none at all. However many passengers there might be, the trains are always the same: three carriages, the first one all third class compartments, the second one a mixture of third and first class, and the third the guard's van, which of course also carries all the goods and luggage."

"Was there much in the way of goods on this evening's train?" asked Holmes.

Huggins nodded his head. "Yes. There were numerous crates, boxes and packages in the guard's van, but they don't appear to have been disturbed in any way."

"Which suggests, of course, that attempted theft was not the cause of tonight's strange events," said Holmes. "Are there any other stations on the branch-line?"

"Yes, just one, Bellbrook Halt, which lies roughly half-way between the two ends of the line. That consists of just a single platform and a waiting-room, and is very little used. Indeed, I doubt it would ever have been built at all but for a generous contribution to its construction made by Viscount Bellbrook, the largest landowner in the district, whose family seat, Bellbrook Castle, is close by. Being a 'halt', as the railway company calls it, trains do not stop at Bellbrook unless there is someone who wishes to board or leave the train there. Anyone already on the train who wishes to alight at Bellbrook must notify the guard in advance – at Fairfield or Parlingham – that they wish to do so, and anyone waiting at Bellbrook hoping to catch the train there must stand on the platform and make a clear signal to the approaching train."

"Do you know if the six-thirteen stopped at Bellbrook this evening?" queried Holmes.

"We really have no idea," returned Huggins with a shake of the head. "I doubt it, because it very rarely does so, so they tell me. But it is possible, I suppose."

"Can you not tell from the tickets issued if anyone intended to alight at Bellbrook?" asked Lestrade.

Superintendent Huggins shook his head. "No-one bought a ticket here – Fairfield – to travel to Bellbrook, but someone could have arrived here from London – or anywhere else – on a through ticket from there to Bellbrook. We haven't yet had chance to look into that possibility."

"We have been told," said Holmes, "that there were certainly no passengers on the train when it reached Parlingham this evening. But is it known if there were any passengers aboard when it left Fairfield?"

"There may have been," replied Huggins, "but I'm afraid that that, too, is a question we have not yet been able to answer."

"That seems a singular state of affairs," observed Holmes, raising his eyebrow in surprise.

"Yes, I know it is a strange thing, not to know if there was anyone on the train or not," conceded Huggins. "But come, I believe the rain has stopped. Let us go and see Mr Thomas, the station-master here. He will explain it to you better than I can."

We therefore left the police van and made our way back to the station building, where Huggins conducted us to the station-master's office. The station-master proved to be an affable man, who was clearly astonished by what had happened.

"The three railwaymen who have disappeared," he began, shaking his head vigorously in disbelief, "they are all so respectable and reliable. Who – or what – can have attacked them? For I can't think for a moment that they would have abandoned their posts voluntarily, and left the train to plough on by itself, completely out of control. Someone could easily have been killed by it."

"Perhaps you could give us some details about the men," said Holmes, "which might help us to understand what could have happened to make them leave their train."

"Certainly, certainly," said Thomas. "All three of them have been working on this line for some years, with – as far as I am aware – no blemish of any sort against their names. The guard, James Morris, is the senior man. He has been a faithful servant of the company for more than thirty years, and his record of safety and diligence is as good as any man I have ever known. He would do anything to preserve the safety of his train. The engine-driver, Arthur Milbank, is also a very experienced man. He used to work the London express, based at Gloucester, and was a real racer in those days. He was disciplined once, I remember, for driving too fast through some station or other – Swindon, I think it was. But he mellowed with age, and some years ago he opted for a quieter life and transferred to the Parlingham branch-line. The fireman, John Turner, is a younger man than the other two, a big strong chap. He was a bit wild in his youth, so everyone says. The usual story, as I understand it: lost his head over some woman, then lost his head even more when she threw him over. He was working at Bellbrook Castle at the time, as she was. He was employed in the gardens there, I believe, but he's been working for the railway company now for nigh on ten years, and so far as I'm aware there's never been any complaint against him. He lost his father when he was quite young, and that may have unbalanced him in his youth, but since he's been working here, old Milbank has been like a father to him, and that has probably helped him find his feet. So," he continued after a moment's silence, "I'm sorry if that doesn't help you at all, but that's all I know."

"Pardon my ignorance," said Inspector Lestrade, as the station-master fell silent again, "but could you tell us how the train could keep going when no-one was aboard, and what would have happened when it reached the end of the line at Parlingham?"

"Certainly," said Thomas. "The branch line is a fairly level one, so it's not difficult to work. They'd have got steam up while they were here, waiting to depart. It's getting going from a standing start that uses most steam up, so they'd have kept the fire stoked up for the first couple of miles, to replace the steam they had used up. After that, they'd close down the regulator a bit, with plenty of steam in the dome to keep them going. By the time they got to Bellbrook, they'd be going pretty slowly, but that's how they'd want it, in case there was anyone waiting on the platform there to board the train. After Bellbrook, the line is level all the way, except for the last half-mile or so, which is a falling gradient, so the fire doesn't need banking up any more. The driver can just let the engine coast along, and it will have enough momentum to take it all the way to the end of the line. So the fact that in this case there was no driver or fireman on the footplate didn't matter from that point of view."

"But what about at the end of the line?" Lestrade persisted. "What usually happens then, and what would be different today?"

"Normally," replied Thomas, "the driver would apply the brake a little way before they reached the station, so that by the time they reached the platform they would be going very slowly. That's a matter of safety. Even at a very slow speed the train will keep rolling – there's so much dead weight pushing it along, you see. Today, who knows what might have happened?" He puffed his cheeks out and shook his head again. "We were very, very fortunate that the station-master at Parlingham, Mr Williams, happened to be on the platform as the train drew in there, otherwise there could have been a dreadful tragedy. As it was, Williams saw the train approaching and thought nothing of it, he says, except that it seemed to be travelling more slowly than usual. But as the engine drew closer to where he was standing, he was, he says, astounded to see that there was no footplate crew aboard her. He realised at once the great danger that the uncontrolled train represented, sprang aboard the footplate, closed the regulator completely, screwed down the brake as fast as he could and managed to stop it just before it overran the end of the platform. Had he not acted so promptly, I dread to think what severe damage the train could have done to the railway buildings at the end of the line – and to anyone who was working or standing there."

"How very fortunate that the station-master was on the platform and not in his office," remarked Lestrade. "I remember an occasion when a heavy passenger train overran the platform at one of the big London stations. It was only creeping along, apparently, but it still managed to cause massive damage!"

"I can well believe it," said Mr Thomas, nodding his head. "Now, is there any other enquiry I can help you with?"

"Yes," said Holmes. "I understand that no-one is sure whether there were any passengers on the six-thirteen tonight or not. Can you shed any light on that, Mr Thomas?"

"Not really, I'm afraid," replied the station-master in an apologetic tone. "That time of day is one of our busiest, and the platforms are often crowded then. You see, the London express arrives at eight minutes to six, and a lot of people alight here. Apart from those passengers whose destination is Fairfield itself, or Parlingham, there are also those who are travelling to somewhere further down the line. The London express doesn't stop again between here and Gloucester, so anyone wishing to travel to one of the stations between here and there will wait here for the slow train to Gloucester, which stops at every station on the way. This stopping train comes in at three minutes past six, and departs again at eight minutes past. After that, the platforms are practically empty again. But between the arrival of the express and the departure of the stopping train the platforms are, as I say, full of passengers.

"Now, the chief porter, Peter Reece, was on the platform all that time, and he says he noticed that at least one man walked over to the other side of the platform, where the branch-line train was waiting. The man was standing over there for some time, says Reece, but whether he actually boarded the train in the end, or had just walked over that way to stretch his legs while he waited for the slow train to Gloucester, he cannot say for certain."

"Was he able to describe this man?" asked Holmes.

"Yes," replied the station-master. "He says he was a tall, thin, scholarly-looking gentleman, possibly elderly, wearing a dark overcoat and silk hat, and carrying a small leather travelling-bag and a walking-stick. Reece says that, although he didn't really give the man much thought at the time, as he was busy and the platforms were crowded, he had the impression that the man might have been a doctor, or some other sort of professional man."

"Did he recognise him?" asked Lestrade.

"No. He doesn't think he had ever seen him before. I think, from what Reece told me, that the only reason this stranger caught his eye at all was because he looked very different from most of the passengers that Reece is used to seeing on the branch-line train, who are, in the main, local, country folk."

"Where was the guard of the Parlingham train at the time the porter saw this stranger?" asked Lestrade.

"Usually," said Thomas, "he would be with his train, preparing it for the journey, stowing away any luggage and so on. But on this occasion, as it happened, he had come to see me about something – nothing very important, but it took several minutes to resolve – so that he was not with his train until just before they were due to leave."

We thanked the station-master for his assistance and made our way out once more to the carriage-yard. It had stopped raining, but it was a dark and chilly night, for the clouds were low and heavy.

"Well," said Superintendent Huggins, with a shake of the head, "you now know as much as I know, which is – to put it bluntly – precious little. At least if we now make our way to Parlingham we shall be in a position to hear any reports that might come in from all the men I have tramping about the district."

"Very well," said Holmes, "but I should like to call at Bellbrook Halt on the way. Of course, we may learn nothing there, but there is a chance we might. The well-dressed man seen by the porter intrigues me, for a number of reasons. In the first place, he appears from what we have heard to be a stranger to these parts, which I imagine is moderately unusual on a line such as the Fairfield to Parlingham branch. His presence is therefore, at the very least, something of an odd coincidence, coming on the same evening as the singular occurrence which has brought us all here. Generally speaking, I have found that when two unusual things occur in close proximity to each other, there is nearly always a connection between the two of them."

"But it is nearly midnight," protested Huggins, "and, from what we know, the man you mention may not even have been on the branch-line train."

"That is, of course, true," said Holmes, "but it is equally possible that he was, and I don't think we should neglect the chance to learn something about him. Furthermore, the porter saw that man standing on the platform by the branch-line train for some time, and it is possible that he was waiting there in order to inform the guard in advance that he wished to alight at Bellbrook – which you told us is the correct procedure. And, from the description the porter gave of him, he sounds perhaps more likely to have been paying a visit to Viscount Bellbrook than visiting the village of Parlingham."

"Very well, Mr Holmes," said the superintendant in a tone of resignation. "I can't imagine we are very likely to learn anything at Bellbrook Halt, but as it is not much out of our way we may as well call there, I suppose."

We had been crossing the carriage-yard as they were speaking, and just as we reached the police van there came a terrific clatter of hooves and rattle of harness, and another police vehicle raced into the yard and drew to a halt beside us. A man in police uniform sprang down, whom Huggins identified for us as Sergeant Maldon. "Sir," said this newcomer in a loud, urgent tone, addressing the superintendent, "there has been a development!"

"What is it, Maldon?" returned Huggins.

"One of the missing men has turned up, sir!"

"Who? Where?"

"James Morris, the guard. In the woods, just the other side of Bellbrook Halt, sir."

"Has he been able to explain the matter to you?"

"No, sir. He's not in a position to explain anything to anyone."

"What! Don't tell me the poor fellow is dead!"

"No, sir, but he's unconscious. He appears to have been the victim of a particularly savage attack. The doctor says he has a fractured skull, and has given him a dose of something to numb the pain, which has put him into a deep sleep."

"How was he found?" asked Huggins.

"It was Pickering, sir, the man who attends to the lamps at Bellbrook Halt."

"Ah!" said Huggins. "I know the man you mean. I'll explain, gentlemen," he continued, turning to us. "From what I told you before about the stations on the line, it will not surprise you to learn that there are no permanent staff at Bellbrook. There is, however, a part-time employee, this man Pickering. He is actually employed as a cattle-man at one of the local farms, which is where he lives. But the railway company also employs him to sweep the platform at Bellbrook, keep the place neat and tidy, make sure there is oil in the station lamps and so on. On dark evenings, like the present, he has also to light the lamps at dusk, and extinguish them after the last train has passed. Now, Maldon, what happened this evening, then?"

"Well, sir, this evening, Pickering was coming along the road, to fulfil his final duty of the day, at about half past six, when he heard the train approaching in the distance. He admits he was a little late in getting there, and by the time he reached the station, the train had already passed through it. He says that by the sound of it, which he could hear quite clearly from a distance, the train had not stopped at the station, but had just passed slowly through. He therefore extinguished the lamps and made his way home. The reason Pickering has come forward to tell us all this is because of something that happened immediately afterwards.

"You may not know, sir, but Pickering has a daughter, Ellie, a plucky girl, about fourteen or fifteen years old, who sometimes accompanies him on his evening walk to Bellbrook Halt. She was with him tonight, and as they left the station she said she thought it would be quicker to walk home through the woods rather than following the road. Pickering said he thought the road was better, so she proposed a contest: he could go by way of the road, she by way of the woods, and they would see who arrived first at the place the two meet again, where the road passes over the railway line. So that is what they did."

"It seems a little careless of him, I must say," interjected Superintendent Huggins, "to let his young daughter go off alone through the woods in the dark."

Maldon nodded his head. "Yes, I thought the same, sir," said he, "but it's not quite as careless as we might think. Ellie is, as I say, a plucky girl, and she had a lantern with her. In any case, she was really just following the railway line, rather than going into the woods at the side of it. Now, just the other side of the thickest part of the woods, the road that Pickering was following curves round and passes over the railway line on a small stone bridge. When he reached this bridge, he found Ellie was there already, waiting for him, as he had expected. He says he knew that she would run, to make sure she got there first, so he wasn't surprised to find her a little out of breath, but he could also see that she was really frightened about something. He asked her what was the matter, and when she had calmed down a bit she told him that as she was coming along the railway line she had heard someone in the woods, thrashing about and 'moaning and groaning' as she put it. She thought it must be the Old Man of the Woods, and was terrified."

"We have heard about 'The Old Man of the Woods' from Superintendent Huggins," Holmes interrupted, as Maldon cast us an interrogative glance.

Maldon shook his head. "They are superstitious folk in these parts," said he, with a chuckle. "Anyway, Pickering told his daughter, Ellie, not to worry about it. He says he thought it was probably just a drunken tramp, so the two of them went home and forgot about it. It was only later, when news reached the farm where they live, about the incredible arrival of the empty train at Parlingham, that Pickering thought that what Ellie had heard in the woods might be connected to whatever had happened on board the train. He hurried to Parlingham to inform us, and I at once sent some men to Bellbrook Halt to look into it.

"It didn't take them long to find the source of the 'moaning and groaning' that the girl had heard. It was no wonder that it had sounded so loud to her, and had startled her so much, for poor Morris lay only a yard or two into the wood beside the railway line."

"Right," said Huggins. "We'll get off to Bellbrook at once, and see the matter for ourselves. We were just about to go there anyway, even before this discovery."

We set off at a brisk trot down the main road from Fairfield, Sergeant Maldon's van following close behind us. After about three miles on this dark, deserted road, we turned off to the right, down a narrow and twisting lane. A further mile or so and we passed through a small, silent village, and came at length to Bellbrook Halt. Upon the station platform, several bright lamps had been lit, and two uniformed policemen were waiting there, who stood to attention as we approached.

"Any fresh developments, Watkins?" asked Sergeant Maldon. "Any sign of the other missing men?"

"No, sir," one of the constables called back.

"Then I'll show you where Morris was found, sir," said Maldon to Superintendent Huggins. "This way, gentlemen!"

He took a lantern from one of the constables and led the way along the platform to the left, and down onto the railway track. Immediately after passing the station, the line began a long curve round to the left, and we followed our guide along this for perhaps two hundred yards. The ground on either side of the track had begun to drop away slightly once we were clear of the station, so that by the time Maldon halted, the line on which we stood was on a raised embankment perhaps eight or ten feet up from the gully on either side. On our left, below us, a lamp had been fastened to a tree.

"This is the place, sir," said Maldon. "It's very slippery, sir, with all the rain we've had, so you have to be careful."

"Thank you, Maldon," returned Superintendent Huggins in an ironic tone, as he began to descend the slope from the line. "I think we can all – " Abruptly, the words died on his lips, as his feet slipped from under him. I was standing the nearest to him, and I instinctively reached out my hand to seize his wrist. But his impetus could not be stopped, and the pair of us slid down the slope, and ended up in a muddy heap in the gully at the bottom.

The superintendent muttered a series of oaths under his breath, as Holmes, Lestrade and Maldon, forewarned by our mishap, made their way with great care down the side of the embankment.

"Are you all right, sir?" asked Sergeant Maldon.

"Yes, I'm all right," returned Huggins in a tone of annoyance. "Are you all right, Dr Watson? Good. Nothing injured, except our dignity, eh? Now, Maldon," he continued, "show us where Morris was found. Was it very far into the woods?"

"No, sir, not at all, just three or four feet. I'm sure that the girl – Ellie Pickering – who heard Morris groaning would have seen him if she had been walking where we are now standing, but, of course, she wasn't; she was up there on the railway track on top of the embankment, and probably running as she passed this point."

"Anything to be seen here?" asked the superintendent. "Any clue as to what might have happened to Morris, or any sign of where the other men might have got to?"

"No, sir. We've been quite a way into the wood just here, and there's nothing to be seen at all: nothing except mud and scrubby undergrowth."

"That's not quite true," interjected Holmes. "There are also several large rocks and stones on the ground just here."

"Of course, that is true," responded Maldon, a mixture of surprise and annoyance in his voice. "I was not intending to give a full list of every little thing I could see here."

"My observation is not irrelevant," persisted Holmes. "What I mean is that Morris's skull-fracture could have occurred when his head struck one of these large stones, as he slipped down the embankment. We have just had a practical demonstration of how dangerous and unstoppable such a slip can be."

"It is possible, I suppose," said Huggins, "although how that helps us shed any light on the matter in general, I confess I can't see, Mr Holmes. Even if what you suggest were true, it doesn't explain – or even begin to explain – what Morris was doing out here in the first place, and why he wasn't sitting peacefully on his bench in the guard's van as usual."

"Indeed," returned Holmes in a placid tone. "But it is a capital error to dismiss from consideration some explanation simply because it doesn't provide an answer to every single point of a mystery. One cannot always alight on the right trail straight away, but, like a hound casting about for a promising scent, must consider every single possibility, however unlikely or trivial each of them may seem. Sometimes, little, apparently insignificant details play a large part in a case. In one murder investigation I handled, it turned out that the whole case hinged on the fact that a woman had called in at the local baker's shop to purchase a Bakewell tart. In another case, the fact that a man had cut himself while shaving one morning proved to be the key point in the solution of the mystery."

"That's all very well in theory, Mr Holmes," said Huggins in an impatient tone, "but how does that help us in practice?"

"In this case, it frees us from wasting our time and mental energies on wondering who it was that attacked the guard so violently, and why on earth he should do so. Instead we can – as you suggest – speculate on the more straightforward question of how the guard came to be outside his van."

"Do you have any suggestions on that subject?"

"It may be that the answer lies in the curvature of the line. It has been curving quite sharply to the left since it passed Bellbrook Halt. The train, so I understand, was quite a short one, so it may be that someone looking out of the doorway of the guard's van could quite easily see the footplate of the engine."

"That's probably true," said Sergeant Maldon. "But why should that have made Morris leave his guard's van?"

"Perhaps," replied Holmes, "because he saw something which made him believe the train was headed for disaster unless he acted quickly."

"Such as ?" asked Maldon.

"Such as that there was no-one there on the footplate, in charge of the engine. Tell me, Sergeant: would there be any way for the guard to communicate with the engine-driver or fireman?"

"Yes," replied Maldon. "There is a continuous cord which runs along the left side of the carriages, above the doors. One pull on that would ring a bell on the footplate of the engine."

"And how might the driver respond?"

"With a short blast on the engine whistle."

"So it is possible, at least, that Morris could have pulled the bell-cord, received no response from the driver by way of a whistle, looked forward and seen that there was no-one on the footplate, and so decided there and then that he would jump down from his carriage – which would not be a dangerous thing to do if the train was travelling as slowly as everyone seems to think it was – run along the side of the line and spring aboard the engine, where he could quickly bring it to a halt."

"But he would have had no need to do that," objected Sergeant Maldon. "There is a brake in the guard's van. He could have applied the brake from there."

Holmes nodded. "I am aware of that," said he. "But perhaps he could tell from the sound of the engine that it was not simply coasting, but was being actively supplied with steam, in which case the brake in the guard's van would have been fighting against the power of the engine's pistons. If so, he might have judged that the only way to bring the train peacefully to a halt was to get aboard the locomotive, close down the steam pipes and then apply the brake from there."

"That is possible," conceded Maldon, "But where does that leave us?"

"I don't suppose you have been able to examine the undergrowth at the side of the line yet," remarked Holmes.

"Not very thoroughly," returned the sergeant after a moment, with a shake of the head. "What with the darkness, the heavy rain we had earlier and the shortage of men, we haven't been able to do much in that respect. Of course, when we were following the directions given to us by Pickering and his daughter, as to where the moaning was coming from, we walked along the line from Bellbrook Halt, just as we have done just now, looking keenly to our left. And when we found Morris, we looked all round him in a wide circle, but there was nothing else to be seen there."

"Very well," said Holmes after a moment. "What I propose then is this, that we return now to Bellbrook and examine the other side of the line carefully as we go."

"I suppose we might as well," returned Maldon, "but it's nearly all just brambles on that side of the line. I can't imagine there's anything there."

"I don't doubt it," said Holmes. "But one can never be certain about anything until one has examined it for oneself."

"Do you have any particular reason for your interest in the other side of the line, Mr Holmes?" asked Superintendent Huggins in a dubious tone.

"There is one indication at least, that something may have happened on that side," returned Holmes.

"I can't imagine what that could be."

"One of the passenger doors on that side was not closed properly," said Holmes, "as you yourself mentioned."

"Oh, that!" said Huggins dismissively. "I doubt if that is of any significance at all!"

"Let us see for ourselves," said Holmes, "rather than debating the matter in the abstract, like a group of mediaeval scholars. As you yourself said, Superintendent, one fact is worth a thousand theories. May I?" he continued, taking a lantern from one of the policemen.

Throughout this exchange, my friend's tone had been a pleasant, almost light one; but I who knew him well could tell that he was growing increasingly impatient with all this talk. Now, as he sprang nimbly up the embankment to the railway line, Superintendent Huggins looked queryingly at Lestrade, then at me.

"Mr Holmes is always keen to examine everything for himself as soon as possible," I said.

"His methods may sometimes seem unorthodox," added Lestrade, "but are generally helpful to us in the end."

"Let's see if he discovers anything, then," said Superintendent Huggins with a shake of his head, as we made our way carefully up the embankment. Holmes was already some distance ahead of us, bent over as he walked along, like some strange bird of prey, as he scrutinised the foliage at the side of the line. Now, as if fate were rewarding him for his enterprise and his determination to get on with the task in hand, the clouds, which had previously been uniformly dark and heavy, were beginning to break up a little and reveal a glimmer of moonlight. It was not much, but it was better than no light at all.

We had been walking along the railway track for about a hundred yards, always keeping about fifteen or twenty yards behind Holmes, when I saw my friend abruptly stop. In a few moments we had drawn level with him.

"What is it?" I asked.

"There's something down there," he returned without looking round. "If you would be so good as to hold the lantern, Watson," he continued, passing it to me, "I'll just hop down and have a closer look."

The ground on either side of the railway line had been gradually rising as we walked along, until it was now just three or four feet lower than the line. Holmes jumped down and bent over again to examine what appeared to be a tangle of undergrowth.

"Aha!" said he after a moment.

"What is it?" asked Superintendent Huggins with heightened interest.

"I can't say for certain yet," replied Holmes. "Some sort of fabric, I should say. Yes, by George! It's the bottom of someone's overalls. And here is a boot – with someone's foot in it!"

We jumped down to join him in the gully at the side of the line, and hold the lanterns nearer.

"Has anyone got a pair of gloves with them?" asked Holmes. "Some of these old brambles are extremely vicious."

"I have," replied Sergeant Maldon. "Here, let me have a look." He pulled on a pair of thick-looking gloves, and bent to the brambles, which he lifted up with a grunt of effort. "Does that help at all?" he asked.

"Yes," said Holmes. "Keep it there if you can, and I'll try to pull this man out."

There followed several minutes of pulling and pushing, and, it must be said, not a few oaths, as the brambles, like some strange malevolent creature, seemed determined to do their utmost to thwart all our efforts, and refuse to yield up their captive. But at length, as Maldon and I did our best to hold back the wild tangle of vegetation, Holmes and the superintendent managed to drag the still figure of a man free from the brambles and onto the strip of bare earth at the side of the railway embankment. I at once bent to him and examined him as best I could by the weak light of the lanterns. "He is alive," I said, "but is in a state of deep insensibility, and does not respond to any stimulus. We must get him to where he can be properly cared for at once!"

"What do you think has happened to him?" asked Superintendent Huggins.

"Concussion of the brain, by the look of it," I responded. "He has a large bruise and a cut above his brow. I think he must have struck his head on something, like the other man – according to Mr Holmes's suggestion – but in this case, probably not a rock, as I don't think there is any evidence of a fracture."

"Do you have any idea who it is?" the superintendent asked Sergeant Maldon.

Thee sergeant bent down lower, and scrutinised the unconscious man's face. "I'm pretty certain it's old Milbank, sir – the engine-driver."

Huggins nodded. "I rather thought it must be. Instruct a couple of your men to get the poor devil to the Parlingham infirmary as quickly as they can!"

Sergeant Maldon blew two sharp blasts on a whistle, and a moment later two constables came running from Bellbrook Halt. In a few words he explained the latest development to them and issued his orders.

"Now," said the Superintendent, when the constables had carried the unfortunate engine-driver away, "what next? Do you have any theory to account for this latest discovery, Mr Holmes?"

"Several."

"Such as?"

Holmes shook his head. "It is too early to decide between different hypotheses," said he, "so there is no point in trying to list them. Some of them may be close to the truth, others may be miles away from it."

"What do you suggest we do then?"

"Continue our examination of this side of the line, back to Bellbrook Halt. I suspect the next 'discovery', as you call it, may be decisive."

"What do you think, Mr Lestrade?" asked the superintendent.

Lestrade shook his head. "Mr Holmes has found one of the missing men for us," he returned. "Perhaps he will find another. I have no better alternative suggestion to make."

"I noticed," said Holmes, "when we were at Bellbrook Halt, that there was a large, flat, open area on the other side of the line there. Do you know what purpose that serves?"

"I haven't the faintest idea," replied Superintendent Huggins.

"I believe," interposed Sergeant Maldon, "that the railway company have used it on odd occasions, when they were loading some unusually large and heavy items onto a goods wagon there. They have a special wagon for that sort of thing, which has a crane on it."

"I see," said Holmes. "There appeared also – unless I am mistaken – to be a narrow track leading away from that flat area into the wood beyond. Would anyone use that to arrive at or leave the station?"

"I shouldn't think so," replied Maldon. "It's a public footpath, but it doesn't go anywhere very useful, except, eventually, to Bellbrook Castle. Bellbrook village is in the opposite direction – we passed it on our way here."

"Well, well," said Holmes. "Let us proceed, then, and see what we turn up." With that, my friend resumed his steady pacing along the track, his keen eyes fixed on the ground at the side. Several times he paused, and bent to examine some mark more closely, before resuming his slow, careful progress. As we drew nearer to Bellbrook Halt, the land on either side of the railway line had continued to rise, until it was now level with the ballast on which the track was laid.

We had almost reached the station when I saw Holmes bend down and examine some mark on the ground very closely.

"What is it, Holmes?" I asked, as I drew level with where he was crouching down.

"A footprint," he replied without looking up.

"There are enough of those to keep us in business all year," remarked Superintendent Huggins in a dismissive tone, most of them made by my men coming and going all evening."

"This one is not the same as those others," insisted Holmes. "The sole is unusually broad, the heel is a different shape, and the boot is going in the opposite direction to many of the other prints. I have been following it all the way from where we found the unfortunate engine-driver, Milbank. Of course, the fact that these prints first appear at the same place as we found Milbank is highly suggestive."

"Suggestive of what?" asked Sergeant Maldon.

"As they appear at the same place, and both men have almost certainly come from the train, which was moving at the time, then they almost certainly came to that spot at the same time. Either these broad prints are those of a stranger, who pushed Milbank from the train – but, then, we must ask 'where is the fireman, John Turner?' – or they are the prints of Turner himself, who fell from the train with Milbank."

"But why should they both have fallen from the train?" asked Maldon.

"Perhaps because they were having a violent quarrel about something," suggested Holmes. "Anyway, whoever he was, the owner of these boots was in a very great hurry to get back to Bellbrook Halt."

"How do you know he was in a hurry?" asked Lestrade.

"Because the toe-end of the boot is generally more deeply marked than the heel, indicating that the man wearing these boots was running. I wanted you to see these prints now, in case we get any more heavy rain and the prints are obliterated. Now, let us proceed!"

I bent down to examine the footprint in question and saw that what my friend had said was true, then hurried with the others to catch him up, for he was now striding out again ahead of us. Presently, we reached the flat, open area he had referred to earlier.

"Keep back," said he. "I am looking to see if – yes, by George!"

"What is it?" asked Sergeant Maldon.

"The next significant piece of evidence," replied Holmes. "I had wondered if someone had hopped off the train at Bellbrook, and it appears that that was indeed the case."

"But the train did not stop here tonight, from all we have heard," protested Maldon.

"No, but if it was travelling as slowly as everyone seems to think, it would not have been particularly difficult or dangerous for someone to hop off just here, pushing the door shut as he did so. See," he continued, beckoning us to come closer, "that narrow footprint with the pointed toe is the one I mean."

"That certainly appears to be different footwear from all the other prints," remarked the superintendent, "but how can you be so certain that it belongs to someone who alighted from the train?"

"Because the first such narrow footprint occurs here," replied Holmes, turning and pointing to a spot closer to the railway track. "As you can see, his foot slipped a little on the mud as he landed, and he steadied himself with his walking-stick, before setting off across the open area, towards that footpath over there."

We all followed Holmes's direction. There was no doubt about it: just to the side of the first, smudged footprint was a small, round indentation which could only have been made by a walking-stick.

"From what we heard earlier from the station-master at Fairfield," Holmes continued, "the scholarly-looking gentleman who was seen standing for some time on the platform there was carrying a walking-stick."

"I believe you are right," said Huggins, "although we don't, of course, know for certain that that man actually boarded the train."

"No," said Holmes, "but, after all, we don't yet know anything much for certain, do we? Let us now follow these narrow-footed tracks and see where they lead us!"

Holding his lantern low to the ground, Holmes set off across the flat, muddy area, and we followed behind him, keeping to the side, as well as we could, of the footprints we were following. Abruptly, Holmes stopped.

"What now?" queried Inspector Lestrade.

"The other man – broad-foot – has now joined us," returned Holmes. "He has run across this open area, as you can see, and turned up the track, where narrow-foot has already gone. I fear this pursuit will not end well, but follow him we must!"

With that, Holmes turned up the narrow track, the rest of us following behind him. After a short distance, the track entered a very dark belt of trees, but we had gone scarcely twenty yards or so through this when Holmes stopped once more. The undergrowth beside the path where he stood appeared disturbed and flattened, and as Holmes bent over to examine it more closely, I heard him mutter something under his breath, then he turned to us.

"Broad-foot caught up with narrow-foot just here," he announced. "One of them is still here, as I feared. Can one of you help pull him out, onto the path?"

I hurried forward to lend a hand. This man was not so tightly caught in the undergrowth as the engine-driver had been, and we soon had him out on the track. But even the very briefest of examinations was sufficient to tell me that this man had passed beyond all human help.

"This man is dead," I announced to the others, "and has been for some time. Like the other two, he has suffered a severe injury to the head. He has a massive bruise across his forehead and brow."

"Who is it?" asked Superintendent Huggins in a forlorn voice.

"By the look of the size of him, and his thick, coarse overalls and shirt," said Holmes, "I should say it is the locomotive fireman – Turner, I think you said his name was."

The others crowded round to see. Sergeant Maldon nodded his head. "Yes," said he, "that's John Turner all right. But how could such a big, powerful man be struck down so completely by the thin, elderly fellow we have heard about? And where is that man now?"

"'The race is not always to the swift, nor battle to the strong', as it is said," returned Holmes. "I think that what must have happened is that when Turner caught up with the other man, the latter, perhaps terrified by Turner's sudden appearance, must have struck out at hazard with his stick and fortuitously caught Turner a heavy blow across the brow. As to the whereabouts of this other man, I imagine he is at Bellbrook Castle, with Viscount Bellbrook."

"What!" cried Superintendent Huggins. "But that is fantastic! How can you know?"

"According to what I was told earlier, this track doesn't lead anywhere except to Bellbrook castle, so it is not such a wild speculation. We had wondered earlier if that was perhaps the destination of the man seen on the platform at Fairfield Junction. It may be that he forgot to inform the guard that he wished to alight at Bellbrook Halt, or was unable to do so, owing to the guard's absence, which we heard about earlier. But – however that may be – it is evident that it was always his wish to alight here, from the fact that when the train did not stop he hopped off it as it passed slowly through the station. It also seems very likely that he has been here before, and knows his way about, from the fact that, having alighted, he set off at once up this narrow track through the woods, despite the fact that it must have been already going dark by then."

Superintendent Huggins stood in silence for a few moments, and it was clear that he was struggling to decide what action we should take next. "What do you think we should do, then, Mr Holmes? he asked at length.

"I think we must go at once to Bellbrook Castle," returned Holmes.

"But it is well after midnight now," protested Huggins, "and it seems to me utterly inconceivable that Viscount Bellbrook could know anything about this business! We can hardly go banging on his Lordship's door in the middle of the night, just because the path we're on happens to go in the direction of Bellbrook Castle!"

"There is a man lying dead here," said Holmes, "and two more lying seriously injured in the infirmary at Parlingham, and Viscount Bellbrook's visitor is probably responsible – either directly or indirectly – for all that has happened. He may be the only man alive who can shed any light on what exactly has occurred here this evening, and therefore we must speak to him as soon as possible."

"What do you think, Mr Lestrade?" asked Huggins.

"It may be," replied Lestrade after a moment, "that everyone at Bellbrook Castle is already in bed and fast asleep, but it is also possible that they may not be, in which case I would agree with Mr Holmes: we should try to interview the man who alighted from the train here, if he is indeed at the Castle."

"As a matter of fact," interjected Sergeant Maldon, "there is a particular reason tonight why they may *not* be already asleep."

"And what is that, pray?" returned the superintendent in surprise.

"Because, sir, there is some special event – a festivity of some sort – taking place there this evening."

"What? Do you mean a ball? I have heard nothing about that."

"No, not exactly a ball, sir. Apparently, Viscount Bellbrook recently celebrated his fiftieth birthday, so he was holding a sort of reception this evening at the castle for all his friends and relations."

"Are you sure about this, Maldon? It's the first I've heard about it!"

"Yes, sir. My wife heard it from someone she knows whose sister works in the kitchens at the Castle."

"Very well, very well," said the superintendent in a tone of resignation. We'll get up to the Castle, then. But first, let's get this poor devil a more dignified place to rest in."

We carried the body of the fireman back to the railway station and laid him down on the floor of the waiting room, with one of the constables to stand guard there and notify the others when they returned of where we had gone. Then the five of us – Huggins, Maldon, Lestrade, Holmes and myself – set off back up the track towards Bellbrook Castle.

As we reached the place where we had found the body of the unfortunate fireman, Holmes cautioned us to avoid walking over the footprints that were already there. "These prints tell the story of what happened here earlier this evening," said he, "so it is important that they are not further disturbed. You will note from the prints, for instance, that the man who struck out at the fireman with his stick was extremely frightened."

"I'm sure he *was* frightened – anyone would be, under the circumstances," interrupted Lestrade, "but how can you tell that from these footprints?"

"Because, having struck out, he did not wait to see what had happened, but dashed off at once. He would probably have known, of course, that his blow had struck home, but not how much damage it had done to his opponent. You can see that he is running here – the heels of his shoes make no mark upon the ground. And now," he continued, pausing for a moment, "he has stopped and looked round, no doubt to see if he is being followed. Now he resumes his hurried progress, and the toe-ends of his shoes are all that touch the ground."

Thus the five of us proceeded in the pale moonlight for some time, Holmes leading the way with his back bent, holding his lantern close to the ground. After a few minutes, we emerged from the belt of trees, and the track continued between two large, open fields.

"He stopped again here," said Holmes after a moment. "I imagine he was out of breath, as he stood here for some time."

"How can you tell how long he stopped for?" asked Sergeant Maldon.

"Because his footprints are all over the place," explained Holmes, "all pointing in different directions, some of them covering up others, and all in a very small area on the ground. He also put down the bag he was carrying."

"Marvellous!" cried Maldon in an appreciative tone. "You read the roughest and scrappiest of signs as someone else might read a book, Mr Holmes! You should have been a tracker in the jungle of some far-flung corner of the world!"

"Thank you, Sergeant," responded Holmes with a chuckle. "But this corner of the world is quite enough to keep me occupied!"

As we reached the far end of the large field, I saw that the land beyond it fell away into a broad vale, and as we passed through a gap in the hedge, a very large, ornate-looking building with turrets and towers came into view below us. Even in the dark of the night, its profile was an imposing one.

"That," said Sergeant Maldon, "is Bellbrook Castle."

"I see there are a number of lights still lit there," I observed.

"Indeed," said Superintendent Huggins. "So we may be in luck after all!"

An easy walk down the hill of seven or eight minutes brought us to a wide, gravel drive which led up to the front of the building, where broad steps rose to the great front door, flanked on either side by bright lamps.

The superintendent banged the heavy door-knocker, and as he did so I heard the sound of gay music from somewhere within the building. Moments later, the door was opened by a tall, dignified-looking man in the livery of a footman.

"Yes, gentlemen?" said he, an impassive expression on his face.

"We have come to see Viscount Bellbrook." said the superintendent.

"His Lordship is engaged at present," said the footman in a firm voice, "and cannot be disturbed."

"This is not a social call," persisted Huggins, "but an official one."

"Yes. sir," responded the footman. "I assumed as much from your uniforms, and from the late hour of your visit. That does not alter the fact that his Lordship is engaged. Might I suggest, sir, that if you call again tomorrow morning – "

"One moment," interrupted Sherlock Holmes in a determined tone. "A man has been killed earlier this evening, near the railway station. Two other men are very seriously injured, and may not survive. We have very good reason to believe that one of Viscount Bellbrook's guests this evening was a witness to what occurred, and we must speak to him at once. I am sure that Viscount Bellbrook would regard this matter as of somewhat greater importance than whatever it is that engages him at present."

The footman hesitated, and it was clear that Holmes's words had plunged him into a state of indecision.

"Indeed," Holmes continued, "I strongly suspect that Viscount Bellbrook would regard it as a positive dereliction of duty were he not to be informed at once of this matter, which is essentially one of life and death."

"Very well, gentlemen," said the footman. "If you will come this way, I will inform his Lordship of your presence."

He stood aside as we passed into a broad marbled hall. From somewhere in the house came the melodious sound of an orchestra playing waltz music. We followed the footman as he led us through a doorway at the side of the hall, into a large antechamber containing a long oblong table and half a dozen chairs. "Please wait here a moment," said he, as he closed the door.

For several minutes we stood there without speaking, as the muffled sound of the music continued. Then the orchestra ceased playing, and silence reigned. Several more minutes passed and I heard the orchestra strike up again. As it did so, the door of our room abruptly opened, and in strode a tall, erect man in evening dress. His hair was grey, his face was wrinkled, but his voice when he spoke belied these tokens of age, for it was strong, firm and decisive, and it was evident that this was Viscount Bellbrook.

"What is this all about?" said he with a frown, his questioning gaze resting on each of us in turn. "I understand there has been an accident on the railway."

"It's not exactly an accident," responded Holmes. "We believe that one of your guests, who alighted from the train at Bellbrook Halt, encountered someone in the woods between there and here. That is the man we wish to speak to."

Viscount Bellbrook frowned again. "I don't believe anyone came that way," said he. "We twice sent a carriage over to Fairfield Junction in the afternoon, to collect various people who had travelled from London and further afield, but I don't think it called at Bellbrook Halt."

"This particular man did not come in a carriage, but on foot," persisted Holmes. "He is, we believe, a tall, thin man, possibly a little elderly."

"That sounds like Professor Sidgwick," said the viscount, an expression of understanding illuminating his features. "He is something of an eccentric," he added with a chuckle. "I can't think that anyone else I know would have walked all the way from the station on such a dark, wet evening. He is – as you perhaps know

– Heppenstall Professor of Moral Philosophy at St Francis's College, Oxford. We were undergraduates together at 'Frank's', as we called it, many years ago. He used to be a regular visitor here in years gone by, although we haven't seen him here now for nearly ten years – until this evening."

"That would be the man," said Holmes. "We knew that the man we wished to speak to, who alighted at the Halt, must be familiar with how to get from there to here by way of the footpath. May we have a word with him?"

"Yes, yes, by all means," said the viscount. "I'll send someone for him at once." He stepped to the doorway, gave instructions to a servant who was waiting there, then turned once more to us. "Someone was hurt, did you say, on the railway?"

Holmes shook his head. "No. A man has lost his life in the woods, near to the railway. Two other men – railway employees – have been seriously injured in what we believe are related incidents."

"Good Lord!" cried the viscount. "What a dreadful business!" He was about to say more when the door of the room opened again, to admit a tall, elderly man in evening dress. "Ah, Sidgwick!" said the viscount. "These gentlemen are looking into something that took place earlier, near the railway station, and believe that you may have been a witness."

The elderly man turned to us with an inquiring expression on his face.

"You arrived earlier this evening on the branch-line train, and alighted at Bellbrook Halt," said Holmes. "Is that correct?"

Sidgwick nodded his head, but did not reply.

"The train did not stop there," continued Holmes, "but was going very slowly, so you dropped down from the carriage onto the flat earth by the line, on the side away from the station platform."

A look of astonishment came over Sidgwick's face. "Were you there?" he asked.

"No," said Holmes.

"Then how on earth do you know what I did?"

"The physical evidence is clear. You then set off up the footpath which ultimately leads here, to the Castle."

"Correct."

"But you had not gone very far when someone sprang at you aggressively, shouting, I imagine."

Professor Sidgwick raised his hands and grasped his head, as he rocked backwards and forwards. He appeared very unsteady, and I feared he might faint.

I stepped forward and took his arm. "Here," I said, "sit down on this chair, Professor. It sounds a frightening experience."

"It was terrifying," returned Sidgwick, sitting down heavily, and resting his elbows on the table. "It was so dark, I could hardly see what was happening. It may sound absurd, but, for a brief moment, I thought it must be 'The Old Man of the Woods' that the country folk all speak of in these parts. This person – this brigand or bandit, or whatever he was – lunged at me, shouting loudly, his face all twisted with rage."

"So you struck out with your stick," said Holmes.

"Exactly," said Sidgwick. "I hit something hard, but as I was already trying to run away, I did not know what it was – whether it was my assailant or a low tree-branch – so I made off as fast as I could, and did not stop for breath until I had gone some considerable distance. Even then I did not linger, but set off running again after just a moment. I could not hear anything from behind me, but could not be sure that he wasn't still coming after me."

"What an awful experience!" said Viscount Bellbrook with feeling. "You didn't mention any of this when we spoke earlier, Sidgwick, although – to be honest – I thought you didn't look quite yourself."

"I didn't mention it because I didn't want to trouble you on such a festive evening," returned Sidgwick.

The viscount turned to us. "Have you found the villain responsible for this outrage?" he asked Superintendent Huggins.

"Yes, sir."

"I take it you have arrested him, then?"

"No, sir."

"Why ever not?"

"He has not been arrested," interjected Holmes, "because he is dead. It seems tolerably certain that the blow from Professor Sidgwick's stick killed him instantly."

"What!" cried Sidgwick, staggering to his feet once more, his face as white as a sheet. "I didn't know. I couldn't tell. I had to defend myself."

"Of course," said Viscount Bellbrook. "No-one could criticize you for that."

"Something I wish to ask you," said Holmes, when Sidgwick had calmed down a little, and had resumed his seat, "is whether you recognized the man who attacked you."

"It's odd you should ask me that," returned Sidgwick after a moment, "because I was asking myself the exact same question earlier. Although I saw it for only a moment, the man's face did look vaguely familiar. Eventually, I remembered why. When I was changing trains at Fairfield Junction, I approached the branch-line train, intending to notify the guard that I wished to alight at Bellbrook Halt, which I remembered from previous visits was the correct thing to do. The guard, however, was not there, so, after waiting some time, I walked to the front of the train, thinking to give the information to the men there. However, the engine-driver was busy doing something round the other side of the locomotive and I couldn't attract his attention. His assistant, a somewhat unattractive-looking young man, gave me a very surly look as I approached, and when I told him that I wished to alight at Bellbrook Halt, he just said 'You'd better tell the guard, then', turned his back on me and began shovelling coal noisily. It was this man that my assailant reminded me of."

"Your memory is correct," said Holmes. "The man who attacked you has been positively identified as the locomotive fireman, John Turner. I take it that after your unpleasant encounter with him at Fairfield, you abandoned the idea of notifying anyone of where you wished to alight."

"Eventually, yes. I did wait a little longer for the guard to appear, but gave up as the time for departure approached, and took my place in the carriage. I saw the guard run onto the platform a moment or two later, but I could not catch his eye, and thus had no opportunity to speak to him. I thought I would probably have to try to hire a cab at Parlingham station to bring me here, but when the train reached Bellbrook Halt, it was travelling so slowly that I decided on the spur of the moment that I could jump from the moving train without any risk of injury. I suppose the fireman must have seen me."

"It's a shocking business," said Viscount Bellbrook. "But why should this railwayman have such a grudge against you? You weren't rude to him when you spoke?"

"No, not at all. If anyone was rude, it was he, and I didn't respond to his rudeness in any way."

"The more we learn of the matter, the more inexplicable it becomes!" observed Superintendent Huggins.

"On the contrary," said Holmes, "it is at last becoming clearer. I rather fancy that the grudge, as Viscount Bellbrook called it, goes back somewhat further than this afternoon's railway journey."

"But how could it?" protested Sidgwick. "I had never seen the man before in my life!"

"So you may believe," said Holmes in a thoughtful voice, "but today's events suggest otherwise. You were a visitor here ten years ago – so I understand from something Viscount Bellbrook said earlier."

"Yes," replied Sidgwick. "That was the last time I was ever here."

"Was there any particular reason for this prolonged absence from your old friend's house?"

Sidgwick hesitated. "Not really," he answered after a moment. "It was simply that I was always too busy to accept Viscount Bellbrook's gracious invitations."

Holmes considered the matter for a moment. It was clear there was something on his mind. "Ten years ago," said he at length, "John Turner, the man who attacked you this evening, was not employed by the railway company, but employed here, at the Castle."

"I don't recall the name," interjected the viscount.

"He was not, so I understand, one of the household staff," responded Holmes, "but worked in the gardens. For all I know, he may not have been here very long. At the same time, there was also a young woman here, in whom he was interested. I do not know if she and Turner were officially betrothed or not, but there seems to have been some sort of understanding between them – in his mind, at least. Then something happened, and she threw him over, so I was informed. We may not know the name of this woman, but – "

"I think I may know who it was," interrupted Sergeant Maldon abruptly. We all turned to him in surprise. "Rose Hilton was her name, if I am right. 'Rosie', everyone called her. She was some years older than me and seemed almost an adult to me when I was still a boy, but her family lived close to my own parents in Parlingham when I was growing up, and I occasionally saw her in the street."

"Can you remember anything about her?" asked Holmes.

Maldon thought for a moment. "She was uncommonly pretty," he replied at length, "with dark, curly hair. Everyone said she was the prettiest thing in the whole of Gloucestershire. Some people said she was stuck up, but I don't think she was, really. Her manner may have seemed a bit superior, if you know what I mean, but that was just because she *was* superior to most folks, and some people were just jealous of her. I can't really remember anything much else about her, except that I did see her once or twice with John Turner, although I don't think anyone thought he really had much of a chance there. I think she left the district completely when she was still quite young, and – to the best of my knowledge – never came back."

While the sergeant had been speaking, there had come a series of low moans from just behind me. Now I turned, to see Professor Sidgwick's head sunk on the table before him.

"What is it, Sidgwick?" asked Viscount Bellbrook, but before the professor could answer, the door opened and a handsome, middle-aged woman swept into the room. From the elaborate and ornate white and gold of her costume, and the sparkling, bejewelled coronet upon her head, I thought she must be the viscount's wife, a conjecture which proved correct when she spoke.

"Charles," said she in an urgent tone, "I don't know what you are all discussing in here, but everyone is wondering where you have disappeared to. Events are coming to an end in the ballroom, and you must come and speak to your guests while they are all still gathered together."

Viscount Bellbrook hesitated. He looked at his wife, at the doorway, at the professor and at us. "Very well," he responded at length. "Gentlemen," he continued, turning to us, "do not go anywhere, and I shall be back in a few minutes!" With that, he and his wife left the room, the door closed firmly behind them.

For several moments we remained in silence, then Holmes spoke. "I believe," said he to Professor Sidgwick, "that you were about to tell us what you know of Rose Hilton."

Sidgwick raised his head and shot Holmes a penetrating glance. "You, sir: who are you?" he asked after a moment. "You seem to know everything, but I do not think you are a policeman."

"Who I am is irrelevant," responded Holmes. "I am assisting the police in this case. You knew Rose Hilton, I think."

The professor leaned back in his chair, an expression of resignation on his features. "'Rosie'," he said at length, as if correcting what Holmes had said. "Everyone called her 'Rosie' – as your colleague said. Yes, I knew her. She was, at the time, employed here as assistant to the housekeeper, and, as I think you may have surmised, she – or, at least, the memory of her – is what has kept me from visiting Bellbrook Castle these last ten years. When I knew her, about ten years ago, I committed the one folly of my otherwise unexciting and well-regulated existence.

"She was – as your colleague remarked – very pretty, but it wasn't simply that: she was also very attractive in a more general sense, attractive and charming – and I fell under her spell. What – if anything – she saw in me, a man some years older than her, and a dull and dusty scholar of old books, I cannot imagine. But she was always very attentive to my needs whilst I was staying here. She would come to my room on some trivial errand or other, and would smile and flash her pretty eyes at me. Sometimes, we would chat a little, and she would laugh at my simple little witticisms. As my stay here proceeded, we began to talk more and more, about all sorts of things, and our conversations were always lightened as much by Rosie's humorous remarks as by my own attempts at wit. She was – so it seemed to me – far too intelligent and lively-minded for much of the routine and menial work she was being asked to do here, and I found her very good company in every way. When I left here to return to London – which was where I was living at the time – I felt more cheerful and light-hearted than I had for several years, and I could hardly wait to return here again.

"An opportunity soon arose, as old Viscount Bellbrook, the father of the present viscount, sent me an invitation to a summer garden party he was throwing here. I had attended such events before, and knew what enjoyable occasions they could be. But this time, my over-riding desire was to see Rosie Hilton again. It may sound absurd for a man of my age, but the truth is that I had fallen madly in love with her, in a way I never had with anyone before.

"We ran across each other quite soon after I arrived here, and I was delighted to find that she seemed as pleased to see me as I was to see her. My stay on that occasion was for only a few days, but, despite all the other events which were taking place then, we still managed to spend many enjoyable moments together. I should like to say, incidentally, that it never occurred to me then that she had any other admirer who might perhaps feel he had more claim upon her affections than I did, and she certainly never gave me the slightest reason for thinking that that might be the case. I don't suppose anyone as madly intoxicated as I was ever considers that possibility, or, if they do, they don't give it any heed.

"She told me then – in response to some trivial observation of mine – that she was bored with her current existence here, and yearned for something different and more exciting. When I asked her what she had in mind, she confessed that it had long been an ambition of hers to live in London, and see something of London Society. I suggested that it might be something of a gamble to give up what was a very good post here for the uncertainties of life in London, but she shook her head, and declared her confidence in her own abilities.

"'So long as I could get off to a good start, I'm sure I would do very well,' said she with a sweet smile.

"'If you are sure that that is what you want,' said I, 'then, if you like, you could stay at my house until you got everything sorted out.'

"'That is very kind of you, Dr Sidgwick,' said she, 'but I couldn't possibly impose upon you in that way. I wouldn't want you to think I come as a beggar.'

"'I wouldn't think that for a moment, Rosie,' said I, laughing, 'but, if it would make you feel better able to accept my offer, you can act as my housekeeper for as long as you wish, and I will pay you accordingly.'

"'Do you not have a housekeeper already?' she asked.

"I shook my head. 'My household is a very modest one. I have a cook and a maid, and that is all. We could accommodate you very easily.'

"Rosie agreed to the proposition then. She seemed very pleased and excited at the prospect of moving to London, and, I don't mind admitting, I was thrilled at the thought of having her in my household. And so, the die was cast. We exchanged a couple of brief letters, and a month later she moved into my house. This, I must say, was a great success in every way. Rosie had such an easy, unpretentious charm that she got on well with everyone she met, no matter what their station in life, and – I need hardly say – I loved having her there. The whole atmosphere of the house seemed to be lifted by her presence. I felt a little guilty for having poached one of Viscount Bellbrook's senior domestic staff, but I thought that he would probably find a suitable replacement without too much difficulty, whereas to me, of course, Rosie was quite unique and irreplaceable.

"Soon after her arrival in London, Rosie began to make enquiries about employment opportunities, and registered with various agencies. I followed her progress in this respect with great interest, and often discussed it with her, but I admit that in my heart I never really wanted to encourage her too much, for, of course I could not bear the thought of her leaving. Weeks passed, then months, during which my feelings for Rosie did not diminish at all, but, on the contrary, intensified. I took her to the theatre, I took her to concerts, I took her to all sorts of interesting places and events. Some times we went for walks on Hampstead Heath and other pretty spots. At length, I resolved to ask her if she would do me the great honour of becoming my wife.

"I remember the day very clearly. Rosie had been out most of the afternoon on various errands, and, my own work for the day being completed, I was sitting with a cup of tea, waiting impatiently for her to return. Each time I heard footsteps on the pavement outside the front of the house, I would look up expectantly, but then sigh with disappointment as they passed by without stopping. Eventually, much later than I had expected, I heard the footsteps pause, and, next moment, heard Rosie turning her key in the lock of the front door. I went out into the hall to greet her. She gave me a beaming smile, and looked, I thought, prettier than ever. I offered her a cup of tea, but she said she would get a fresh pot for us both, so I told her to bring it into the drawing-room, when she could tell me all that she had been doing that afternoon. In my mind, this was all just a preamble to my proposing marriage to her, but – alas! – that part of my plan was never to be fulfilled.

"She came into the drawing-room with excitement and happiness on her features and in her voice. I remarked that she looked pleased about something, and asked her what it was. She thereupon described to me how, following a preliminary interview three days previously, of which I was aware, she had now been interviewed for a second time by a nobleman who kept a large household in Belgrave Square. The result of this was that he had offered her the post of housekeeper, to start as soon as she was able. Rosie was naturally as thrilled at this as she could possibly be, and I congratulated her with as much enthusiasm as I could muster. Inside, though, I felt more forlorn than I have ever felt in my life, as my own private hopes were dashed. I told her to keep in touch with me, and that if she ever found that her new life was not quite so happy as she had hoped, she would always be welcome to return to my humble household at any time.

"Several weeks passed, and, as I had heard nothing from Rosie, I ventured to write her a letter, describing some trivial details of my own daily life and asking how she was getting on in her new circumstances. After a week or two, I received an extremely brief reply, saying that she was too busy to respond in any detail at the moment, but would write again later – although she never did. Many months then passed without a word from her, until, eventually, I wrote again, on some pretext or other, expressing the hope that she was thriving and that things were going successfully for her. To this letter I received a prompt reply, but it was not from Rosie. It was, rather, from someone called George St John-Wallington, who described himself as secretary to Lord Margrave. In it, he informed me that Lord and Lady Margrave were not at home at present, but were spending some time at their house in the south of France. However, he informed me, he had been authorised to thank all those who had kindly written to express their best wishes on the recent happy occasion of the wedding of David, Lord Margrave, and Rose Hilton.

"After that letter, I made no further attempt to communicate with Rosie. My life continued as before, at least in its external appearances, but with – from my point of view – a permanent shadow of sadness hanging over it. I wrote many essays, I wrote a book, my name became well known in my field and I was, five years ago, offered and accepted the chair in Moral Philosophy at St Francis's College, Oxford." Professor Sidgwick paused. "But," he continued after a moment, "I would willingly give all of that up this instant if I could have Rosie Hilton back again."

Professor Sidgwick paused for a few moments. "So, gentlemen," he said at length, with a sigh and a shake of the head, "as it seems likely from what you have told me that the man who accosted me earlier – John Turner – wished simply to give me a piece of his mind, as people say, and upbraid me for stealing away his sweetheart, then, if he had been less violent, aggressive and frightening in his manner, I could have informed him that the exact same fate as he wished to complain about had, in turn, befallen me."

We all remained in silence for some time after the professor had finished speaking. I do not think that any of us could think of anything that would be worth saying after such a very personal and heart-felt account. Out in the hall, the sound of the viscount's many visitors, talking and laughing, had been growing louder in the last few minutes. Abruptly, the door opened, and Viscount Bellbrook himself entered. He looked enquiringly at our no-doubt solemn faces, and frowned.

"We have just finished going through it all," said Holmes, with a glance at Professor Sidgwick's tired and melancholy features.

"Yes," responded Sidgwick. "I'll give you the gist tomorrow morning," he said, addressing the viscount, "if that is all right. You don't need me to go anywhere tonight do you?" he continued, addressing Superintendent Huggins.

"No, sir," replied the latter. "That won't be necessary. We can take a formal statement tomorrow morning."

As the three policemen, Holmes and I made our way back down to Bellbrook Halt, where the police vehicle was waiting for us, the clouds in the sky broke up completely, and, by the time we reached the station, the moon was shining brightly.

"What a business!" said Superintendent Huggins with feeling, which brought forth murmurs of agreement from everyone. "I've never known anything like it," he continued. Then he turned to Sherlock Holmes. "Mr Holmes," said he, "I would just like to say that I had my doubts about you when you first arrived, and didn't think we should need your assistance. But everything that has happened since has proved to me that I was quite wrong. You have led us from darkness to light, from complete ignorance to full knowledge of the case, in a way I have never seen before in my entire police career. It is the finest display of detective-work I have ever witnessed." With that, he put out his hand and shook Holmes's hand vigorously.

"I agree with every word the superintendent has spoken," said Sergeant Maldon, and he, too, shook Holmes's hand.

"Thank you," said Holmes, visibly taken aback by this generous appreciation. "I am grateful for your compliments, gentlemen. But, really, I have no special talents. I have simply trained myself to always observe the details of a case, and never to rely merely on general impressions. For it is almost always in the details that the solution of a problem is to be found."

The engine-driver, Arthur Milbank, and the guard, James Morris, both recovered from their injuries after some considerable time, although neither ever worked again. When they had recovered sufficiently to answer questions, their testimony shed light on what had happened on that fateful evening. What was particularly striking about this was that on almost every point, their account confirmed Sherlock Holmes's speculations.

"When we were preparing the engine for the evening run to Parlingham," said Arthur Milbank, "Turner told me that he thought he had just seen the man that he regarded as having ruined his life by luring Rose Hilton away to London. I told him to forget it. 'All that is long gone,' I said, 'and in any case, it's probably not the same man. Don't dwell on it.' But he wouldn't let the matter drop, and told me, five minutes later, that the man had just approached him – 'as bold as brass' said Turner – and asked him about getting off the train at Bellbrook. Turner said he had told the man to let the guard know if he wanted to get off there. 'Well,' says I to Turner, 'if the guard gives us the signal, I'll stop there, and if he doesn't, I won't.'

"When we reached Bellbrook Halt, we hadn't had a signal, so I didn't stop, but I was going slowly in case a signal came late. Turner was bobbing about, looking first out of the nearside, then out of the offside. Then he said 'There he is! He's just jumped out! I'm going to tell him exactly what I think of him!'

"I told Turner not to be such a fool. 'It won't do any good!' I told him. I took hold of him then to stop him jumping off the footplate, but he was driven mad with anger and hatred, and I could hardly hold him. We wrestled like that for a few moments, then with a lunge he tried to pull away from me, but as I was clinging onto him, we went flying off the engine together, and onto the ground. I think I must have banged my head, because I don't remember any more until I woke up in broad daylight in a bed in the infirmary at Parlingham."

The guard of the train, James Morris, gave the following additional testimony: "I was late getting back to the train at Fairfield Junction. No-one had told me that they wanted to alight at Bellbrook, but as we were passing slowly through the station there, I thought I heard one of the carriage doors slam. There was no-one on the platform, so I quickly looked out of the window on the other side. A tall, thin man was standing there, dusting himself down, and it was clear he had just jumped down from the train.

"As I was standing there, wondering who he was, and why he had adopted such a dangerous course of action, I saw both Milbank and Turner fall together from the engine footplate ahead of me. I had no idea what was happening, but realised that the train was now in a very dangerous state. I started to apply the brake, but it didn't seem to achieve much, so I thought the only thing I could do would be to run along the side of the line and climb aboard the locomotive footplate, and then bring the train to a halt. I opened the door on the onside, jumped down and set off. The train was going so slowly that I made good progress and had almost reached the engine when my feet suddenly slipped from under me. For a second I was skidding about uncontrollably, then I must have struck my head on something because I remember nothing more but darkness and pain."

When the inquest on John Turner was finally concluded, having been adjourned twice so that the above testimony could be included in the evidence, it was adjudged that the blow from Professor Sidgwick's walking-stick was undoubtedly the cause of death. No charges of any kind were laid against Sidgwick, however, the court accepting that he had acted entirely in self-defence while in a state of extreme fear.

As Sherlock Holmes and I travelled back to London the day after the dramatic events I have described above, my friend remained in silent thought for some considerable time. At length I asked him what he was thinking about.

"I was hoping," he replied, "that I never fall in love."

"Why so?" I asked in surprise.

"Just consider, Watson, the misery inflicted upon all concerned in this case by that simple-sounding notion: one man dead before his time, several others whose lives or careers have been adversely affected."

"I don't think falling in love always involves such dire consequences," I remarked.

"Perhaps not," said Sherlock Holmes, "but you cannot be certain of that, Watson, and it is not a risk I would wish to take."

THE HUNGARIAN DOCTOR

DURING THE TIME I shared chambers in Baker Street with Mr Sherlock Holmes, the well-known criminal investigator, our visitors came from almost every walk of life. In itself, this meant little to Holmes, for as his interest lay entirely in the problem a client might bring to him for solution, the client's particular rank or station in life was perfectly irrelevant to him, except insofar as it might affect the case. For myself, however, I must say I found this panorama of human life endlessly fascinating, not least because it was almost impossible to predict from a client's appearance or antecedents what strange tale he or she would recount.

Being a trained medical man myself, it was perhaps understandable that I should feel a heightened interest when a fellow medico called to consult my friend, and I was always fascinated to hear what others had done when they had completed their medical training. One man, I recall, had joined the Army Medical Department, as I had, although his subsequent experiences had been quite different from my own. Another had sailed for a season as surgeon on a whaling ship in the Arctic seas. Yet others had served their first years of general practice in places as far apart as Cornwall and the north of Scotland, and most of the cases they laid before Sherlock Holmes were as different from each other as their professional experience had been geographically different. Any one of a dozen such cases would make a worthy addition to this series of tales, but none was perhaps so striking in its details nor so surprising in its outcome as the strange case of Dr Kazinczy and the bandaged man. This case may not have provided Holmes with any great opportunities for the exercise of those powers of observation and inference for which he was noted; but it nevertheless contained features which made it exceptionally memorable, especially for me, as the reader will see.

It was a cold, damp period in February 1885, the sort of weather which always made the old wound in my leg ache painfully. It was particularly bad that morning, I remember, and after breakfast I had pulled my chair closer to the fire and attempted to distract myself with the morning papers, but they contained little of interest. Holmes, meanwhile, curled up in his chair with his old mouse-coloured dressing-gown wrapped around him, had lit his pipe and pored for some time over the personal columns of *The Times*, groaning loudly with annoyance from time to time. At length, with a snort, he had cast the paper aside, sprung from his chair and paced about the room, eventually ending up by the window, where he stood for some time, surveying the scene in the street outside.

"I believe I have some talent, Watson," said he abruptly, turning from the window.

"Of course," I replied.

"And yet, day after day, I have no work to do, nothing to which I can apply that talent. Another day as barren as the last few and I believe that, like some powerful engine which is not connected to any useful work, my racing thoughts will wrack my brain to pieces!"

I was about to make some mollifying remark, when, all at once, there came the sharp jangling of the door-bell.

"Perhaps this is a client for you," I remarked in as cheery a voice as I could muster.

"I sincerely hope so," returned my companion, in a sceptical tone.

A moment later, a pleasant-faced, smartly-dressed man was shown into the room. He was, I judged, in his late thirties, and his neat black frock-coat and silk hat indicated a professional man, perhaps a doctor, a suggestion all but confirmed by the small leather bag he carried in his hand.

"Come in, come in," said Holmes, casting off his dressing-gown and pulling his chair back a little from the hearth. "Pray take a seat and tell us what we can do for you on this damp and dreary morning."

"My name," began our visitor when he had seated himself beside the fire, "is Laszlo Kazinczy. My family home, as you might guess from my name, is not in England, but in Hungary, where I trained as a physician."

"And yet," said Holmes, "you have lived here some time. Your clothes, your shoes, your hat," he explained in answer to a querying expression from the other: "they are all, I should say, of English manufacture, and although of good quality, are clearly not new. Your medical bag in particular, handsome though it is, shows signs of some years' wear. My colleague, Dr Watson, here," he continued, nodding in my direction, "is also a medical man, and his bag regrettably shows exactly the same pattern of wear."

"You are quite correct," said Kazinczy with a smile of appreciation at Holmes's observations. "If your colleague is a medical man, he may find my account of particular interest, for it does have a medical aspect to it. But, first, I shall tell you how I came to be here. For a few years after qualifying, I worked in a large hospital in Budapest, increasing my knowledge and skill in all branches of medicine. At length I became particularly interested in the diseases and problems of the human eye, and resolved to increase my knowledge of this subject as much as I could.

"At that time, the greatest eye-expert in Europe was your Professor Whitburn, here in England, so I wrote to him, expressing my interest in his work. His response was a very friendly one. He invited me to attend a series of lectures he was about to give in London, and when I arrived here he put me up in his own house for a while. Fortunately, I was already able to speak English, although not so well as I do now. Anyway, to cut a long story short, I became very friendly with my host – who is a most generous man – and with his family, too, including his pretty daughter, Elizabeth.

"At length, Elizabeth did me the honour of consenting to be my wife. I had by then been working for some time, in a part-time capacity, as a dispensary assistant to an elderly physician, Dr Gildersleeve, in Hackney, but saw that I should have to secure a more lucrative position if I were to support a wife. I therefore entered into correspondence with the Royal College of Surgeons to see what would be required of me if I were to practise here, and having at length satisfied the Royal College as to my qualifications and abilities, I went into partnership with Dr Gildersleeve. His practice was certainly not the most fashionable in London, but it has kept me busy for a few years now, especially since Dr Gildersleeve himself retired. My patients are, I must say, as varied as anyone could wish for. One minute I will be attending to the medical requirements of a well-off financial manager from the leafier parts of the northern fringe of Hackney or Stoke Newington, the next I will be consulted by a coal-heaver or street-sweeper from down Whitechapel way – and each of them brings his own unique problems to me for solution."

"Your practice sounds somewhat like my own," observed Holmes with a chuckle. "And the interesting thing, I find, is that one can never predict with any accuracy which of these very varied clients will bring an especially interesting problem. Indeed, the cases of the poorer clients are not infrequently more fascinating than those of the wealthy!"

"Absolutely," returned our visitor with a smile. "To hear you speak as you do gives me confidence that you will not simply dismiss my story as of no interest."

Holmes shook his head. "I never dismiss what a client has to tell me," he remarked in a vehement tone. "But, come! I believe we understand your circumstances now. Pray tell us what has occurred to bring you here today."

"It all happened last night," replied his client after a moment. "It was about ten minutes to six and my evening surgery-hour was almost over. I had not been especially busy, and I was tidying my consulting-room and thinking about what I was shortly going to have for my supper when there came a tap at the door.

"'Come in!' I called, and in walked a tall, gaunt-looking man I had never seen before, wearing a heavy black overcoat. He had dark, deep-set eyes, and a large, hooked nose, which gave him the appearance of a fierce bird of prey. There was a purposefulness in his tread as he came to the desk which caught my attention. I think it passed through my mind, the way such thoughts do, that, if the firmness of his step was anything to go by, there didn't seem to be much wrong with him. 'Take a seat,' I said. 'What can I do for you?'

"'It is not for me,' he replied as he sat down, 'but for the one I represent.' Although his English was perfectly good, it was delivered in an odd accent, which I could not place. I dare say I myself have an accent which native English-speakers notice but of which I am unaware, but this gentleman's accent was, I think, considerably stronger than my own.

"'I see,' said I after a moment. 'Is there some reason why the gentleman in question cannot come here himself?'

"'There are two reasons,' said he. 'In the first place, he is very ill and in some considerable pain. In the second place-' He paused. 'I must be discreet when I speak of this, doctor. You should know that the gentleman I serve is not from this country. In his own land he is most eminent, both an aristocrat and a scholar. He has tried to educate his fellow-countrymen, to lead them away from their old barbarity, to take their place in the modern world. But this mission has aroused the enmity of some, who are, for their own selfish reasons, opposed to his benign reforms. They call themselves The League of the Golden Ribbon, but should call themselves "The Scarlet Ribbon" for all the bloodletting they have caused. When his Excellency became ill, it was thought advisable that he leave the country for a time until he had recovered. This recovery has not occurred naturally, and it is feared that he needs medical assistance. Meanwhile, his enemies are looking for him all over Europe and the latest information we have is that they are here in England. As you will perhaps now realise, his presence here in England is a secret, known only to his closest and most trusted allies. If his whereabouts were known to his enemies, his life would not be worth two farthings. He therefore instructed me to bring a doctor to examine him, a doctor, he stressed, who is as discreet and trustworthy as he is skilled in all branches of medicine. I have therefore made numerous searching inquiries, Dr Kazinczy, and your name has been mentioned to me several times as someone who is as discreet as he is skilful.'

"'I am flattered,' I said, 'but a little surprised. I had no idea that my name was known to anyone outside my own parish. May I ask who it was that recommended me?'

"My visitor put his finger to his lips. 'I would rather not say,' he replied. 'You will understand, I believe, that inquiries as to the discretion of someone are themselves subject to discretion.'

"'Yes, of course,' I said. 'Can you tell me, then, something of the patient himself – his age, for instance, and general health?'

"'He is about forty-five years of age,' my visitor replied. 'He has a very strong constitution, and his health has always been first class – until, that is, his present illness.'

"'What are the symptoms of his affliction, then?'

"'The chief one is a great pain in his left side. Here,' he added, indicating with his finger-tips a place between his ribs and his waist. 'Because of this, he finds it very difficult to find a position in which he is not in pain. Even walking, which you might suppose would not be affected in any way, is so painful as to be almost impossible.'

"'I see,' I said, thinking to myself that it sounded like a kidney stone. 'Well, I will certainly go and examine him, but you must understand that I may not be able to solve his problems straight away. When would he like me to visit him?'

"'Immediately,' said my visitor in a firm tone. 'I have a cab waiting outside.'

"'Very well,' I said, 'but you must give me five minutes to get ready. This my visitor agreed to, and I hurried upstairs to tell my wife I should be going out. I took the opportunity to fortify myself with a slice of bread and cheese, then, packing everything I thought I might need into my bag, and picking up a volume of medical reference, I informed my visitor that I was ready. 'May I take your name?' I asked. 'Just for my records,' I added, as he seemed to hesitate.

"'You may call me Ferdinand,' said he at length.

"'Is that your first name or your last name?' I asked.

"'First name, last name – what does it matter?' said he with a shake of the head. 'From your point of view, Dr Kazinczy, it is my only name.'

"As he shook his head, my eye was drawn to a curious scar on his upper cheek, just below his left eye, which was in the shape of a large 'X'. I had noticed it earlier, without really thinking about it, but now my gaze must have rested on it a little, for he put his hand up to it and touched it with his finger-tips. 'It is not pretty, that,' said he. 'But at least I came out of the encounter alive; the other man was not so fortunate. Put my name down, then,' he continued in an irritable tone, 'and we can be off.'

"'Very well,' said I, writing his name on one of my sheets of paper. A minute later, we were in the cab and rattling away in the darkness.

"As I watched the street-lamps passing us by, as we turned south and made our way down towards Bethnal Green, I wondered how far we should have to go, and I asked my companion.

"'That I cannot tell you,' he returned. 'Where my master is in hiding is a closely guarded secret.'

"'Oh, yes, of course,' said I quickly, fearing I had been indiscreet in asking the question. 'I understand. Well,' I added with a smile, 'I don't mind, so long as I can get back home before bed-time!'

"My companion regarded me with a cold look, and did not return my smile. '"Before bed-time,"' he repeated in a sombre tone. 'Yes, that should be possible.' After that, he lapsed once more into complete silence.

"From Bethnal Green we made our way down to Shoreditch, and so across the river, at length pulling up before London Bridge station. Without a word, my companion opened the door, stepped from the cab, and held the door open for me to follow him. I assumed that we were about to take a train to somewhere in Kent, and hoped that it would not be too far, but, to my surprise, we passed the front of the station without pausing, and walked round the side. There, a private closed carriage stood. At our approach, a man who had been sitting on the pavement edge, smoking a pipe, sprang to his feet and pulled open the carriage door.

"In a moment we were in the carriage, whereupon, to my surprise, my companion drew the curtains and pulled down the blinds on all the windows 'It is better for you if you don't know where we are going,' said he. 'When I say "better", I mean "safer",' he added after a moment in a grim tone. 'Our enemies are very violent men, who would slit your throat as soon as look at you. What you do not know, you cannot be forced to divulge.'

"'I see,' I said, feeling a little unnerved at the thought of these violent, desperate men.

"After that, we did not speak again for a long time. But the silence in which we passed the journey had a surprising consequence. In the absence of conversation or any other distraction, I found myself listening with unusual attention to the noise of the traffic in the street and the sound of our carriage wheels upon the cobbles. Round a sharp right-hand corner we rattled, the carriage swaying as we turned, then round a second corner, then a third. I had almost completely lost my bearings by this time, but I felt fairly sure that we were not making our way down into Kent, as I had at first supposed, but perhaps to somewhere in the south-western suburbs. Further corners followed, this way and that, until I felt quite bewildered by all the changes of direction. But then a different sound came to my ears, which surprised me so much that I fear that my mouth fell open. I glanced at my companion and saw that he was watching me closely.

"'The traffic is very dense at this time of day,' I remarked, to conceal, as I hoped, what I was really thinking. For what I had heard was the distinctive sound that vehicles make when crossing one of the long bridges over the Thames. If I was right – and I felt sure that I was – then we were heading north again, back the way we had come! Clearly, these people were prepared to go to great lengths to keep their whereabouts secret and throw any pursuers off the scent.

"After several minutes of what seemed like very slow progress, we abruptly lurched forward and the horse broke into a rapid trot. Presumably, we were through the City and making our way out into the suburbs again. We then raced along with scarcely a pause, for some considerable time, our carriage swaying alarmingly at times with the great speed at which we were travelling, until at length we slowed a little, and I thought we must be reaching our destination. Where we were I had no idea, as I had no way of knowing which road we had taken north from the City, but I judged that we must be at least as far as Highbury or Dalston, and perhaps much further than that. For all I could tell, we might even be in the vicinity of my own surgery.

"My companion lifted one of the blinds a little and peered out. I could not imagine what he could see, as the night was a black one, but he evidently saw something, for as he lowered the blind again he turned to me and spoke.

"'We are almost there,' said he in a lugubrious tone. 'I must warn you not to say anything unless you are asked, doctor. My master does not like idle chatter, and he is in such grave distress that his reaction is likely to be an irritable one.'

"'I understand,' I replied. I felt a little insulted that he should consider that I, a professional man, would engage in 'idle chatter', as he put it, but I said nothing. Perhaps, I reflected, in the country from which they came – wherever that might be – such insulting language was commonplace.

"'We have had to secure the assistance of one or two local people,' continued my companion. 'They have been sworn to secrecy as to my master's whereabouts, and have been made to understand that any loose talk could cost the lives of all of us, but other than that, they know little. The best thing for you to do is to ignore them. If you wish to request anything you need, you should do it through me.' I nodded, but that was evidently insufficient affirmation, for he fixed me with a piercing stare. 'Do you understand?' he demanded, in what I can only describe as a threatening tone.

"'Yes, certainly,' I replied. With every pronouncement my companion made, my spirits sank a little lower. I began to wonder what on earth I had let myself in for. I hope I don't sound too mean or selfish, but I confess that my sense of anticipation, the focus of my thoughts, had already shifted from the patient I was about to see to the moment when I would have done my duty as a physician and could get away from these people and go home again.

"Presently, I heard the driver call something to the horse as he reined him in, and we came to an abrupt halt.

"'We are here,' said Ferdinand, rising to his feet. 'Don't forget what I have told you!'

"I followed him from the carriage and along a narrow, muddy path. Ahead of us in the darkness, the yet darker shape of a large house loomed up. A small lantern by the front door threw a weak, yellowy light upon the path, and it was well that it did, for there was not the tiniest speck of light from any other source in any direction. Clearly, wherever we were, we were well away from the public roads and streets of the north London suburbs.

"As we approached the lantern, I saw that it was fixed on a large, heavy-looking porch at the front of the house, the sort of porch which is a common feature of very large old houses. Within the dark recess of this porch was the front door. My companion thumped on the door with his gloved fist, and after a moment it was opened a crack. 'Let us in,' commanded Ferdinand in an imperious tone, at which the door was pulled back a little and we made our way into a dimly-lit hallway. 'Dowse that light out there!' said Ferdinand. 'It's not needed now, and it gives our position away! This way, doctor!' he continued, turning to me.

"I followed him along the hall, and up a dark, uncarpeted staircase. On the wall near the top, just where the stair took a sharp turn to the right, a small candle was flickering fitfully in a sconce, in front of an old enamelled religious picture of some sort. When we reached the landing at the top of the stairs, it was almost pitch black, but Ferdinand was evidently familiar with the layout of the house, for he pressed on without pause, and I followed him as well as I could in the darkness. Abruptly, we halted, and a narrow slit of light near the floor indicated that we had reached a door.

"'My master is in here,' said he in a low tone. 'He may be asleep, for he has taken something to relieve the pain which kept him awake most of last night.'

"'Paregoric?' I asked.

"'No, that was too weak, so we got him a stronger tincture of opium.'

"'What, laudanum?'

"'Yes.'

"'I hope you are aware that laudanum is very dangerous stuff,' I said. 'There is only a small difference between an effective dose and a fatal dose.'

"'Don't you worry about that, doctor,' said Ferdinand in a dismissive tone. 'You just concentrate on healing your patient!'

"'But I must worry about it,' I insisted. I was, I admit, irritated by his condescending manner. 'There is not much point in my solving the problem of his pain if he then kills himself with laudanum.'

"'Very well,' said Ferdinand after a moment. 'I shall keep an eye on him.' He rapped with his knuckles on the wooden panelling of the door, then pushed it open.

"The room beyond was dimly lit by two oil-lamps, both turned down very low. The air was thick and heavy with a sweet, burnt smell, which I recognized at once.

"'Someone has been smoking opium in here.' I said.

"'My master asked for it, to ease his pain.'

"'What, on top of the laudanum? He will surely kill himself, sooner rather than later, at this rate! We must open the window, and get some fresh air in here at once, or I myself shall pass out and then I shall not be able to help him!'

"Somewhat reluctantly, it seemed, Ferdinand helped me pull down the top half of the window, and a strong gust of cold air blew into the room. There was a loud groan from behind me, and I turned to see that the man on the bed was stirring. 'I'll examine the patient now,' I said to Ferdinand. I asked him to bring one of the lamps to the bedside and turn it up. Then, just as I was bending over him, the man on the bed threw back his covers, turned my way and began to raise himself up.

"With an involuntary cry, I stopped and took a step backwards. For a moment, I could not make out in that dim light what it was I was looking at. Where I had expected to see my patient's face, there was nothing but a grimy, featureless lump. Then, as Ferdinand brought the lamp closer, I was just able to see that the sick man's head was wound round and round with dirty-looking bandages, so that it was completely covered, and nothing could be seen of his face or his hair. From two narrow slits in the bandage, a pair of sharp eyes looked out at me, reflecting the light of the lamp.

"Abruptly, I felt Ferdinand's hand on my arm. 'You are unnerved by your patient's appearance,' he whispered, his mouth so close behind me that I could feel his breath upon my ear. 'Do not concern yourself, doctor. He had an accident with some boiling water, and his face is covered to protect his raw skin. It is irrelevant to the malady for which he requires your aid.'

"'Who is this?' interrupted the man on the bed, in a deep, unpleasant voice.

"'It is the doctor,' responded Ferdinand. 'He has come to attend to you.'

"Without warning, the man on the bed shot out his hand and seized my arm in a vice-like grip. 'Let me see,' he said, drawing me closer to him. 'Do you know what will happen to you if you break your trust?' he demanded of me.

"I hesitated, unsure as to his meaning. 'I know that everything must be kept secret,' I responded at length. I would have said more, but at that moment he let out a loud cry of pain, released his grip on my arm and collapsed back onto the bed.

"I signalled to Ferdinand to bring the lamp closer, and then proceeded to make a general examination of the man on the bed."

Dr Kazinczy paused and ran his fingers through his hair. "Was any medical examination ever conducted in such strange circumstances!" said he with a shake of the head. "I felt I was living through some horrible dark nightmare from which I hoped I might soon wake up. But, for the moment, I knew I must carry on. I will not weary you with the details of my examination. No doubt you are familiar with it, Dr Watson," he continued, addressing me.

I nodded. "Familiar enough," I replied, "although I have never been called upon to do it myself since I qualified."

"Suffice it to say, then, that the result of my examination was that I was practically certain that the patient was indeed suffering from a stone, just as I had thought when I had first heard his symptoms. I gave them my opinion, and Ferdinand drew me away, as the man on the bed fell back into his opium-induced sleep. 'What should we do, then, doctor?' he asked me in a low tone.

"'You must get him to a hospital as quickly as possible.'

"'Impossible!' he cried. 'Whatever needs to be done, must be done here, and by you!'

"I explained to him that, in such a case, surgery was always a last resort, and that however severe the pain might be at the moment, it could pass away as abruptly as it had started. I asked him how long the patient had suffered from the pain in his side.

"'About three days,' said he. 'The first day was weak pain, yesterday and today is severe pain.'

"'Then this is not what drove him from his homeland?'

"'No. That was something else. Never mind about that. It has cleared up now. We thought it was all part of the same ailment, but perhaps it is not. What is bothering him now is what you have seen. You must do something about it.'

"I considered the matter. I was not sure that I believed anything now that this man who called himself Ferdinand was telling me. First he had said that his master had been ill for several weeks, now he was saying it was a matter of a few days. Just as he had said earlier that their presence in England was a closely-guarded secret, known to no-one, but had also told me that their enemies were in England, looking for them. All I really knew for certain was what I had learnt with my own eyes and my own finger-tips, that the man on the bed was suffering from a stone, probably in or near his kidney. 'Can you get a lemon?' I asked Ferdinand.

"'It may be difficult at this time of the year,' he replied dubiously. 'I will try.'

"'Get three or four,' I said. 'You must get your master to drink a glass of water every hour or two, and into every glass you must squeeze a quarter of a lemon. That is likely to do him as much good as anything I can do for him.'

"'But if that doesn't help, you must cut him open and remove the stone.'

"I shook my head. 'You need a specialist for that. You will find one in a hospital.'

"He insisted that they could not risk going to a hospital, and insisted that I must perform the operation. 'You are a qualified surgeon, are you not?' he demanded. Then he took my arm and led me out of the room, onto the dark landing. 'You must do this,' he said in a harsh tone, the sort of tone which admitted no possibility of contradiction, 'or you will surely have his Excellency's blood on your conscience forever – and perhaps the blood of all of us.'

"He took a firm grip of my elbow and propelled me forward, along the corridor and down the stair. When he spoke again, at the foot of the stair, it was in a louder, threatening tone.

"'If, for whatever selfish reason of your own, you refuse to help us, you may find your decision turns out to be an unfortunate one. In short, you may regret it. Indeed, your whole family may regret it – your wife, for instance.'

"I stopped. 'Are you threatening me?' I asked.

"'No,' said he. 'I am simply warning you, Dr Kazinczy. The warning is for your own good. I have told you of the League of the Golden Ribbon, who would cut your throat for sixpence, and think nothing of it. But there are others, too, faceless men and women who may be all around us even now, as we speak. Some of these are supposed to be on our side, but I cannot control them, and thus cannot answer for them. For your own sake, and that of your family, you must do as I ask.'

"He paused. 'I shall come for you at the same time tomorrow. Please be ready, with everything packed that you might need. Now, Simpson will show you where you can wash your hands.'

"As he spoke, a man materialised out of the darkness in the hall. I think he had been there all the time, but I had not seen him. 'This way,' said he, in a low, guttural voice, and I followed his grey shape along the hall in the darkness. He pushed a door open, and we passed into a plain, bare room, evidently a kitchen, illuminated by a single small lamp which stood on a wooden table in the centre of the room. 'There's the sink,' said my guide.

"I washed my hands under the cold water tap, and, without speaking, the man handed me a piece of rag which was evidently meant to serve as a towel. 'Is there any hot water in the house?' I asked him, as he stood there in silence, watching me.

"He shook his head. 'No. To get hot water, we would have to light the fire here, and I was told not to, in case the smoke from the chimney gave our position away.'

"'Well, if I come again tomorrow I shall need plenty of hot water. Can you tell them?' There was a grunt of assent. 'How did the man upstairs hurt his face?' I asked as I finished drying my hands. 'I heard he scalded it.'

"'"Scalded it"?' the man repeated in a tone of surprise. 'No, there's nothing wrong with his face. Didn't they tell you? He just doesn't want anybody to see it, in case they recognise him.'

"'Yes, of course; I know all about that,' I said quickly. 'I must have just misheard something about his face.'

"'Anyway, I'm not supposed to talk to you,' said the man.

"I nodded, and held my hand up in a gesture of acceptance. 'Of course,' I said. 'I understand.' After that we did not speak again. In my own mind, however, I noted that this was yet another example of contradictory information that I had been given. It almost sounded as if the man who called himself 'Ferdinand' had just been making things up on the spur of the moment, and I began to wonder if anything at all that he had told me was really true.

"My guide led me back to the darkness of the front hall. 'Wait here,' he said, and I heard a door open and close as he disappeared into the darkness.

"I had been standing there for what I suppose was just a minute or two – although in that silent darkness it felt more like a quarter of an hour – when a door opened at the side of the hall, and a figure emerged. As there was a lamp lit in the room beyond – although not a very bright one – I could see it was a young woman with dark hair. As the light was behind her, I could not make out her face very well, but I could see that she was of slim build and carried herself in an elegant sort of way. 'Hello,' I said, more from a sort of instinctive politeness than for any other reason. For a moment, she stopped, and looked at me with piercing eyes and a rigid expression. Then she closed the door behind her, passed on down the hall without replying, and disappeared into the darkness. I was still thinking about her, and wondering who she was, when another door opened, further along the hall, and the man calling himself Ferdinand emerged.

"'I am sorry to keep you waiting,' said he. 'Are you ready to leave now?'

"I said I was and, without further comment, he led the way to the front door. Someone again seemed to materialise out of the darkness, who unbolted the front door and opened it for us.

"As we stepped out of the house, a very sharp, cold wind was blowing, and there were drops of rain in the air. 'Just follow close behind me,' said Ferdinand, and we set off along the muddy path. My eyes had become so accustomed to the inky darkness within the house that the darkness outside now seemed almost light by comparison, and I could see through the murk that a horse and carriage awaited us at the end of the path. Into this carriage we climbed, and away it rattled, into the night.

"Again, we rambled about for thirty or forty minutes, until I was at last discharged at the side of London Bridge station. 'Remember,' said Ferdinand, as I stepped down onto the pavement, 'be ready with everything you will need when I call for you at six o'clock tomorrow evening. In the meantime, not a word to anyone about anything you have seen or heard this evening. Not a word – do you understand? You may be being watched, Dr Kazinczy. And if you break your trust, we shall certainly know about it.' His voice was full of menace as he spoke these last words, and I don't mind admitting to a certain nervousness and apprehension at his threats. I certainly didn't want to risk provoking any of these people to violence."

"And yet," said Sherlock Holmes, "despite his threatening manner, and your own fears and anxieties, you have come to consult us."

"I could hardly sleep at all last night," said our visitor after a moment, "and lay awake for hours, going over and over the matter in my mind, trying to decide what to do. Eventually, I decided that, despite what Ferdinand had said to me, I must tell someone of what I had become involved in, someone, ideally, who had some familiarity with London's darkest and most mysterious happenings. I could think of no-one known personally to me who might be suitable, and was for a time at a loss, until I thought of you, Mr Holmes. Although I don't generally follow the criminal or other sensational news very closely, I have from time to time read of your involvement in fascinating investigations of all kinds, and I thought you might be the very man."

"You have done the right thing, Dr Kazinczy. It is a remarkable account you have given us, and certainly a dark and mysterious one. Do you believe you have been followed on your way here?"

"I cannot be sure. This morning I saw a man across the street from my surgery who appeared to be watching the house, and I thought it might be one of Ferdinand's men. It is for that reason I have brought my medical bag with me, so that I can always say I was here to visit an old patient who has moved from Hackney to the West End."

Holmes nodded. "I take it from what you have told us," said he, "that you did not tell your wife about your evening's adventure."

"Only in the very broadest of terms. I did not wish to recount the matter to her in any detail, as I knew she would become so anxious about it. More than that, I knew she would do her utmost to prevent my going to see these strange, menacing people again."

"But you are determined to go?"

"I must. Quite apart from Ferdinand's threats, I don't see that I have any choice, Mr Holmes. I may feel less than enthusiastic about Ferdinand and the others, and more than a little concerned about all their vicious and violent enemies – the League of the Golden Ribbon and the others – but, when all is said and done, I now have a patient there who has clearly been in severe pain. I have diagnosed what I believe to be the cause of that pain, but the oath I took as a medical man is worth less than nothing if I don't at least try to do something to alleviate his suffering."

"Bravo!" said Holmes with enthusiasm. "Well said!"

"Are you confident," I asked our visitor, "of performing the appropriate surgery on your patient if necessary?"

"I very much hope it doesn't come to that, Dr Watson, but if I have to do it, then I shall."

"Your patient will need anaesthetic. Which do you favour?"

"Ether. I regard it as safer than any of the alternatives."

"I am inclined to agree with you. I have a suggestion to make, then," I said. "What I propose is that I accompany you tonight, and act as your anaesthetist."

Our visitor's features expressed surprise. "That is an extremely generous offer, Dr Watson," said he after a moment, "but I could not possibly accept it. I feel there is danger in that house."

"No doubt, but I have faced greater danger before. You cannot both perform the surgical procedure safely and also be responsible for the anaesthetic. That is too much to ask of anyone. Nor can you with much confidence ask anyone else to do it. I, on the other hand, have considerable experience with anaesthetics. I absolutely insist on coming. Besides, if I come with you, that gives you a better excuse for calling in here today than visiting some old, mythical patient. You can tell them that you must have someone with you who is experienced in the use of anaesthetic, and that you at once thought of me, whom you met some years ago. Have you ever spent any time in Bart's?"

"What, St Bartholomew's Hospital? Yes, I spent over six months there, assisting one of the best surgeons in England. That was part of what I had to do to convince the Royal Society of my fitness to practise medicine here."

"Excellent!" I cried. "That is where I did much of my initial training. When were you there?"

"About ten years ago."

"So was I. So, if anyone asks, that is where we met! I take it you have all the equipment you need? Good," I said, as he nodded his head. "Then that is settled."

Sherlock Holmes had been sitting without speaking for some time, a frown of concentration on his face.

"What do you think, Holmes?" I asked.

"What I think," responded Holmes after a moment, "is that there is indeed very great danger in that house. I am very reluctant to allow you to go, Watson. On the other hand, if you don't go, I shall feel just as uneasy at Dr Kazinczy going there alone. At least if the two of you are there together, you can, in a sense, share the danger, and each keep a watch over the other."

"What will *you* do?" I asked.

"I shall try to learn a little more about these singular people and the house they are occupying."

"I cannot think where you could possibly start," remarked Kazinczy. "It seems an impossible task."

"Come, come," said Holmes. "As a man of science, doctor, you must appreciate that there is very little which is truly impossible to learn if a man sets his mind to it. The situation is not as hopeless as you make out. In seeking to learn new information, we must start with what we already know. You are convinced that the house you were taken to is to the north of London, rather than the south?"

"Certainly. I have no doubt we crossed the Thames after leaving London Bridge station, and then crossed it again on the way back."

"Then that information will be my starting-point."

"But that still leaves dozens of square miles!"

"Don't let that concern you," said Holmes with a chuckle. "You will go to the old house again this evening at six o'clock, with Dr Watson here. That is enough for you to have to think about. I must warn you again, however, that I fear there is great danger in that house. Do what you are asked to do by these people, and do not speak out of turn in any way that might anger them. Do not under any circumstances mention my name, nor this meeting we have had. Be alert the whole time and keep a watch on each other, but do not be tempted to have any private conversations with each other while you are there, for you will almost certainly be watched closely by these people."

Dr Kazinczy gave me detailed instructions as to how to find his surgery in Hackney, and then, after a brief further discussion of the medical aspects of the matter, he took his leave. Sherlock Holmes went out shortly afterwards without saying where he was going, and I turned to my medical books to refresh my knowledge of the ailment from which Dr Kazinczy's patient was suffering.

At four o'clock in the afternoon I left our chambers with my medical bag in my hand. Holmes had not yet returned nor sent any message, so I had no idea where he had got to, nor whether he had managed to learn anything about the man calling himself Ferdinand and the others.

I took a Metropolitan train from Baker Street to Liverpool Street, and a Great Eastern train from there to Hackney Downs, as Kazinczy had suggested. The trains were very busy, and as I looked round the crowded platforms and packed carriages, I wondered to myself where everyone was going. From their appearance, I imagined that most of them were returning home after a day's work. I doubted if any of these hundreds of people who surrounded me were on an errand quite as strange as mine, bound for that dark and isolated house with its atmosphere of menace, inhabited by people who, according to Kazinczy's account, scarcely seemed to speak at all. I glanced again at my fellow-travellers in the railway carriage, some chatting, others immersed in their evening papers. So familiar and commonplace did it all seem, that for a moment I could scarcely believe my own memory of the account which Dr Kazinczy had given us that morning. With a shake of the head, to try to clear my thoughts, I told myself to concentrate on the medical questions involved, and push all the other aspects of the matter to the back of my mind. Perhaps things would become clearer, perhaps they would not, but at least I could play my part as well as I was able. Then, whatever happened, I should know that I had done my best.

The directions Dr Kazinczy had given me were very clear, so it was a simple task to find his surgery, which I reached at a quarter to six. The maid had clearly been told to expect me, for upon giving her my name, I was at once shown into a room at the back of the house and offered a cup of tea, which I declined.

As I sat there in silence – for the sounds from elsewhere in the house reached me only as faint murmurs – I regret to say that my thoughts had wandered once more from the medical aspects of my prospective journey to the people in that dark house which Dr Kazinczy had visited the night before. Who were they? Where had they come from?

My thoughts were interrupted by the sudden opening of the door, and Kazinczy put his head in.

"If you are ready, Dr Watson, we had best be off. Our guide is here."

"Ferdinand?"

"Yes. I have managed to convince him, with some difficulty, that I need you there this evening to administer the anaesthetic, but he wishes to see you before we leave."

I followed Kazinczy into his consulting-room. A tall, thin-faced man was standing by the desk, a grim, almost menacing expression on his features. He cast a cold, calculating eye over me as I entered.

"What is your name?" said he, without preamble.

"Watson," I replied.

"Do you have experience in what you will be required to do this evening?"

"Yes."

"Where are you in practice?"

"I'm not. I was an Army surgeon, but was badly wounded in Afghanistan, and was eventually pensioned off."

"Where do you live, then? I may need to get in touch with you again, so I must have your address."

I hesitated. I did not feel inclined to give my private address to this stranger just because he demanded it. On the other hand, I did not wish to arouse his suspicions in any way, or create any difficulties for Kazinczy. "221b, Baker Street," I said at length.

"Baker Street is not the cheapest place to live in London," he remarked, "especially for someone getting by on a wound pension."

"That is true," I returned, "but living close to the centre of town does have its advantages. I can get to most places on foot, and thus save on travelling costs."

"Where did you qualify?" he asked abruptly, as if he had not listened to my previous response.

"Here, in London."

"And where did you meet Dr Kazinczy?"

"At Bart's – St Bartholomew's Hospital."

"I know what Bart's is. What year did you meet him?"

I pretended to think for a moment, as if trying to recollect when it was. "I'm not sure," I said. "About '76 or '77, I think – nearly ten years ago."

"My problem, you see, is this, Dr Watson: I told Dr Kazinczy to be discreet, and tell no-one what he had seen or heard last night, but he went straight off and told you about it. How do I know that you will not do the same? For all I know, you may already have done so."

"I can assure you I have told no-one anything," I responded. "In any case," I added quickly, "I have nothing to tell. All I know, other than the patient's symptoms and Dr Kazinczy's diagnosis, is that the patient is from abroad and does not wish his whereabouts to be generally known."

For a long moment, Ferdinand regarded me in perfect silence, his rigid, cold eyes fixed immovably on mine, as if he would peer into the deepest recesses of my soul. Then, without further remark, he picked up his hat from the desk and turned to the door. "We must go now," he said. "We're late as it is."

A four-wheeler was waiting for us outside, which set off at a fast clip as soon as we were aboard. The journey we took through the dark streets was exactly as Kazinczy had described to us that morning. We alighted at London Bridge station, where a closed carriage awaited us, then set off once more. Throughout the lengthy journey which followed, neither Kazinczy nor I spoke, save only once, and that only very briefly, to discuss some technical questions concerning the anaesthetic. This silence – on my part, at least – was because I feared that if I fell into general conversation I might inadvertently let something slip which would reveal to Ferdinand that I had only met Kazinczy for the first time that very morning, and that had it not been for the chance of my sharing chambers with Sherlock Holmes, whom Kazinczy had come to Baker Street to consult, I should never have met him at all. What thoughts were passing in Kazinczy's mind, I could not, of course, say, but from his silence, I fancied that they were not too dissimilar from my own.

Eventually, after what seemed an absolutely interminable length of time, our carriage abruptly turned off the road into softer, quieter ground, and proceeded vey slowly for some considerable distance before coming to a final halt.

"We are here, gentlemen," said Ferdinand, in a low, sepulchral voice, as he put up one of the window-blinds. The night outside was pitch black. "Follow me."

The man waiting inside the door had evidently been told to look out for us, for he opened the door as we approached along the footpath. "Any news?" demanded Ferdinand in a gruff tone, to which the other man gave a negative reply.

We followed Ferdinand into the dark hall and up the stairs, our feet clattering and echoing on the bare, uncarpeted boards.

"I think you will find that my master is in somewhat better health today," said he as we reached the landing.

"Oh?" responded Kazinczy in a tone of surprise. "You did not say anything about that when we spoke earlier, in my surgery."

"I did not wish you to make any difficulty about coming, perhaps using that as an excuse."

"You had no need to worry on that score," said Kazinczy in an indignant tone. "Once I had examined him last night and made my diagnosis, he became in a sense my patient, and I took on full responsibility for him. Whatever you had told me of him this evening, good or bad, I should still have wanted to come, to assess the matter for myself. Did you manage to get hold of any lemons for him?"

"Yes. He has been having lemon juice all day."

"Good. Let us examine him, then."

Ferdinand pushed open a door and we followed him into a dimly-lit room. Other than a bed, a small table and a single chair, the room was bare, with no carpet on the floor, and no curtain at the window. The air was thick and heavy, and it did not surprise me that Kazinczy stepped immediately to the window and pulled it open. "You can shut it again when we've gone, if you wish," he said to Ferdinand, "but I can't conduct an examination in this atmosphere – I can hardly breathe!"

At the sound of the window's opening, the occupant of the bed stirred and raised himself up a little. I don't mind admitting that, despite being forewarned by the account Kazinczy had given us that morning, I still felt a sudden thrill of horror at the sight of this strange creature rearing up before us, seemingly covered with dirty bandages from head to foot, and with no discernible human features, like something from an evil dream. Kazinczy approached the bed, as the figure subsided once more, and began his examination. He asked several questions concerning the strength of the pain and its position, and how it compared with the pain of yesterday, but the answers were given in such a deep, gravelly whisper that it was clear he could not hear them. Ferdinand then leaned close over the bandaged figure and interpreted his responses for us. "He says the pain is lessened slightly," he related, turning to us, "but is still bad. It has also moved. It is now lower in his side."

"That is very good news," said Kazinczy, "and is what I had hoped for. It often happens after three or four days of static pain. If it is lower down today, it should be even lower tomorrow, and less painful. Surgery will almost certainly not be necessary."

Ferdinand regarded my companion suspiciously. "You're not using what I've told you as an excuse not to do anything, are you?" he demanded in a menacing tone.

"Of course not," returned Kazinczy dismissively. "But I thought I'd made it clear to you last night that surgery is a last resort. The operation is a difficult and dangerous one."

"What does your friend think?" demanded Ferdinand in an unpleasant tone.

"I agree with Dr Kazinczy in every respect," I said.

Ferdinand stood in silence for a moment, his face grim. Then he opened his mouth as if to speak, but whatever he was about to say I was never to learn, for at that moment there came a terrific racket of banging and crashing from somewhere downstairs.

"What the –!" cried Ferdinand, then sprang for the door.

I turned to Kazinczy. "Have you any idea what is going on?" I asked in alarm.

"Absolutely not. The house was as quiet as the grave last night. I can't imagine what is happening."

Even as he spoke, there came a final deafening crash from downstairs, as if a door had been violently burst open. This was followed by a lot of shouting, a woman's screaming, and what sounded like a pistol shot.

"What on earth can it be?" I cried.

Kazinczy clapped his hand to his head, an expression of terror on his face. "The League of the Golden Ribbon!" he cried.

Ferdinand had yanked the door open and raced out onto the landing, but as we made to follow him, the creature on the bed behind us, no doubt roused by all the noise, lurched up again. Before I knew what was happening, he had seized my wrist in a grip like iron, his finger-nails digging deep into my flesh like the talons of some dreadful bird of prey, so that I could not move.

Kazinczy had reached the open doorway, but he got no further. He stepped back in alarm as a large figure in dark clothing abruptly appeared in the opening, barring his way. An instant later, I saw that it was a police constable. "Not so fast, you!" said he in a loud voice, then, turning, he called out to someone further along the landing, "There's more of them in here, sir!"

A moment later, the first policeman was joined by another, in the braided uniform of an inspector. "Who are you?" he demanded of Kazinczy.

"My name is Kazinczy. I am a doctor."

"Who is he?" the inspector asked, indicating me.

"He is a medical colleague of mine. His name is Watson."

"What are you doing here?"

"Attending to this man, who is ill."

The inspector stepped forward with a frown. He had evidently not noticed our patient before. As he came closer, the bandaged man released his grip on my wrist and moved away slightly. The inspector turned up the lamp on the table, and peered closely at this strange figure. "Ah!" said he. "I believe this is who we are after!" He reached forward, and as he did so, the bandaged man at first shrank back against the wall to the side of the bed, leaning over as if reaching for something behind the bed, then, with a fierce, animal cry, sprang forward, a long-bladed butcher's knife in his hand, and launched a violent attack on the policeman.

"Oh, would you!" cried the latter, as he managed to avoid the knife, seized the man's arms, and wrestled him to the floor. "Constable! The cuffs!"

In a moment, the bandaged man was subdued, handcuffed and led away. Then the inspector dusted himself down and turned to us. For myself, I confess I was in a state of stunned confusion at these sudden events, and, to judge by the expression on his features, so was Kazinczy.

"Do you know who any of these men are?" the inspector asked.

"No, I've no idea," I replied, as Kazinczy shook his head. "I understood that some of them were from abroad."

The inspector snorted. "Oh, did you?" he remarked with a harsh laugh. For a moment he regarded us in silence. "For all I know," he said, "you may know nothing, or you may know something. I can't tell yet, so you'll have to come along with the rest of them, until we get it all sorted out."

I picked up my medical bag and followed the others downstairs. Two lamps had been lit in the hall, and the bright light shining up the stair revealed for the first time the bare, dirty floorboards and the cracked and flaking plaster on the walls, which were festooned with filthy-looking cobwebs. The front door stood wide open, the wood cracked and splintered, and in the hall a large number of uniformed policemen were standing guard over several handcuffed prisoners. These included, I observed, the bandaged man, the man calling himself Ferdinand, and a woman I had not seen before. As we reached the hall, the inspector asked his men if every room in the house had been searched, and when he was satisfied there could be no-one else lurking anywhere in the house, instructed his men to take the prisoners out to the vans which were waiting outside.

"What about these two?" asked one of the constables, indicating Kazinczy and myself. "Shall I put the cuffs on 'em?"

"I don't think that will be necessary," returned the inspector, shaking his head. "I doubt they'll give us any trouble. Just put them in the van with the rest of them."

I was thus, for the only time in my life, marched to a police van and pushed inside, where I sat down with three of the most disreputable-looking individuals imaginable, watched over by four large policemen.

It was a very bumpy ride until we reached the main road, and not much better after that, but eventually, after a journey of little more than ten minutes, the van drew to a halt, the door was opened, and we stepped out into a cobbled courtyard. Through a wide doorway we were ushered, and it soon became apparent that we were in a fairly large police-station, although where it might be, I had no idea.

After standing around in a reception area for several minutes, we were taken, in ones and twos, into a corridor which led to the cells. Just as I was turning into this corridor, a door at the back of the main room opened, and two tall men in plain clothes entered, walking quickly and talking as they went. I stopped in surprise. The first man I recognised at once as Inspector Gregson of Scotland Yard, who had often called in at our chambers in Baker Street to consult Sherlock Holmes, but the second man, to my utter amazement, was Holmes himself. What he might be doing here – wherever we were – I could not imagine. I tried to catch his eye, and thought for a moment that I had done so, but he seemed to look right through me, as though he had not recognised me, and followed Gregson through another doorway, and so out of the room. Moments later, I found myself locked in a cell with Kazinczy.

"I have just seen Holmes," I said, "but I don't think he noticed me."

"That's a pity," Kazinczy replied. "He might have been able to get us out of here. I wonder what he's doing here, anyway."

"I haven't the faintest idea," I said. "Do you know where we are?"

Kazinczy shook his head. "We weren't in the police-van for very long, so we can't be all that far from that dilapidated old house." He shivered. "It may not be very enjoyable being arrested, but I think that, on balance, I'd rather be here than there, in that gloomy old house with those menacing people."

"I'm inclined to agree," I said. "I take it you had the bandaged man and Ferdinand in your van, as they weren't in mine. I just had three other men that I'd not seen before, who spent the journey looking sulky and not saying anything."

"Yes, I had the pleasure of their company – and that of the woman, too. But you were fortunate, Dr Watson, if your journey was a quiet one. We had a fight in the van I was in."

"Was that Ferdinand, or the one he calls his 'master'?"

"Neither. They were quiet enough. It was the woman. She produced a devilish-looking little knife from a pocket somewhere in her skirt and went for one of the constables with it. He had to wrestle it off her, while she was biting him and kicking him and calling him every name under the sun. I don't think I've ever heard a woman speak like that before."

I shook my head. "I wonder who she is," I said, "and what she was doing at the old house."

Thus we talked, in a desultory sort of way, for some considerable time, hearing footsteps coming and going in the corridor outside the cell, and doors being opened and closed, until at length the footsteps stopped outside our cell, a bolt was drawn back, and the door was opened. The police inspector we had seen at the old house put his head in, introduced himself as Inspector Raynor, and asked us to accompany him to his office. There he offered us a cup of tea, which we accepted. "Now," said he, "tell me exactly how you became involved with these people."

I made a gesture to Kazinczy that he should do the talking, which he did, describing to the inspector the events of the previous evening much as he had related them to us that morning in Baker Street. From time to time, the policeman made notes of what was said, and when Kazinczy's account was finished, he nodded his head.

"Well, well," said he. "I can see it has been an anxious twenty-four hours for you. I'm sorry I've had to prolong the anxiety by keeping you here, but I didn't know for certain who you were, and couldn't risk your slipping away to warn others whom we might wish to arrest in connection with this business. Fortunately, your account is precisely confirmed by what I have heard from Dudley and the others, so you are free to go. I dare say you are looking forward to your supper."

"Who is Dudley?" I asked. "And where are we now?"

"I'm sorry. I forgot that you don't really know any of these people, or what has been going on. Where you are, doctor, is Stoke Newington police station. You should be able to pick up a cab in the High Street outside, to take you home. As for Dudley: he's the one with the scar on his cheek, the one who told you to call him 'Ferdinand'."

"I see," said Kazinczy. "But who exactly is he, and why was he pretending to be somebody else?"

"Vivian Dudley is a criminal," said the inspector, "and one of the most vicious and violent I have ever known. You are very fortunate to come out of their clutches in one piece, I can tell you. Just as you are, by profession a doctor, so he is, by profession, a criminal. As far as I am aware, he has never done anything in his life which was not criminal. As to what he's been doing for the last few days, I'd rather not say. Our investigation is not yet concluded, and there are some others still at large that we wish to question on the matter. The fewer people who know what's afoot, the less chance of the people concerned being forewarned. You will find out soon enough what it's all about."

With that less than entirely satisfying explanation, our interview was concluded, and a minute later Kazinczy and I found ourselves in a dark and deserted Stoke Newington High Street, where a cold rain was falling. But if I had thought that the evening's surprises were at an end, I was mistaken. A short distance away, a four-wheeled cab stood beside the kerb. We were walking in that direction, and I was just wondering if the cab was free, when the door was opened and, for a brief moment, someone leaned out and beckoned to us.

"Careful," I whispered to Kazinczy as we approached the cab. "It may be a crony of Dudley's, hoping to get some information from us."

As we came closer to the cab, however, the door opened again and, to my surprise, a familiar figure leaned out.

"Holmes!" I cried. "What on earth are you doing here, sitting in the dark?"

"Waiting for you," he replied in that brisk and business-like tone I was so familiar with. "I began to fear you would never get away at all!"

"I saw you earlier with Tobias Gregson, in the police station," I said. "Why did you ignore us?"

"Get in, out of the wet," said he, pushing the door further open. "Then we can be off, and I'll explain it to you as we go."

We climbed in, thankful to be out of the rain. Holmes rapped with his knuckles on the roof of the cab, which set off at a brisk trot, then settled himself back in his seat.

"You ask me why I ignored you earlier, Watson," said he, "and the answer is, I was doing you a favour."

"What!" I cried. "It seems an odd sort of favour, I must say, to ignore two perfectly innocent men being held in a police station!"

"Nevertheless, it *is* a favour," returned my friend, leaning forward and lowering his voice slightly. "You were surrounded at the time, Watson, by a selection of the worst villains in London. These men are hardened criminals, ruthless and violent. If they had suspected for even a moment that you or Dr Kazinczy had been responsible – even partly responsible – for their capture, they would not leave you in peace. They would come to exact their vengeance, if not now, then later – next week, next month, next year. It was therefore vital that there should be no discernible connection between you and the forces of law and order. I had therefore already decided that if I saw you I would ignore you, and I had told Gregson to do the same."

"I see," said I. "In that case, thank you for your forethought and consideration, Holmes! And forgive my short temper – it's been a trying evening!"

"Yes, thank you," echoed Kazinczy, nodding his head. "It has certainly been an odd experience! But what is this business all about, Mr Holmes? Inspector Raynor wouldn't tell us anything, except that the real name of the man who told me to call him 'Ferdinand' is in fact Vivian Dudley."

Holmes hesitated. "I regret that any explanation will have to wait for a few days, doctor," he replied at length. "I have promised Raynor that I shall keep the matter to myself for the moment. However, I shall write to you in a day or two, to explain some aspects of the matter, at least."

We left Kazinczy at his house, where Holmes paid off the cab. Then he and I walked on to the railway station at Hackney Downs, my friend explaining that he was breaking up the journey in this way in order to make it more difficult for anyone to follow us without being seen. There were still plenty of people about, especially at the stations, and Holmes thought it better not to speak in public of the business which had taken us to that part of town. It was therefore not until we had reached our lodgings, finished our supper and filled our pipes as we sat before a blazing fire, that we returned once more to the case which had provided such an anxious and hair-raising twenty-four hours for Dr Kazinczy.

"It will perhaps be simplest, Watson," my friend began, "if I tell you how it seemed to me as I listened to Dr Kazinczy's singular account this morning. He described the man who came to his consulting-rooms as tall and angular, with a large hooked nose, and – most crucially from my point of view – with a distinctive scar upon his cheek, near his left eye. Now, I do not have such an encyclopaedic knowledge of London's criminals as you sometimes credit me with, but I do try to follow the careers of the most notorious of them, and when I heard about this man's scar and his general demeanour, I at once thought of Dudley. The more we heard, the more convinced I became that this identification was indeed correct. Dudley is an odd character, Watson: he has a certain degree of intelligence and cunning – more so, certainly, than most of the men he mixes with – and might, one feels, have made a worthwhile contribution to human life; but his character is a warped one, and he seems to see his fellow human beings only as people who can be intimidated or cheated out of whatever they possess. And if they possess nothing? Why, he will intimidate or cheat them anyway, just for the pleasure of doing so. His usual method is the use or threat of violence, in the employment of which he is perfectly ruthless."

"He sounds a thoroughly unpleasant individual," I remarked.

"He is. He rules the lives of all those unfortunate enough to cross his path with a mixture of physical violence and terror. Everyone is frightened of him, and he himself is frightened of no-one save only the one man who is worse than he is, a man by the name of Muldownie – but I will come to Muldownie in a moment. If Dudley could have got what he wanted from Kazinczy simply by the application of brute force and violence, then I have little doubt that that is the method he would have employed. But as the situation clearly demanded a different approach, he fell back on his other chief talent, which is a great facility for lying. I have it from many sources that Dudley is the most accomplished and convincing liar they have ever encountered."

"Does that mean that there is no truth whatever in what he told Kazinczy last night?"

"Very little. But if I was right, and it was indeed Dudley who visited Kazinczy's surgery last night, then what, I wondered, might he be up to? For that he was up to something, I could scarcely doubt: whenever Dudley shows his face outside his usual haunts – which is not very often – it generally spells trouble for someone.

"The first thing I considered was whether it was really just chance that Kazinczy had been chosen, out of all the medical practitioners in London, for this mysterious consultation. I have generally found that when some event appears to have happened purely by chance, it is always worth looking into the circumstances surrounding it, for you often find that what appeared at first just a matter of chance has occurred for quite specific reasons. In this instance, Dudley himself had suggested that Kazinczy had been chosen because he had a reputation for discretion, but I rather doubted that that was really the case. It sounded a little too much like the sort of flattery a man like Dudley would employ to get someone to do what he wanted. There were, I thought, at least two other more likely explanations as to why Kazinczy had been chosen, either of which – or both – might be true. In the first place, Kazinczy's practice is in the eastern quarter of London, where Dudley and most of his associates live, so it was quite possible that Kazinczy was already known to some of them as a physician who concentrated on the medical condition of his patients and did not ask too many inconvenient questions. In the second place, although Kazinczy has been resident in England for more than ten years, and speaks English fluently, he is nevertheless a foreigner by birth, and as such might be presumed to have a smaller circle of relatives and acquaintances than a native-born doctor might have, and who was also unlikely to follow the intricacies of the English news very closely. If this were true, it suggested that there might have been something in the news recently of which Dudley and his associates hoped that Kazinczy had no knowledge.

"Now, the only really significant points to arise from Kazinczy's account concerned the whereabouts of the decayed old house in which these people were staying, and the fact that an unidentified man there was suffering from what Kazinczy had diagnosed as a kidney stone. With regard to the whereabouts of these people, it seemed likely to me that the meandering journey which our client had been taken on, both going to and returning from the old house, was not so much to throw pursuers off the trail as to prevent Kazinczy himself from learning where it was. Thanks to his alertness, however, and the mistake they made in crossing the Thames, this was not entirely successful, and, despite the lengthy detour to London Bridge station, it seemed certain that their destination was not to the south of London, but to the north."

"Yes," I agreed. "That seemed clear enough from his account."

"Now," Holmes continued, "the man that Kazinczy spoke to in the kitchen of the old house informed him that he had been forbidden to light a fire, in case the smoke from the chimney gave away their position."

"Yes, I remember that."

"But that is strange, is it not? At this time of the year, and in this weather, every chimney in London will be puthering out smoke. That the people in the house were so concerned about it suggested to me that they were not simply keen to prevent anyone from learning that they themselves were staying there, but that anyone at all was staying there. That in turn suggested that there was something odd or distinctive about the house, for if it had been simply an ordinary empty house, what would be so surprising about someone's renting it, moving in there, and lighting as many fires as he wished? It suggested, I thought, that the house had not only been empty before these people moved in, but was known to have been so for some considerable time. It might even have been abandoned and practically derelict, possibly even half in ruins. The description Kazinczy gave us of the interior – or as much of it as he could see – as uncarpeted and almost devoid of furniture, also supported that speculation.

"All in all, it seemed to me most likely that the occupants of the house were not renting it in any normal legal way, but that it was indeed an abandoned building, which they had simply broken into. If we were to find this house, therefore, we should need to look for a dilapidated and abandoned building, and probably one which was very isolated, as our client saw no other houses nearby, nor any lights anywhere near it. This latter point, that no lights were visible anywhere about, suggested to me that the house was probably not only isolated, but stood in a very low-lying position. For it was not very late in the evening when Kazinczy first arrived there, and if the house were in an elevated position, one or two lights would surely have been visible somewhere about, on one of the many roads leading to the north. Now, much of the land to the north of London is very hilly, so most of it could, I thought, be safely ruled out. My best initial conjecture was that the old house lay somewhere in the flat marshlands of the River Lea, which separates the north-eastern suburbs of London from the county of Essex."

"Your reasoning seems clear and convincing," I remarked.

"Thank you. Now, what I proposed, to try to confirm my reasoning, was to equip myself with a large-scale map of the area, borrow a pony and trap, and drive back and forth over every road and track I could find in the Lea valley until I had identified the house. Given a little time, I was confident that I could find it. First of all, though, I wanted to learn something more of what the people in the old house were really up to."

"I can't imagine what that could be," I said with a shake of the head, "nor how you could possibly have hoped to find out."

Holmes chuckled. "I agree that the whole business appeared somewhat opaque," said he. "However, the way I reasoned it was this: the bandaged man's illness was really the only significant and indisputable fact in the whole business. I wondered, therefore, if this could possibly be somehow related to the item of news which, I suspected, Dudley and the others were hoping Kazinczy had not seen in his daily paper. On the face of it, it sounded a little unlikely, I admit, but I had no other starting-point, so after our client had left us this morning, I took myself round to Scotland Yard, to see if I could learn anything there.

"Fortunately, Inspector Gregson was in his office. I have been able to do him one or two small favours in the last couple of years, so he is always willing to oblige me when I come to him for information.

"I came straight to the point. 'Do you happen to know of anyone of interest to Scotland Yard who might be suffering from a kidney stone?' I asked him.

"At this, his mouth fell open in surprise. 'Now, how in Heaven's name do you know anything about that, Mr Holmes?' he asked in a puzzled tone. 'Of course, it was in the local papers down there, but we tried to keep it out of the big national dailies. We didn't want anyone to get in a panic about it.'

"'Who is it, then?' I asked, intrigued by his very cautious manner, and wondering why anyone's illness might cause a panic.

"'Do you know anything of Albert Muldownie?'

"I nodded. 'Before his imprisonment, he was perhaps the most brutal and ruthless criminal in London in the last twenty years, with a gang he controlled with terror. He is almost certainly a murderer, and only cheated the gallows because of the mysterious disappearance of the chief witness for the prosecution.'

"'That's the man,' said Gregson, 'although you forgot to mention that the jury at his trial were also seriously intimidated. We knew that for a fact, but couldn't prove it. At least we got him on a lesser charge, and he was given a fairly stiff prison sentence, which he has been serving in Dartmoor.'

"'Is he the one with the kidney stone?'

"Gregson nodded. 'Yes. Prisoners get ill sometimes, like the rest of us, and have to receive treatment. If it had been a trivial complaint, he would have been seen to in the prison's own infirmary. But as it was a more serious matter, which might have needed surgery, it was decided to send him down to the Royal Naval Hospital at Plymouth. Unfortunately, his gang somehow got wind of this, intercepted the prison van between Dartmoor and Plymouth, attacked the guards and spirited Muldownie away. How it was arranged, how they got him away from Plymouth, and where he is now, we have no idea.'

"'I believe he may be in London,' I said.

"'You may be right. We've been keeping an eye on former members of his gang, just in case he is here, but we've learnt nothing so far. We were particularly watching Vivian Dudley, who used to be Muldownie's right-hand man, and who has taken over the gang in his absence, but he seems to have dropped out of sight altogether recently. You'll appreciate why we've tried to keep Muldownie's escape out of the papers, though. There are a lot of people in the East End who were terrified of him in the past, and if they thought he was out of prison, they'd be terrified of him all over again. Dudley is bad enough, but Muldownie was even worse. But you haven't told me how you've heard anything about it, Mr Holmes.'

"'It's soon told,' I said, and gave him a brief account of Dr Kazinczy's experiences last night.

"'Well, I never!' said Gregson, when I had finished my account. 'That certainly sounds like Dudley and the rest of them, and the man in the bandages must be Muldownie. They must be hoping to cure him of his kidney stone, so he can resume his previous reign of terror, perhaps in disguise and with a new name. If only we knew where that old house is!'

"'I think I do know,' I said, and described to him my reasoning as I have explained it to you, Watson. He agreed with my conclusions, but was less enthusiastic at first about my plan to drive back and forth across the marshlands until I found the house. However, I managed at length to convince him – and his superior, Superintendent Satterthwaite, who was in charge of the investigation into Muldownie's escape, and who joined our discussion – that if they flooded the Lea Valley with uniformed policeman in daylight it might only serve to give an advance warning to Dudley and the others, who might then be able to make their escape. We therefore arranged that they would assemble their men at Stoke Newington Police Station, as that was the nearest large station to the likely location of the house, I would meet them there as soon as I could, and they would then proceed, once darkness had fallen.

"As it turned out, it took me very little time to find the house in question, an abandoned, decaying old building, which stands in isolation on the Hackney Marsh. The recent carriage tracks on the lane approaching the house were as clear as day, and my suspicions were confirmed when a slight movement at one of the windows caught my eye as I drove by. I was therefore at Stoke Newington Police Station long before Satterthwaite's men were there, and spent an anxious couple of hours kicking my heels, as I waited for them. Although the policemen had agreed with my proposal to approach the house after nightfall, you will imagine that I was also keen that they got to the house before Kazinczy was obliged to commence any surgery. That they just managed, and the rest you know."

"I heard a shot as the police stormed the house," I remarked after a moment. "Do you know if anyone was hurt?"

My friend shook his head. "The woman had a pistol," he replied, "and let off a wild shot. Fortunately it didn't hit anyone, and she was quickly disarmed."

"Who is she, anyway?"

"Some connection of Muldownie's, I believe. But I gather that just as Dudley took over Muldownie's gang after his imprisonment, so he took over the woman, too."

"It makes you wonder why Dudley was so keen to get Muldownie out of Dartmoor," I observed. "Surely he'd be better off with Muldownie locked away and himself the unrivalled king of the castle."

"So you would think," said Holmes, nodding his head in agreement. "But some of the gang are known to be loyal to Muldownie, so perhaps Dudley, for all his power, felt obliged to go along with the plan. After today, all being well, the question will be a purely academic one, as these villains should all be removed from the world of honest folk for some considerable time."

That, then, is how I came to play a part – minor though it was – in the capture of some of the most violent and dangerous men in England. I made a detailed record of the matter at the time, while it was still fresh in my memory, even though I knew I should not be able to share the story while the villains involved were still alive. A couple of years later, however, we heard that the former gang-leader, Muldownie, had fallen ill again in prison, and had subsequently died. Then two or three years after that, I read with surprise in my newspaper one morning that Dudley, who had recently been granted an early release from Portland Prison on the grounds of ill health, had been shot dead the previous evening in a public house in Shadwell. No doubt his assassin – who was never apprehended – was one of the many people in the East End who had had good reason to hate him for many years. Although any unnecessary loss of life is usually regarded as a tragedy, I doubt very much that Dudley's passing elicited much sorrow in those parts of London where he was known.

As for Dr Kazinczy, he continues to practice and flourish in Hackney, where, as far as I am aware, he lives still. I have met him once or twice since our alarming adventure together, when he has never failed to bring vividly to my mind once more the memory of that strange old dark house and the singular bandaged man.

THE VON STRAUFFHAUSEN PAPERS

AMONG THE MANY CASES of which I kept a record during the time I shared chambers with Sherlock Holmes, there were some in which, although successful, he was unable to demonstrate his view of the matter with that absolute logical precision which was so dear to him. It might be that conclusive evidence was lacking, that a vital witness could not be found, or that the delicate circumstances of those involved prevented his inquiring too deeply into the matter. In such cases, the conclusion necessarily depended, to a greater or lesser extent, upon conjecture and surmise. But there were some among these cases in which subsequent events, or the private words of those intimately involved in the matter, left little room for doubt that Holmes's analysis of the problem had been the correct one.

Especially memorable among such cases were the mystery surrounding the fate of the steamship *Anna Kilmartin*, the disappearance at a garden party given by the Marquess of Ord and Lindsey of the necklace known as 'the Kesteven Rubies', and the affair of the von Strauffhausen papers, in which Holmes's intervention in the matter was of the utmost significance to the well-being of the country. It is this last case I now propose to describe. I should certainly have done so before were it not that in giving a true and accurate account of the matter I should undoubtedly have laid myself open to an action for defamation of character. That threat having been removed by the recent death of one of the chief actors in the drama, a suitably guarded account of the case can now be laid before the public.

It was in the third week of July, 1886, that I descended to breakfast one fine sunny morning to find a long cream envelope leaning against the marmalade-pot, addressed in a large, flowing hand to Mr Sherlock Holmes. The envelope was an expensive one, of smooth, stiff paper, and the red sealing-wax upon the back flap was impressed with what appeared to be a noble coat of arms.

Holmes was late to rise that morning, and by the time he appeared at the breakfast-table I was sitting in the bright sunshine by the window, immersed in the morning papers.

'You have a letter from some high-ranking quarter,' I remarked, looking up as he seated himself at the breakfast-table.

'Well, the stationery is high-ranking, at least,' returned my companion with a chuckle, tearing open the envelope as he spoke. 'But, come,' he continued after a moment, as he read the letter; 'my correspondent is indeed of the highest! There can be few more eminent subjects of the crown! Well, well, well! It is Lord Woolmer, Watson,' he added, in answer to my query. 'He wishes to consult me professionally.'

'Lord Woolmer?' I cried. 'Why, there is a report in this morning's newspaper of a speech he gave at the week-end, in Manchester!'

'The subject?'

'The need for the Houses of Parliament to scrutinise keenly the actions of the Government.'

'I understood that Lord Woolmer himself held some post under the present administration,' said Holmes in surprise.

'So he does. He holds a junior position at the Board of Trade, his particular responsibility being that of European trade.'

Holmes chuckled. 'Every administration must of course prepare itself to receive a hail of criticism from the opposition benches from the moment it takes office. That is part of the natural order of things. To receive such reprobation from someone who is himself a member of that administration is somewhat more unusual!'

'His argument is not directed solely at the present administration,' I returned, 'but at all and any. His view is that all governments, however well-intentioned, have a tendency to lapse somewhat from the highest standards from time to time - "cutting the corners of democracy", he calls it - and that it is the duty of all members of Parliament, of whatever hue, to be ever vigilant for such lapses, not least when those lapses occur on the side they themselves support.'

'I see,' said Holmes, nodding his head. 'Of course, that is a theme he has addressed before. He is a man of quite unusual integrity and honour, not afraid to speak his mind, to friend and foe alike.'

'Does he say why he wishes to consult you?' I queried.

Holmes shook his head. 'Only that the matter is one of the utmost urgency. He proposes to call at ten, so I had best make a start on these two rather antique-looking boiled eggs!'

As Holmes busied himself with his breakfast, I finished the report I had been reading. Lord Woolmer was a fine speaker, both vigorous and eloquent. His strict adherence to truth and to the principles of democracy shone like a beacon from every sentence of his speech. Such a man undoubtedly merited both the support and the admiration of all parties in the country, wherever their sympathies might lie on specific details of public policy. What on earth could have occurred, I wondered, to bring such an eminent public figure to our humble lodgings, to seek the advice of the criminal specialist? As I pondered the question, I recalled what I had read of Lord Woolmer over the years.

His life had certainly been a curious one, I reflected. Born in poverty on a small moorland farm near Whitby, to parents who could neither read nor write and knew little of the world beyond the moors, he might have passed his entire life in herding sheep, had not the vicar of the parish, visiting the village school one day, detected in the little lad signs of quite unusual intellectual gifts, and recommended that he be allowed to pursue his education further afield. This he had done, afterwards becoming himself a teacher of small children, in Scarborough and Huddersfield, and other places in Yorkshire, until he had won a scholarship to read History at London University. So outstanding had been his record there, that upon graduation he had been offered a teaching post, and the opportunity to pursue his studies yet further. Secure at last in a position worthy of his talents, he had then begun to produce the series of historical studies which had made his name a byword in educated circles for profound and impartial analysis. Within a very few years he had come to occupy a uniquely respected position in public life, had served by invitation on numerous

Government commissions, for which work he had received a knighthood, until, in recognition at last of his outstanding contribution to public life, he had been elevated to the peerage and a seat in the House of Lords. This, then, was the man from whom my friend had that morning received a letter.

'It should be an interesting interview,' remarked Holmes, breaking in upon my thoughts, as he rang for the maid to clear the breakfast-table. 'Will you stay?'

'I should be honoured to be present,' said I; 'if Lord Woolmer has no objection.'

A few minutes before ten there came a peal at the door-bell, and a moment later the noble lord was ushered into our little sitting-room. He was a tall man, both dignified and imposing, with a high domed forehead, old-fashioned mutton-chop side-whiskers, and thick, straggling eyebrows, from beneath which a pair of keen, intelligent eyes shone out. He shook hands with us both, and then got briskly down to business.

'Something quite dreadful has occurred,' he began. 'Even now, I can scarcely credit it. It is an odd fact, but the worst blows in life seem always to fall when one is least expecting them.' As he spoke these last words, there was a slight tremor in that measured, sonorous voice, and he paused for a moment, as if in the grip of some powerful emotion which he was striving by force of will to master. 'I have never in my life,' he continued after a moment, 'sought to take undue advantage of my position. I am a member of the House of Lords, I have been a member of three separate administrations, but, let it rain or shine, I will take my turn in the queue for a cab like anyone else. I have only contempt for those whose puffed-up self-importance demands special consideration for themselves. Now, however- '

Lord Woolmer paused, and shook his head.

'Now, I don't mind admitting,' he continued after a moment, 'I thank the Heavens that I am who I am. Were I not so well-known, I doubt that I would be free to walk the streets today, and to go where I please. Most likely, I should already be behind bars, awaiting trial for treason!'

'Surely you exaggerate, Lord Woolmer!'

'I think not, Mr Holmes. As it is, I suspect that I have only been allowed my freedom in order that I might incriminate myself further in some way. I have been followed this morning, I believe. No doubt the hope is that I will inadvertently lead the authorities to my supposed criminal confederates.'

Holmes stood up and stepped to the window, where he peered cautiously round the curtain.

'There is a man standing near the corner,' said he.

'Yes, that is he,' said Lord Woolmer, who had joined him by the window.

'Do you know him?'

'I have seen him somewhere about - in Downing Street, I believe. He is certainly a government agent.'

'I confess,' said Holmes as he resumed his seat, 'that I find these suspicions utterly incredible, Lord Woolmer.'

'Thank you,' said the great statesman, bowing his head. 'Nevertheless, it is true.'

'The details, then, as precisely as possible!'

'You are no doubt aware, gentlemen, that I currently hold the position of junior secretary at the Board of Trade. I have held similar positions before. I have never sought high public office, and nor, in truth, have I ever been likely to achieve it. My own modest talents are perhaps not best suited to positions of great power. Besides, the principles with which I endeavour to conduct my life - however inadequately - no doubt make me a somewhat troublesome bed-fellow for those who regard decisiveness and action as more important than impartiality and fairness. However, I have, as I say, been granted junior office, and in that capacity I am honoured to serve.

'I was away over the week-end, returning to town on Sunday evening. On Monday morning, I received a note summoning me to the Prime Minister's private office in the House of Commons. Upon his desk as I entered, I saw a sheaf of papers, marked "Confidential".

'"I have had His Excellency, Gottfried von Strauffhausen as a guest over the week-end," he remarked.

"'Not a difficult guest, I trust," I returned with a smile. I was aware that von Strauffhausen was in England, acting as plenipotentiary for the German Emperor, although on what errand, I did not know. I was aware, too, that he had something of a reputation for being a rather prickly companion.

"'Von Strauffhausen would not be my first choice of cabin-mate on a long sea-voyage," returned the Prime Minister with a wry smile. "However, he is in England for business, not pleasure, and from that point of view our discussion was quite fruitful. His particular brief at present is trade, as you may know, and he has brought several interesting proposals from the German Chancellor. Our discussions ranged over many aspects of our mutual trade - the general principles, you understand. However, he has elaborated the matter in considerably greater detail in these papers here."

'The Prime Minister tapped his finger on the documents I had observed before, on his desk. "I haven't the time to read through it all - even if I wished to, which I don't - and nor has the President of the Board of Trade. I should therefore be obliged, Woolmer, if you would set aside whatever else you have been working on, and devote yourself for the next few days to a close study of von Strauffhausen's proposals."

"'Certainly, Prime Minister," said I. "I am honoured and flattered to be given the commission; but would it not perhaps be more appropriate for someone more senior to consider the matter? I have, of course, some knowledge of Anglo-German trade, but I am by no means an authority on the subject."

'The Prime Minister shook his head. "All your superiors at the Board of Trade are otherwise occupied this week, Woolmer. We are passing through a period of upheaval in Parliament, as you can scarcely fail to be aware, and with each day that passes there seems yet more which must be attended to. I am sure you will do a good job, Woolmer. The document is of course in German, and it is well known that your command of that language is superior to that of anyone else in the department. When I was discussing the matter with von Strauffhausen, your name cropped up, and he seemed to think highly of you. I certainly have the utmost confidence in your abilities. He returns to see me on Thursday, incidentally, so I look forward to having your précis of the proposals, with whatever comments you deem appropriate, on my desk on Thursday morning!"

'"Very well," said I, as I took the papers from his hand.

'"One further point," said the Prime Minister. "These proposals are highly confidential, Woolmer. Some of them are fairly innocuous, but there are others which would, I imagine, cause great irritation to some of our Continental neighbours. We don't want to give rise to strained relations - especially as we may well not take up any of von Strauffhausen's suggestions anyway - so you must give no hint in any quarter of anything contained in these documents. And it is not only our own relations with our neighbours that we have to consider, but those of the German Empire, too. Were any of Germany's neighbours to learn of these proposals at this stage, it would cause the German government considerable embarrassment, as von Strauffhausen stressed to me. Is that clear?"

'"Perfectly so, Prime Minister," said I, and left his office, clutching the papers he had given me. Now, as you will imagine, I have got used to carrying confidential papers about with me in recent years, but I was aware that these documents were of unusual importance and confidentiality, and I determined to take especial care of them.' He paused. 'I could not have conceived then of the dreadful calamity which was about to befall me!'

'You have lost the papers?' queried Holmes.

The great statesman nodded his head forlornly. 'But it is worse than that. I am under suspicion of attempting to pass them to a foreign agent.'

'"Attempting", you say? The papers have been recovered, then?'

'Yes. So, to that extent, no harm has been done.'

'Very well. Pray proceed.'

'I took the papers to my own room and looked them over for a while, then put them in my dispatch-box, which I took home with me that evening, placing it upon the desk in my study. I have a house in St Peter's Street, which is only a few minutes' walk from the Palace of Westminster.'

'One moment,' interrupted Holmes. 'Did you verify before you left the Palace of Westminster that the papers were still in your dispatch-box?'

'No. I had been busy during the afternoon and early evening - there was an important vote in the House - and the dispatch-box had lain untouched for several hours on the desk in my office. As I came to leave, I simply called in there, picked it up and left.'

'The case was locked, presumably?'

'Certainly.'

'Does anyone else have a key?'

'No. There are only two. One I carry about with me, and the other is in the bureau in my study at home.'

'Was your office in the House of Lords left unoccupied while you were elsewhere in the building?'

'Not for any very long period. I share the room with Lord Belgrove. He was there for most of the day, working at his desk.'

'Is Lord Belgrove a close acquaintance of yours?'

'Not especially. He is, as it happens, distantly related, by marriage, to my wife; but the fact that we share an office in the House is simply coincidence.'

'At the time of the vote you mentioned, Lord Belgrove would also, presumably, have been in the Chamber, in order to vote.'

'That is true. Our room would have been unoccupied then, for an hour or more.'

'Does the door lock?'

'No.'

'Very well. Pray proceed with your account.'

'When I reached home, at about seven o'clock, I put the dispatch-box on the desk in my study, then sat in conversation with my wife in the drawing-room for the best part of an hour. She has had a long-standing invitation to visit cousins of hers in Wales which she had decided to fulfil this week, and we were discussing the arrangements for that. She then reminded me that our dinner-guests would shortly be arriving, and I hurried upstairs to change. About fifteen minutes later, I was informed that the guests had arrived, and had been shown into the drawing-room. Five minutes later, I joined them there, and ten minutes or so after that we went into dinner.'

'Who were your guests?' queried Holmes, taking his notebook from his pocket.

'Sir Marcus and Lady Devereux, who have just returned from Japan, Lord and Lady Yelland, and the Italian ambassador and his wife. About half-way through the meal, there was a ring at the door-bell, and Jeffers, my butler, informed me that Viscount Hardigate had called, on a matter, he stated, of some urgency. Do you know anything of Hardigate, Mr Holmes?'

'Only that he is a young man whose political star is said to be in the ascendancy.'

Lord Woolmer nodded. 'That is true enough. He certainly has the ear of the Prime Minister at the moment. He is at the centre of a group of like-minded young men, who are impatient for change, and dismissive of the traditional way of doing things. I gave him every encouragement a few years ago, when first he came into the House, for I recognized in him a young man who possessed both intellect and ambition. He and his friends spent many evenings at my house, in earnest discussion of this or that point of public policy. I respected his views even when they did not entirely accord with my own, and he, I believed, granted me the respect which my experience, at least, merited. But now - alas! - circumstances have changed. I fear that he and his circle regard me as something of a fossil, a relic from a bygone age. I have argued consistently, as you may be aware, that change simply for its own sake is pointless, that any change which increases the liberties of our fellow-countrymen is good, and that any which confines or restricts those liberties, by howsoever small an amount, is bad, whatever other merits it may possess. These opinions, I regret to say, are increasingly regarded with more or less open contempt by Hardigate and his circle, and on the rare occasions in recent months when he has deigned to acknowledge my existence, his tone has been one of impertinence and insolence.

Aware of this, and thinking it likely that his errand on Monday evening was somewhat less urgent than he made it out to be, and that it would do him no harm to wait, I sent word from the dinner-table that I would be with him in five minutes.

'When I joined him in the drawing-room, in what, I confess, was nearer ten minutes than five, he was standing by the hearth, his hat and his umbrella in his hand, a look of intense irritation and impatience upon his face.

'"I understood you to say that you would be here in five minutes," said he, consulting his watch.

'"I have some very important guests- "

'"The Prime Minister requests your presence at once. He has instructed me to take you to him now."

'With that, he clapped his hat on his head, and made for the door. In a moment, I had donned my coat, explained matters hurriedly to my wife and our guests, and joined Hardigate where he stood impatiently tapping his umbrella on the front-door step, like a peevish, overbearing martinet.

'"What is it about?" I inquired.

'"I am not at liberty to say," said he, in a peremptory tone; then, turning on his heel, he set off across the street. It was a dark, dismal night, for the clouds were thick and heavy, and it had started to rain. I speculated as to what could have occurred to make the Prime Minister summon me in this fashion. My modest brief in the Government is, as I explained, not one which touches upon any great matters of state, and I was therefore at a loss to understand the meaning of it. Viscount Hardigate, meanwhile, was striding out briskly ahead of me. So quickly was he walking, indeed, that I was forever some distance behind him, and struggled to keep pace with him. As he strode along the street, looking neither to right nor left, and forever tapping his umbrella pompously on the pavement, it struck me that he resembled nothing more than the puffed-up beadle in *Oliver Twist*, and that I was cast in the role of the poor chastised orphan boy, obediently following in his footsteps.

'In a matter of minutes, we had reached Downing Street, and having delivered up his charge, Hardigate took himself off somewhere. Moments later, I was in the Prime Minister's study, where he sat at his desk, an enormous pile of documents in front of him.

'"Take a seat, Woolmer," he began. "Have you any idea why I have called you here?"

'"No, sir; I have not."

'For a moment, he looked at me, with that penetrating gaze of his, as if he would read the innermost secrets of my soul.

'"Very well," he continued at length. "A very serious incident has occurred this evening, Woolmer." Again he paused. "Do you know the present whereabouts of the documents I gave you earlier today?"

'"Von Strauffhausen's proposals?"

'"Precisely."

'"Why," I cried in surprise, "they are in my dispatch-box, on the desk in my study at home."

'"No, they are not," said he in a grave tone. "They are here before you now." He tapped one of the piles of papers on the desk in front of him.

'"What!" I cried. "But that is impossible!"

'"Unfortunately, Woolmer, it is not only possible, it is true. See for yourself."

'In a state of stunned confusion, I took the papers he passed to me. A swift glance was sufficient to tell me that what he said was true. These were undoubtedly the papers he had handed to me in the House that afternoon.

'"Have you anything to say, Woolmer?"

'I shook my head dumbly, my mind still reeling.

'"When did you last see these papers?"

'"Shortly after you first gave them to me, Prime Minister. I had a quick glance at them, then locked them securely in my dispatch-box. I have not yet had the time to look them over properly."

'"You have not taken them out of your box again for any reason - any reason at all?"

'"No. My dispatch-box has remained locked ever since I put the papers in it."

'He then picked up a small, ragged-edged square of paper from his desk, about the size of a quarter of a sheet of note-paper.

'"Do you recognize this hand?" said he, passing the little slip of paper to me.

'On it, written with a broad-nibbed pen, were the words "Take these - usual route - 142 VS - must be returned tomorrow". I shook my head.

'"I don't believe it's a hand I've seen before," I answered at length.

'"It looks tolerably like yours, to me," said the Prime Minister in a dry tone.

'"What!" I cried. "I assure you that it is not, sir!"

'"But it is not dissimilar."

'"I cannot deny that," I conceded after a moment, as I looked again at the slip of paper. "Where was it found?"

'"Pinned to the top sheet of von Strauffhausen's papers," he returned. "Have you any observation to make on the matter?"

'"None whatever. I can hardly credit what has happened. Someone must have slipped into my little office in the House, when both Lord Belgrove and I were out of the room for a moment, and somehow managed to unfasten my dispatch-box, extract the papers, and lock the box up again."

'"I should say that that was highly unlikely in the House of Lords, Woolmer. What of your household servants? Can you trust them?"

'"I certainly believe so."

'"Hum! It is an odd chance, is it not, Woolmer, that the person that wrote that note - presumably the same person as extracted the papers from your box - should have handwriting so similar to your own?"

'"Undoubtedly, Prime Minister. It is a strange coincidence."

'"Hum! I am not sure that you realize the seriousness of your position, Woolmer! If it were anyone but you, I should not have sent young Hardigate to fetch you, but the sergeant-at-arms, and you would now be in a police-cell."

"'I thank you for your consideration," I ventured. "I assure you that I am perfectly innocent of whatever it is I am supposed to have done. Might I inquire how and where these papers were discovered?"

'He explained to me that word had recently reached the authorities from an anonymous source that Axel Schnelling, a known foreign agent, against whom, however, nothing has ever been proved, would shortly be in receipt of some most valuable and confidential documents. It had therefore been decided that plain-clothes officers would keep a watch upon his house, which is at 142, Vincent Square, in Westminster. At about twenty to nine that evening, a shabbily-dressed man had been seen to approach this address in a furtive, suspicious-looking manner. He had almost reached the door when he appeared to see that he was being observed, took panic, turned and ran. The plain-clothes officers thereupon gave chase and apprehended him before he had gone fifty yards. One of the officers then recognized the man as Alfred Davis, a petty criminal who has been sought recently in connection with a burglary in Clerkenwell. He was unable, or reluctant, to explain what his business might be at 142, Vincent Square, and the officers deeming that this was sufficient reason to question him further, he was taken at once to Cannon Row Police Station, where he was searched and found to have official-looking papers concealed within the lining of his jacket. From the embossed crest atop the pages, and the seals and signatures at the end, it was recognized at once that these were important state papers. The senior officer took them at once to the Foreign Office, whence they were passed to the Foreign Secretary, who in turn passed them to the Prime Minister, so that in less than half an hour from the apprehension of the man Davis, they were upon the Prime Minister's desk in 10, Downing Street. A few minutes later he dispatched Viscount Hardigate to my house.'

'What explanation did this man, Davis, give of how he came to be in possession of the documents?' queried Holmes.

'He denies any wrongdoing. He says that on Saturday night he had been approached by a man he did not know as he was leaving a pub in Pimlico, and told that if he wished to earn two guineas for half an hour's work, he was to be outside Victoria Station at half past eight on Monday evening, when he would be given the money and a parcel to deliver. This he agreed to do, and on Monday, at the appointed place, he was approached by another man, who gave him a packet of papers to deliver to the address in Vincent Square, and paid him. He says he understood that it was simply a matter of urgency and convenience, and he did not know that the papers had been stolen.'

'Is he believed?'

'No; but it would be difficult to prove that he was lying. He has been charged with handling stolen property; but, frankly, I suspect that the case against him will be quietly dropped, to save embarrassing the Government.'

Holmes nodded. 'There is little likelihood, I imagine, of following the trail from that end, so we must follow it from the other. What is your own position now?'

'It hovers somewhere between that of a despicable traitor who has deliberately passed state secrets to our enemies, and an incompetent bungler who has simply given insufficient care to the documents entrusted to him. Neither charge is one I should welcome, but I will with reluctance accept the latter if I can be cleared of the former.'

Again Holmes nodded. 'It is not clear to me,' he remarked after a moment, 'why papers which deal only with matters of trade should have attracted such attention, nor why the degree of confidentiality attaching to them should be so great.'

'I have not yet had time to study them to any great extent, as you will have gathered,' replied Lord Woolmer in a dry tone; 'but I understand that the proposals contained within them would tend to favour some aspects of trade between the German Empire and ourselves, at the expense of trade between the German Empire and certain other nations. Generally speaking, we do not care for any special arrangements of this sort. They are usually more trouble in the end than they are worth - when they are worth anything at all, which is not very often. It is unlikely, therefore, that we should ever commit ourselves to any such arrangement, and our considering the proposals at all is largely a matter of simple courtesy to the German government. But there are those on the Continent who would seize upon the proposals to stir up enmity and discord.'

'Anyone in particular?'

'France for one, Russia for another; but the real danger lies in the Balkans. That whole region is like a rumbling volcano at present, and one day the volcano will erupt. Who can say what the incident will be which will finally cause the eruption? As any student of history will attest, it is as likely to be a trivial but annoying agreement on the international trade in rubber galoshes as anything else.'

'I take it that as the British Government neither sought nor encouraged these proposals from Germany, it would be they rather than us that would be the more embarrassed by their premature publication.'

'That is undoubtedly correct.'

'Hum! Who knew that the papers were in your possession?'

'No-one, apart from the Prime Minister and myself, as far as I am aware; but of course there may be a traitor on Herr von Strauffhausen's own staff who guessed that I would have them.'

'You did not speak of them to anyone?'

'No. I mentioned to my wife that the Prime Minister had given me a rather thick wad of papers to read through, but I did not specify what they were.'

'And Lord Belgrove, with whom you share a chamber in the House of Lords?'

Lord Woolmer shook his head. 'I had the papers spread out on my desk for some time, whilst he was in the room, but he was engrossed in his own work at the time, and the few words we exchanged had no reference to them.'

'Did anyone look in upon you whilst the papers were on your desk?'

'Yes. Lord Savours and Lord Kelling-Lynche both stopped by at different times. Neither stayed for very long.'

'But they could have seen what you were reading?'

'I suppose so; yes. But I don't believe that either of them reads German.'

'Hum! And did you leave the chamber for any reason whilst the papers were spread upon your desk?'

Lord Woolmer hesitated. 'Yes,' said he at length. 'I remembered a message I had to pass on to one of my colleagues; but I was only out of the room for a minute or two.'

'So someone might have entered the room in your absence and seen the papers lying there?'

'Possibly, although I believe that Lord Belgrove was present throughout my absence, and he did not mention to me that anyone had called.'

For several minutes Holmes sat in silent thought, his chin cupped in his hand, and a frown upon his face. 'Tell me frankly, Lord Woolmer,' said he at length: 'Is there anyone among your colleagues in the House that might perhaps wish to see these documents published?'

'I really cannot say. I certainly do not believe so.'

'Do you yourself have any personal enemies?'

'I do not care for Kelling-Lynche, nor he for me, but I should hardly class him as an "enemy". I have, also, had numerous heated disagreements with Lord Prestwich, as you may have read in your newspaper. His ideas and mine are perhaps as utterly opposed as it is possible for two men's ideas to be, but it is inconceivable that he would attempt to purloin Government papers. Some of the younger elements in Parliament regard me as something of an antique, as I mentioned earlier, but as my influence upon anyone else's opinions is distinctly on the wane, I don't imagine they care tuppence for what I say or do.'

'Very well. Pray continue with your most interesting account.'

'The Prime Minister cautioned me that it was of the utmost importance that the Press did not get any idea of what had occurred:

'"If von Strauffhausen himself, or anyone connected with him, were to get wind of this," said he, "it would be disastrous for Anglo-German relations. And of course once the gentlemen of the

Press get hold of such a story, they are like a dog with a stick, and will not let go of it. And, you may be sure, Woolmer, that they will use the stick to beat us with. They will show no mercy, and any reputation for integrity which you may have managed to acquire over nearly thirty years of public service will count for nothing. I will not be able to shield you."

'I assured him that as I was perfectly innocent I had not the slightest desire to be "shielded", as he put it.

'"It is not so straightforward as that," returned he in a grave tone. "The Government's position, as you are aware, is a delicate one - as is likely to be the position of any administration in the immediately foreseeable future - and the slightest hint of scandal would be disastrous. I confess, Woolmer, that I find it difficult to believe that you could be guilty of deliberate treachery, which is why you are sitting here now in my study, rather than in a police-cell. But I cannot warrant that the rest of the Cabinet will take such a benevolent view of the matter. Moreover, even if your word is believed, and no treacherous intentions are imputed to you, you can scarcely escape a charge of culpable carelessness. That in itself is enough to require the dismissal of a public servant."

'"I am sure I took all the usual precautions- "

'"Which, in this case, were clearly insufficient."

'I could hardly deny the truth of this observation. I left Downing Street with the feeling that the world had fallen upon my head, and for some time wandered aimlessly about the streets of Westminster, turning these sudden, dreadful events over and over in my mind. By the time I reached home, my guests had departed, for which I was most thankful. My wife saw at once from my face that something terrible had occurred, but so forlorn and hopeless did I feel that I could scarce bring myself to tell her of the shocking position I found myself in, or of the shameful stain which, it seemed, must fall upon our family name. Poor Margaret! She did her best to comfort and reassure me, but I was, I am afraid, inconsolable.

'The following morning I received a message from the Prime Minister's office, informing me that I should remain at home, and that a senior detective officer from Scotland Yard would be calling to examine the premises. At half past nine, he arrived.'

'His name?' interrupted Holmes.

'Inspector Gregson.'

'I know him well. He is a competent officer. Pray proceed.'

'He examined my dispatch-box with some care.

"'These cases are not very secure," he remarked.

"'The lock is a solid one," I returned in surprise.

"'Quite so, sir," said he. "The lock is undoubtedly sufficient to prevent the case from falling open and your papers from falling out, and perhaps sufficient, also, to prevent a chance passer-by from opening it and removing the contents. But it is not, if I might say so, sir, sufficient to prevent a determined thief from gaining access."

'So saying, he took some small metal tool from his pocket, and applied it to the lock. In a trice, there came a sharp click, and he had opened the dispatch-box before my very eyes.

"'You see, sir," said he, as he lifted the lid. "It is a sad fact, but gentlemen often believe their possessions to be safe when they are not!"

"'Good Lord!" I cried. "I should never have believed it possible! That must be how the thieves got at the papers!"

"'Perhaps," said the policeman, in an enigmatic fashion; "and perhaps not."

"'Do you see any suspicious marks on the case or the lock?" I asked him.

"'I can't in all honesty say that I do," was his reply.

"'Is there no indication that someone has opened the case in the same way as you have just done, Inspector Gregson?" I persisted.

"'Not that I can see, sir," he replied, shaking his head; "but one cannot always tell."

'He then made a tour of the ground-floor rooms of the house, examining carefully every window. I suppose he was looking for signs of a forced entry.'

'Did he find any?'

'No,' replied Lord Woolmer, shaking his head. 'He then went outside. We have a small back garden, and he stood in this for some time, surveying the back of the house. Then he proceeded to examine all the windows again, this time from the outside.'

'Did he find anything suspicious?'

'I think not. When I asked him if there were any signs of an intruder, he replied that he did not in all honesty think that there was. As he finished his examination, he took me to one side and questioned me about the servants.

'"Do you think they are to be trusted, sir?" he asked.

'"I trust them as I would trust my own family," I returned with some warmth. "The maids have all been with us for between three and five years, the cook nearly a dozen, and Jeffers, the butler, for almost twenty."

'"You don't think it possible, then," he asked, "that any of them might be tempted by a large sum of money to betray your trust?"

'"Certainly not," said I.

'"Very well. If you say so, sir," said Inspector Gregson. Thereupon, he closed up his note-book, bade me good-day, and left. That was yesterday, and I have heard nothing more since then. My wife offered to cancel her visit to Wales, saying that she must stay with me in my hour of trial, but I wouldn't hear of it, and insisted the visit went ahead as planned. Yesterday evening, I dined at my club, and got into conversation with a very old friend of mine, Lord Clenchwarton. Upon my intimating to him - without of course giving any details - that I was in some difficulty, being suspected of having done something which I had not done, Clenchwarton at once mentioned your name to me, Mr Holmes. He says you are the one man in London that might be able to help me.'

'I am honoured by his recommendation. It is gratifying to know that he remembers favourably the little service I was able to render him. Do you recall the Clenchwarton Substitution Case, Watson?'

'Indeed I do,' I returned. 'It was a most interesting case.'

'Interesting, perhaps, but not especially difficult,' remarked my friend. 'Lord Woolmer's case, I suspect, will present somewhat greater difficulty.'

'You see my situation as hopeless?' queried Lord Woolmer in a resigned, mournful tone.

'Certainly not,' returned Holmes with emphasis. 'One must never confuse difficulty with hopelessness, Lord Woolmer!'

'No, of course not. I appreciate that, but- '

'As my friend, Dr Watson will attest, I prefer to be associated only with those cases that do present some difficulty. A man will never progress in his chosen career if he chooses always that which is easy and avoids that which is difficult.'

'A sentiment with which I would undoubtedly concur,' remarked our visitor.

'Excellent!' said Holmes in a cheery voice, taking up his pipe and beginning to fill it with his dark shag tobacco. 'Then we are agreed, Lord Woolmer. We have before us a difficult, and, therefore, a stimulating problem. Let us then address the problem in the round before moving on to a more detailed consideration of it.' He paused and put a match to his pipe before continuing:

'Some confidential papers have been purloined. They have, however, been recovered inside an hour or two, and within a mile or so of the place from which they were taken. Now, it seems more than likely that neither the man Davis, who was arrested in possession of the papers, nor the policeman who questioned him and found the papers, will have had any real idea of what they were. On the face of it, therefore, it would appear as you say, that little harm has been done.'

At this point, Holmes abruptly stopped speaking, and stared for several minutes into the empty fireplace, an expression of the most intense concentration upon his face, as if he were struggling by force of intellect to grasp and hold some train of thought which was proving elusive. Presently, he came to himself once more, re-lit his pipe, which had gone out, and continued:

'As I was saying, little harm would appear, on the face of it, to have been done to the national interest. You, however, Lord Woolmer, are in a position of some difficulty, and this is what we must address. Now, if we take into account the time taken in passing the papers to Davis at Victoria Station, the time he himself took in getting to Vincent Square, the time taken by the policemen in arresting him, taking him to the police-station, searching him, finding the papers and taking them to the Foreign Office, whence they were passed ultimately to the Prime Minister, and finally the time taken by the Prime Minister in summoning Viscount Hardigate and sending him to your house, and if we further allow that the actions of all these various people were conducted, for various different reasons, with some degree of urgency, it would appear that the papers were taken at least an hour before Hardigate arrived at your house.'

'Perhaps considerably earlier than that if they were taken from Lord Woolmer's office in the Palace of Westminster,' I suggested.

'A little earlier, perhaps,' returned Holmes, 'but not a great deal earlier. Whoever was responsible for the theft would have wanted the papers to reach Vincent Square as quickly as possible, and yet, it appears, they had reached Davis only ten minutes or so before he was apprehended.'

'I cannot really understand why this man, Davis, was involved at all,' interjected Lord Woolmer.

'It is frequently how such people operate,' returned Holmes, 'by employing a host of small fry to do the routine work, who will generally be ignorant of the significance of what they are doing, and will thus, if caught, be unable to supply the authorities with any worthwhile information. But there may well be other reasons in this case: an obvious one, for instance, is that whoever stole the papers may have suspected that Axel Schnelling's house in Vincent Square was under observation, and did not wish to be seen to be a visitor there.'

'I understand that,' said Lord Woolmer; 'and as you yourself remarked earlier, we can not expect to make any progress in the matter from that end of the problem. But the other end of the problem, it strikes me, is equally as likely to prove a barren field. I have absolutely no idea how or when the papers were taken from my dispatch-box, and I can see no way in which we could possibly discover it now.'

'Well, well' said Holmes in a reassuring tone; 'I have faced greater puzzles than this, Lord Woolmer. Let us not give up hope before we have even begun! The papers were in your dispatch-box on Monday afternoon. They were therefore taken at some time between then and around half past eight that evening.'

'So much is plain.'

'They were taken either from your chamber in the House of Lords, or from your study in St Peter's Street. Now, the Prime Minister thinks the former possibility highly unlikely. Whether his conviction on this point is justified remains to be seen, but let us accept it for the moment, for the sake of the argument. If the papers were not taken from your office in the House of Lords, then they were taken from your private study at St Peter's Street. If so, they must have been taken by you yourself, Lord Woolmer, or by one of your domestic staff, or by an intruder. Now, Inspector Gregson, after an examination of the property, apparently convinced himself that there had been no intruder. He therefore questioned you as to the trustworthiness of the servants. You said, in so many words, that you were prepared to vouch for them.'

'That is correct.'

'And you therefore succeeded in establishing beyond doubt that you yourself were the chief suspect in the matter.'

'No doubt I did, but I should not have spoken differently had the policeman questioned me for a thousand years. I could see perfectly well what was in his mind, Mr Holmes, and I certainly was not prepared to cast unpleasant and unwarranted suspicions upon my staff simply to get myself out of a difficult position!'

'Well said!' cried Holmes with a smile. 'Of course, I was not suggesting that you should have spoken other than as you did; I was merely pointing out the logical consequence of your own words.'

'All the logic in the world might indicate that I have betrayed my trust,' said Lord Woolmer in a firm voice; 'but the fact remains that I have not.'

'Quite so,' returned Holmes in an emollient tone. 'Let us now consider the little note which was found pinned to von Strauffhausen's document when it was discovered, in the possession of Davis. Can you shed any light upon that, Lord Woolmer?'

'None whatever.'

'It stated, if I remember aright "Take this to Vincent Square - must be returned tomorrow" - or words to that effect. Unfortunately, this, too must cast suspicion specifically upon you, Lord Woolmer.'

'Why ever so?'

'Because the implication of the instruction to return the document the next day is that it was to be studied and no doubt copied by the spies, and then returned so that no-one would know it had been purloined for a time. There would be no point whatever in returning it if its loss had already been discovered.'

'Yes, of course; I follow that.'

'But if it was taken by a stranger, he could not have presumed that you would not attempt to study the document - and thus discover its loss - for a period of twenty-four hours. But the implication of the note is that the writer is confident that the loss will not be discovered before the document is returned, some time on Tuesday. A prosecuting counsel would argue, Lord Woolmer, that only you yourself would have the requisite confidence to send such a message.'

Our noble visitor stroked his chin and considered the matter for a moment. 'I can see that what you say is true,' he remarked at length in a sombre voice. 'I had not considered that aspect of the matter.'

'And the fact that the handwriting on the note appears remarkably like your own scarcely helps your cause.'

'There is little need for any prosecuting counsel, Mr Holmes,' rejoined Lord Woolmer, a wry expression upon his face. 'You appear to be making out a very strong case against me on your own. I should say that my view of the matter, and of my own position in it, is somewhat more pessimistic now than it was when I entered your chambers!'

'It is of the first importance,' returned Holmes, 'that we state the matter clearly, and recognize all the difficulties that we face. I should be doing you no service, my dear sir, were I to disguise the difficulties, and arouse premature hopes of success. It is by no means an easy problem, and I sense that the most fruitful line of approach may be a tangential one.'

'You do have some hopes of success, then?'

'Oh certainly, certainly! And remember, Lord Woolmer, as the old proverb has it, "It is always darkest just before the dawn"! Tell me, is Herr von Strauffhausen still in London?'

'No - thank goodness! So at least there is little likelihood of his getting wind of what has happened to his precious proposals. He has been in Paris, I understand, for the last couple of days, paying a visit to the French President. He returns to London tomorrow, by which time I was supposed to have studied his proposals, and reported upon them to the Prime Minister.'

'A task which has now been assigned to another?'

'Indeed so: Harry Tomlinson, one of the Prime Minister's own secretaries.'

Sherlock Holmes nodded his head. 'Very well,' said he. 'I shall devote my undivided attention to your problem, Lord Woolmer, and let you know of any progress I make.'

'When might I hear from you?'

'It will not be today.'

'I hardly expected so!' cried Lord Woolmer in surprise.

'But it may be tomorrow.'

'What!'

'Of course, it depends on what I am able to discover.'

'Very well, then, Mr Holmes. I leave the matter entirely in your hands.'

'A pretty little problem, eh, Watson?' said Holmes to me when our visitor had left us.

'Indeed,' I concurred. 'The matter seems perfectly insoluble.'

'Oh, I should not put it so strongly as that!' cried my friend in a light-hearted tone. 'The case has certain suggestive features, and I am confident of solving it before too long. The real difficulty may lie in saving Lord Woolmer's reputation, which has sustained something of an injury in the last couple of days.'

'Surely the one implies the other,' I protested. 'If you solve the case, surely you will also thereby clear Lord Woolmer's name?'

'It may not be so straightforward as that,' responded my friend in a thoughtful tone. 'But, still,' he continued, springing from his chair; 'let us see what we can do!' In a moment, he had thrown on his coat and clapped his hat upon his head, then with a cheery salute he was gone, and I heard his footsteps clattering down the stair.

I confess I had no notion in what direction my friend's inquiries might lie. For myself, I could not think where any such investigation might even begin. As far as I saw the case, it seemed practically impossible for anyone other than Lord Woolmer himself to have abstracted the papers and passed them, either directly, or through an intermediary, to Davis, the man who was caught in possession of them. It was true that he had sought the assistance of Sherlock Holmes to help prove his innocence, but this in itself proved nothing: Holmes had on more than one occasion in the past been consulted by those who were indeed guilty of the crimes with which they were charged, in the vain hope that he would publicise all those circumstances which were favourable to their case, and suppress those which were not. The mistake such people had made was to misunderstand my friend's calling, which was not to prove the truth of some view which he had decided beforehand, but to discover the truth, whichever view of the matter such discovery might favour. Was this, too, such a case? Had Lord Woolmer consulted my friend simply in order to appear more innocent than he really was? Certain it was that there was little enough in the case to inspire any great confidence in his innocence. And yet, although I had never met the man before, I had known of him for many years, and had read a fair number of the many speeches he had made during that time. If there was one man in all the country whose name stood for honesty, probity and integrity, then that man was Lord Woolmer. Indeed, it was undoubtedly his unwillingness to compromise his principles in the slightest degree which had cost him the possibility of high government office. He was, moreover, known to be a great patriot, of the very finest, noblest type. No easy tap-room boasts and heroics for him, but a profound knowledge and understanding of his nation's history, of its merits and strengths, and, it must be said, of its occasional weaknesses and failings. Some of the younger men in politics might express impatience, and affect a yawn, when he quoted sentences to them from the Magna Carta, or the Bill of Rights, but they would learn in time that the future of a country is only safe when it has its roots in the past, and that Lord Woolmer's wisdom was not that of a man in his dotage, but of a man whose experience of life was far greater than their own.

Could such a man be guilty of the treachery of which he was suspected? It seemed utterly inconceivable. But if it seemed morally impossible that Lord Woolmer should have purloined the papers, it also seemed practically impossible that anyone else could have done so. What, then, was the explanation for the events of Monday evening?

The reader will surmise from this record of my reflections on the case that I reached no worthwhile conclusions. From whichever way I examined it, the whole affair seemed fantastic and improbable. With a shake of the head and a sigh, I resolved to put the matter out of my mind altogether, so far as I was able. It was a fine summer's day, with scarcely a cloud in the sky and only the gentlest of breezes, so I took myself off to the Park, where for several hours I strolled about, observing the graceful horses and carriages which were there in abundance.

Sherlock Holmes was out all day, but returned in time for supper. His manner was genial and cheery, and I surmised that his day's work had not been entirely unsuccessful; but he would not be drawn on the matter, and our discussions that evening, I recall, although they ranged over many topics, from the cuneiform writing of ancient Babylon to the design of ships' propellers, never once touched upon the Woolmer case.

At length, late in the evening, my friend took up his violin and began to play a series of old airs. But there was an expression of intense concentration upon his features as he did so which seemed unrelated to the music, and I suspected that even then, while his fingers were remembering the melodies, his brain was engaged upon Lord Woolmer's problem.

The following morning, I descended to breakfast to find Holmes seated already at the table. He greeted me cheerily, and it was evident that he was in the very best of spirits. Clearly he had formulated some plan of action, and I found myself wondering what it might be. I was soon to discover.

'I shall be paying a visit to Lord Woolmer this morning,' said he; 'or to his house, at least. Would you care to accompany me?'

'With the greatest of pleasure!'

'I have asked Inspector Gregson to meet us there at eleven o'clock,' continued my friend with a glance at his watch, 'and as I wish to examine the premises before he arrives, we had best be getting along there as soon as you have finished your toast.'

An hour or so later, therefore, our cab deposited us outside Lord Woolmer's house in St Peter's Street. Our ring at the bell was answered by a sombre-looking butler, who conducted us to a drawing-room on the left of the hallway, and said he would inform his master of our arrival. A few moments later he returned, declared that Lord Woolmer would receive us now, and led us directly across the hallway and into the study. Lord Woolmer was seated at his desk, writing, but he stood up as we entered, and we shook hands.

'I am composing a letter of resignation to the Prime Minister,' he remarked in a grave tone, indicating the sheet of paper upon his blotting-pad. 'I have given the matter considerable thought since last we spoke, and I realize now that my position is untenable. Of course, I am guilty of no crime, and certainly not of the treachery of which I am suspected in some quarters; but I am guilty, perhaps, of carelessness - culpable carelessness - in respect of the confidential papers which had been entrusted to me.'

'It is a nice point,' responded Holmes, 'as to when a charge of carelessness becomes justified. A man may take all reasonable care - as much care, say, as any other in his place might have taken - and still be defrauded or robbed, if the criminals are determined enough.'

'That is true,' observed Lord Woolmer, nodding his head in agreement; 'but I do not intend to argue the point in my own defence. My resignation, it seems to me, will simplify the position enormously. I will be no great loss to the Board of Trade, and, in truth, the Board of Trade will be no great loss to me; for I have felt recently that my work there, trifling though it has generally been, has taken up too much of my time, and kept me from pursuing matters which I regard as of greater importance. Of course, if any serious charges are laid against me, then I shall defend myself most vigorously. Otherwise, I shall let the matter drop. I can bear the discredit of being thought careless, even if it is not truly warranted; I could not bear the disgrace of being thought a traitor. The former should not seriously hamper my work; the latter would of course destroy it utterly.'

'That has, if I might say so, been my own train of thought precisely,' remarked Holmes. 'If a charge of carelessness is laid against you, it may be that I am unable to rebut it to any effective degree, that charge being always, as I remarked, somewhat nebulous, and largely a matter of personal judgement. It is therefore upon the other, if less likely charge, of treason, that I have concentrated my energies.'

'Have you been able to discover anything?'

'Nothing conclusive, but one or two things that are suggestive.'

'Might I know what those are?' the nobleman inquired, as Holmes gave no sign of enlarging upon his answer.

'I had rather not enter into any detail at the moment.'

'Very well. What do you intend to do next?'

'To conduct a little survey of these premises - especially of the windows accessible from the ground outside - to determine if there is anywhere an intruder might have gained entry on Monday evening.'

'The Scotland Yard man has already made such an examination,' observed Lord Woolmer in a doubtful tone.

'There may be something he overlooked.'

'His examination seemed a very thorough one.'

'Nevertheless, I should wish to take a look for myself.'

'Of course,' said Lord Woolmer, nodding his head. 'I'll ring for Jeffers to show you round the downstairs rooms.'

For twenty minutes, then, I watched as Holmes carefully examined every one of the downstairs windows. The windows of the drawing-room and the study overlooked St Peter's Street, at the front of the house. They were separated from the pavement by a wide area, however, which would have made an unseen forced entry there so unlikely as to be practically impossible, and they were, besides, very securely fastened.

At the rear of the house was a small garden, which like the gardens of the adjacent houses, was at a lower level than the street at the front. Overlooking this was the broad bay window of the light, high-ceilinged dining-room.

'I imagine,' said Holmes, addressing the butler, as we stood by the dining-room window, looking out into the garden, 'that this room was the scene of considerable activity early on Monday evening, when you were preparing for dinner, and for the arrival of Lord Woolmer's guests.'

'That is so, sir,' responded the other. 'There is always much preparation to be attended to on such occasions.'

'So that the room was probably not left unoccupied for more than a minute or two at a time.'

'That is so, sir.'

'How does one get down to the garden from here?'

'This way, gentlemen,' responded the butler, leading us from the room, and forward into the front hall. There he drew aside a heavy curtain on our left, to reveal a curving flight of steps down to the basement. At the foot of this staircase was a door to the outside. The butler took down a key which hung on a hook by this door, and unlocked it.

'Was this door locked on Monday evening?' Holmes inquired.

'Oh, undoubtedly, sir.'

We passed through and found ourselves at the side of the house, in a narrow alleyway which sloped down gently from the level of the street to that of the garden. At the top, near the street, was a high wooden gate, bolted shut. Holmes looked this over for a few moments, then we descended to the garden. This consisted of a rectangle of lawn, surrounded by raised flower-beds, bright with pinks and geraniums. Surrounding the garden was a brick wall, atop which was a wooden trellis, through which various plants twisted and twined. For some time, Holmes walked about the lawn, looking back at the house and its neighbours from various angles. Below the bay window of the dining-room was an area, not so deep as the one at the front of the house, within which was another window.

'I take it that that is the window of the kitchen,' remarked Holmes to the butler.

'Indeed so, sir.'

'And the little oblong sash window to the left, with the frosted glass?'

'One of the pantries, sir. It is not one we use very much.'

'Does it open directly into the kitchen?'

'No, sir; into the basement corridor.'

'Near the bottom of the staircase we passed down?'

'Yes, sir.'

'Is the house next door occupied?' Holmes then inquired, indicating the next house on the left. 'Some of the shutters appear to be closed.'

'It is the residence of Count d'Ambrosio of Italy,' Jeffers replied. 'However, he is not at home at present, but is away on a visit to Scotland.'

'And the house on the other side?'

'Belongs to Viscount Dudeney, sir.'

Holmes nodded. 'I see. Thank you for your assistance, Jeffers. I think that will be all. We should be able to manage by ourselves now.'

'Very good, sir. Should you require any further information, I shall be in the servants' hall.'

As soon as the butler had left us, Holmes lowered himself into the shallow area at the back of the house, and proceeded to examine the little pantry window with great care. He took some small tool from his pocket, with which he prodded and poked in the narrow gap between the two halves of the sash window. After a while, he climbed back out of the area again, and glanced at his watch. There was an expression of intense concentration upon his face.

'I am going to have a look at this window from the inside,' said he. 'You had best remain here, Watson, in case Gregson arrives early.'

He disappeared up the little alleyway at the side of the house, and moments later I saw his shadow on the inside of the pantry window, and heard him moving the catch back and forth. Presently, he flung up the sash, and put his head out.

'It is a narrow gap for a full-grown man,' he remarked with a frown.

'You think that someone entered by this window on Monday evening?' I queried, but he did not reply directly.

'Let us see if it is possible,' said he, speaking more to himself than to me. So saying, he inched himself through the open lower half of the window. 'It is only one's shoulders that present any difficulty,' he remarked as he squeezed through the gap. 'There,' he continued, as he reached a point where he was hanging half out of the window; 'once the shoulders are through, the rest follows as straightforwardly as a proof in Euclid!'

He reached forward across the area and grasped the top edge with his hands, then worked his legs out until his feet were upon the little window-sill. From that position he was easily able to pull himself up and over the little edging wall at the top of the area, until he stood once more with me upon the lawn.

'If someone had entered that way on Monday,' I remarked, as my friend dusted down the knees of his trousers, 'would he not have been seen or heard by the kitchen-staff?'

'It would certainly be a risky enterprise,' returned my friend, nodding his head; 'but a man with ice-cold nerve might succeed. Once inside the pantry, he would have to wait until all was quiet in the corridor outside, and hope that no-one came from the kitchen to the pantry for anything. If anyone did, he would be discovered at once, for there is nowhere to hide in there. He would be able to hear quite clearly when anyone passed up or down the staircase, for the bottom step is just outside the pantry door, and could wait until one of the servants had descended, then quickly make his way out and up the stair, hoping that he did not encounter anyone else on the way up. Once at the top, and in the hall, his way would be relatively clear: avoiding the dining-room, he could slip along the hall, and so into Lord Woolmer's study.'

'You appear to have demonstrated the possibility very clearly,' I remarked.

'Not quite,' returned my friend, an expression of wry amusement upon his features. 'I have demonstrated that it is perfectly possible to leave the house by this little pantry window. Now I must demonstrate that it is also possible to enter in this way, which may, I think, prove a sterner challenge. If you would be so good as to go round and lock the window from the inside, I shall prepare myself for the task!'

I did as he bade. The door to the pantry was in a dark corner at the foot of the servants' stair, and the pantry itself was a narrow chamber with large shelves on either hand, stacked with old tins, bottles and jars. As I pulled the window down to shut it, I noticed that the catch shook slightly, and as I examined it I saw that the screws holding it appeared to have been loosened a little. I remarked on the fact, but my friend appeared not to hear me. A sharp snick came to my ears as he opened his pocket-knife, then he began to work it through the gap between the two halves of the window, a task rendered easier, as I could see from inside, by the looseness of the catch. In a matter of moments, he had forced the catch back, and pushed up the window.

'Now,' said he with a chuckle, as he closed up his knife, and replaced it in his pocket. 'Which way to enter? If I go in head first, I risk getting stuck half-way, or falling rather painfully onto the floor; if feet first, there is a distinct possibility of putting my back out of joint. Still, I think it will have to be feet!'

He had wriggled his way three-quarters of the way in without mishap when one of his waving feet caught an old biscuit-tin on the edge of a shelf, and sent it crashing to the ground. Then, as he succeeded in getting his shoulders in through the window, and put his weight upon his feet, he trod upon the tin, and bent the lid.

'I don't believe, Watson,' said he, as he closed the window, and dusted himself down once more, 'that you have ever fully appreciated my skills as a contortionist! On reflection, I think that head first might have been the less painful option! Ah!' he cried, as the sound of the front-door bell came to our ears. 'That may well be Inspector Gregson. Let us renew our acquaintance with our old friend!'

It was indeed the policeman. We all three shook hands, then Holmes suggested that we repair to the garden. There were a couple of benches set at the corner of the lawn, and we seated ourselves on these, in the warm sunshine.

'I am glad to see you, Mr Gregson,' said Holmes, as he began to fill his pipe.

'I am sure I am glad to see you gentlemen, too,' responded the other; 'but what is it all about, Mr Holmes? I got your note, but I don't know what it is you want of me.'

My friend did not respond directly. He put a match to his pipe, and puffed away gently at it for a few moments.

'I consider it a stroke of great good fortune,' said he at length, 'that you were assigned to this case, Gregson. We have known each other some years now, have we not?'

'Indeed we have, Mr Holmes.'

'And I have managed on occasion to make myself useful, and to offer you some assistance?'

'I cannot deny it.'

Holmes nodded his head. 'Good. Because today I wish to ask a favour of you.'

'You have only to ask,' returned the policeman in an affable tone. 'If it is within my power- '

'Oh, it is within your power all right; but whether you will be inclined to agree to it is another matter!'

'Oh?' said the policeman in a bemused tone. 'You have lost me, Mr Holmes! What is it you wish to ask of me?'

'First of all,' responded Holmes, 'I must ask you what you know of the case that has brought us all here.'

'I know only that some Government document was found upon a petty criminal, Alfred Davis, who was arrested not far from here on Monday evening, and that the document may have been taken from this house. The document - whatever it is - is now back safe and sound where it belongs, so I understand, so there's no harm done. However, there is still the question of how Davis came to have it in the first place. That's why I was sent round here on Tuesday, to see if there was any evidence of a forced entry. It was clear to me that there was not, as I put in my report, so if the document was stolen at all, it must have been stolen from somewhere else.'

Sherlock Holmes nodded his head. 'I have no doubt that that is how it appears to you,' he responded after a moment. 'Unfortunately, it is regarded as unlikely that the document was stolen from anywhere else, either, so by reporting that in your opinion there was no burglary here, you have inadvertently helped to cast suspicion upon Lord Woolmer himself, or upon his domestic staff.'

'I cannot help where suspicion falls,' the policeman remarked with a shake of the head. 'I can only report matters as I find them. What is the favour you wish of me?'

'I should like you to admit that you have made a mistake.'

'Eh? In what respect, pray?'

'That you were perhaps a little hasty in arriving at your conclusions on Tuesday.'

'I don't believe that I was.'

'Perhaps not, but it is possible, is it not? Come, Gregson! We all fall into error upon occasion!'

The policeman chuckled. 'It is good to hear you admit it, Mr Holmes! Of course, in my twenty-five years in the force I have made my share of mistakes. But I don't believe that this occasion is one of them! What grounds have you for believing otherwise?'

'I have been looking into the possibility that someone broke into the house by the little pantry window, to the left of the kitchen,' said Holmes, pointing with his pipe to the window in question, 'and it seems perfectly possible to me.'

'Show me then,' said Inspector Gregson in a sceptical tone, rising to his feet.

The three of us climbed down into the shallow area at the back of the house.

'You see,' said Holmes, drawing the policeman's attention to the edge of the window: 'there are signs there that someone has recently forced the window open: the paint is chipped, and the wood is indented slightly.'

Inspector Gregson bent down to have a closer look. 'I am sure these marks were not here when I inspected this window on Tuesday,' said he in a tone of puzzlement.

'Well, they are there now. Is it not possible that you could have been mistaken?'

'No, Mr Holmes, it is not. As it happens, I gave particular attention to this window the other day, because it struck me as the likeliest place for a burglar to try to gain entry. These marks were certainly not here then. Someone has made them since last I was here.'

'Hum! You sound very sure.'

'That is because I am sure.'

'You do not allow that you could have been mistaken?'

'Certainly not.'

'Hum! I did say, Gregson, that it was a favour I required of you.'

The policeman turned and regarded my friend for a moment with an expression of curiosity upon his face. 'You know more about this business than you have admitted,' said he at length.

'I would not deny that.'

'Mr Holmes!' cried the policeman in a tone of sudden enlightenment. 'You have made these marks yourself!'

'I should be obliged if you would lower your voice,' responded Holmes with a frown. 'Let us return to the bench and discuss the matter further.'

'What you wish me to say,' said Gregson, when we had resumed our places on the garden benches, 'is that those marks upon the window-frame were there all along, and it is therefore possible that someone did break into the house?'

'Precisely.'

'But that would be untrue. I have been in the force now for a quarter of a century, and I have never once falsified any evidence.'

'I do not doubt it for an instant; and nor are you being asked to do so in this case. I am not suggesting that you state categorically that anyone did in fact enter the house through that window on Monday evening, but simply that someone might have done so. And the possibility that someone might have done so clearly includes both the possibility that someone did and the possibility that someone did not.'

Inspector Gregson was silent for a minute. 'I have already submitted my report,' said he at length.

'Call it back. Say you made a mistake.'

'I should appear a fool.'

'Well, that is a fate that befalls us all at some time or other,' observed Holmes with a chuckle. 'I doubt that your reputation will be tarnished forever, Gregson. Why, the whole matter will likely be forgotten inside of a fortnight!'

'Perhaps it will, but I am uneasy about it nevertheless.'

'I understand that, but it will harm no-one, I assure you. I ask the favour not to throw the suspicion of guilt onto anyone, but, rather, to remove the shadow of that suspicion from a perfectly innocent man.'

'Is it his lordship's reputation you are concerned to protect?' asked Gregson after a moment.

'Yes,' said Holmes, nodding his head. 'Lord Woolmer has conducted his life to the very highest standards of conduct. Now, through no fault of his own, his reputation stands besmirched by the false accusation of treason. If we cannot rebut that accusation, then, even if he escapes a trial, his name will be forever stained, and his benevolent influence, once so great, will dwindle to nothing.'

Inspector Gregson sat in silence for several minutes, considering the matter.

'Between you and me, Mr Holmes,' said he at length, in a very low tone; 'why are you so certain that his lordship is innocent of the charge?'

'Because I know who is guilty.'

'Then why have you not reported the matter, or laid a charge against this man?'

'I have no evidence.'

'Will you be able to get the necessary evidence in due course?'

'No. It is impossible.'

'I see. And if I were to alter my report, it would not implicate anyone else directly?'

'No.'

'Nor indirectly?'

'No. You have my word on that, Gregson.'

'Very well, Mr Holmes,' said the policeman in a tone of decision. 'I cannot promise anything, but I shall do what I can.'

'Good man!' cried Holmes. 'Incidentally, Gregson, there is a biscuit-tin in the pantry which has suffered somewhat from being trampled on, which might be considered yet further evidence of an intruder.'

'More of your handiwork, I take it,' said the other chuckling.

'Footwork, more like, in this case,' returned Holmes.

'Gregson is a sound fellow,' remarked Sherlock Holmes in a cheery voice, as we crossed St James's Park in the sunshine. 'I am confident he will not let us down.'

'I wish I understood as much of the case as you evidently do,' I remarked. 'To me it appears only as a confused tangle of separate threads, every one of which leads to a conclusion so improbable as to be beyond belief!'

'All will become clear shortly,' returned my companion. 'I am sifting and clarifying my own thoughts on the matter even as we walk, Watson. I can tell you this now, though: that unless I am very much mistaken, we are rapidly approaching the final act in this little drama! Incidentally,' he continued in a lighter tone;

'did you observe the nasturtiums in Lord Woolmer's garden? Were they not delightful, twining in orange profusion upon the walls and trellis! I sometimes think, Watson, that the nasturtium, above all other blooms, not even excepting the rose, displays to us the very soul and essence of the summer!' Having delivered himself of this surprising pronouncement, my friend fell silent once more, and I knew it was pointless to question him further.

When we reached our chambers, Holmes seated himself at his desk and spent some time in composing a long letter. Later, he went out, taking the letter with him, and I saw no more of him until tea-time. Our landlady had provided us with scones and freshly-made strawberry jam, and I remember that Holmes spoke at surprising length about the excellent quality of these home-made comestibles as he drank his tea; but he appeared nervous and tense, and immediately he had cleared the plate he donned his old brown dressing-gown, lay down upon the couch, and closed his eyes. His rest was destined to be a short one, however, for it was scarcely twenty minutes later that the door-bell sounded, and, a moment later, Inspector Gregson was shown into our room.

'The sleep of the just, I hope, Mr Holmes,' remarked he with a chuckle, as Holmes looked up. 'Yes, I will take a whisky and a cigar, Doctor Watson. Just a little soda in the whisky, if I may. I am on my way home, but I thought I would call in, as I have some news that will please you, gentlemen, which I did not wish to commit to paper!' He took a sip from his glass, and a long, satisfied pull on his cigar.

'You have managed to amend your earlier, inaccurate report,' said Holmes, helping himself to a cigar.

'I have indeed, Mr Holmes,' returned the policeman with a chuckle. 'Better than that, I was able to do so without having to explain or excuse myself to anyone. When I looked in at the superintendent's office, the first thing he said to me was that he had been so busy that he has not yet found time to read my report. I said I wished to have another glance at it, to make sure that I had put everything in it, and he raised no objection. When he does find the time to read it, he will now learn that there are distinct signs of a forced entry at the pantry window at Lord Woolmer's house, indicating that someone might recently have entered the premises that way.'

'Which is, of course, perfectly true,' interjected Holmes, laughing heartily. 'The ache in my back is testament to how recent it is! I must say, this is excellent news, Gregson! I think you have discharged in full any debt you may have owed me for my occasional assistance in your professional work!'

'Now,' said the policeman, after a moment, 'you must tell me, Mr Holmes, what it is all about. That is surely only fair. I have gone out of my way to assist you, without really knowing what lies behind it.'

'It is a reasonable request,' returned Holmes, in a more serious tone. 'I could not possibly deny it! However, my dear Gregson, I am afraid I must ask you to preserve your soul in patience for a little while longer. If my reading of the affair is correct, as I am sure it is, then events in this drama are now moving towards their end. The last act, however, remains yet to be played, and I had rather keep all the facts together in my own head until I am quite certain that the final curtain is down. The next time we meet, I promise I shall satisfy all your queries on the matter.'

'That is good enough for me, Mr Holmes,' said the policeman in an affable tone. 'I know you like to keep your cards close to your chest until the last round is played! I must be off now,' he continued, rising, and putting his empty glass on the table. 'I'll thank you for the whisky, and look forward to hearing more about the St Peter's Street business next time we meet!'

'He is a good fellow,' said Holmes, when Gregson had departed; 'and I certainly owe him an explanation. But I really could not begin it this evening. I know the man well, and he is like a dog gnawing upon a bone: he would have so many questions that we should very likely have spent all evening in answering them, and I have hopes of a slightly different evening's entertainment! Ah! Speaking of bones, here come the chops that Mrs Hudson promised us!'

For some time we ate in silence. I could see from the expression of concentration upon my friend's face that he was still turning the matter over and over in his head, and I feared to speak, lest I break his train of thought. At last, however, when we had almost finished the meal, he himself broke the silence.

'I have often had occasion in the past to remark to you,' he began, 'that however tangled a case may appear, there is generally a loose thread to be found somewhere in it. Grasp that thread and follow it carefully, and it will eventually lead you to the heart of the mystery. In this case, however, matters have been somewhat different. True, there were threads aplenty, but none of them, as you yourself remarked earlier, seemed to lead one very much further. The heart of the problem seemed to be in impenetrable darkness, and it was only when a light, like the dawn, seemed to break upon the whole affair at once that all became clear to me, and I could see that all the separate threads were tied together in one central knot. I will tell you now, Watson, how the light dawned, and how I came to realize the nature of that great central knot.

'When Lord Woolmer was first speaking yesterday of the von Strauffhausen papers, and of what they contained, it occurred to me, as it must have occurred to you, that they seemed scarcely worth the trouble of stealing. Of course, they were confidential government documents, and as such might have attracted the attention of a casual thief; but the trade proposals they contained did not represent the official policy of either the British Government or the German Government. They were proposals only; neither side had agreed to them, and nor was very likely to, from what we had heard of them. If details of the proposals had become generally known, either party to them could at once have declared that they had no intention of adopting them, and the matter would have been at an end. Their theft, then, seemed hardly worth the effort of such a careful and complex plan.

'That the theft was indeed carefully planned beforehand seemed evident from the arrangements which had been made for passing the papers on, including the use of the petty criminal, Davis, as a courier, and from the fact that the spy, Axel Schnelling, was expecting the papers at his house in Vincent Square.

'That Davis was apprehended, and the papers recovered so promptly, appeared a stroke of good fortune. It depended, if you recall, on an anonymous message which had been received, warning the authorities that Schnelling would shortly be in receipt of some important document. Now, this "stroke of good fortune" struck me as almost too good to be true, and made me wonder who had sent the message, and why.

'We further learnt that a note had been pinned to von Strauffhausen's papers, the handwriting upon which was remarkably similar to Lord Woolmer's own. This seemed a curious coincidence, to say the least, and I found myself speculating as to what it might mean.

'Lord Woolmer had remarked to us that as the papers had been recovered so quickly, no lasting harm had been done, and as I reflected on that point I was struck all at once by another thought. You are familiar, no doubt, with the Latin phrase *cui bono?*'

'Certainly. The meaning is "to whom the benefit?", or, in other words, "who is it that stands to gain from some action or other?".'

'Precisely. I have found it a useful little principle from time to time when faced with a puzzling case, in which the motive for the crime is obscure. But there is also another little principle - or, if there is not, then there should be - which one could call the *cui malo?* principle. In other words, "who is it that suffers, or is disadvantaged by some particular action?". This principle is especially pertinent in this case, for although Lord Woolmer declared that no lasting harm had been done by the theft of these papers, that was not in fact quite true. The prompt recovery of von Strauffhausen's proposals had of course saved both the British and the German governments from mild embarrassment, but Lord Woolmer's reputation stood on the brink of a precipice. At the very least, he was likely to be accused of gross carelessness, and at the worst, of treachery to his country. To the question *cui malo?*, the answer was undoubtedly Lord Woolmer. What if, I speculated, the whole purpose of the plot all along had been to discredit Lord Woolmer?

'This, Watson, was the dawning light which broke all at once over the whole knotty problem. Suddenly, all was bathed in clarity, and the different, perplexing strands seemed as clear as day. On this reading of the matter, the message received by the authorities concerning Schnelling's house in Vincent Square had obviously been sent by the plotters themselves. They wanted the petty criminal, Davis, to be apprehended, because they wanted the papers to be recovered. They were not interested in the papers themselves, but only in discrediting Lord Woolmer. Furthermore, the note found with the papers had been deliberately written in a hand like Lord Woolmer's. Of course, they knew that he would deny vehemently that he had written it, but it would still serve to make darker the suspicions against him.'

'I follow your reasoning,' I interrupted. 'The way you describe it, it all seems very clear, although scarcely credible for all that; but I still do not understand how the plot could be made to work. How and when were the papers abstracted? Nor do I understand why Lord Woolmer should have been selected to be the victim of such a cunning and despicable plot. He holds only a minor post under the present administration, as he himself remarked; and his general influence, considerable though it may have been in the past, is not now so great as it was.'

My companion had been finishing his meal as I spoke, and now removed himself from the supper-table to the basket-chair by the hearth, where he filled and lit his pipe before replying.

'To answer your second question first,' said he at length, 'as to why such a devious and deceitful plot should have been laid against Lord Woolmer, who is, on the face of it, relatively unimportant to the government of the country, it is necessary to understand that there has been a serious error of judgement.'

'By the plotters?'

'No, by Lord Woolmer himself. It is an error of judgement which, I confess, I was guilty of following myself.'

'I do not understand.'

'I will make it clear. Lord Woolmer remarked to us that he considered his influence in political life to be distinctly on the wane, and said that he feared that the younger men regarded him as something of a fossil, a relic from a bygone age. Now, Lord Woolmer is a very modest man. With him, modesty is not a false affectation, as it is with some men, but a genuine and sincere part of his character, and this should be borne in mind when evaluating his own remarks about himself. I admit that, not used to encountering such sincere and courteous modesty, I accepted his self-judgement as accurate. But he is wrong, and so was I. While his immediate influence upon the daily routine of the Government may be negligible, his enduring influence upon the philosophical and political discourse of the country has been, and remains, immense. There are cabinet ministers now, and high-ranking ones, too, whose names and deeds will scarcely be remembered five years after they have left office, whereas Lord Woolmer's speeches and writings will live on, to inspire future generations. For he represents a persistent - one might go so far as to say, eternal - strand in political thought, the focus of which is the liberty of the common man.'

'I understand what you say. But surely that makes it all the less likely that Lord Woolmer could be the focus of anyone's animosity? Here is a man who does not say "income tax should be this or that", or "there should be a tax on biscuits", but whose arguments are largely above and beyond the everyday fray of party politics. Surely Lord Woolmer's arguments, abstract and general though they may be, are such as would be accepted by almost all shades of political opinion? Why, if a man denounces or seeks to discredit such principles, which are the very foundation-stones of the nation and the rule of Law, surely he is as good as declaring openly that he is in favour of tyranny!'

'Ha! There you fall into error, if I may say so, Watson. For you suppose that what politicians propose to those who vote for them is always self-evidently clear from the outset. This, unfortunately, is not the case, and it is not unknown for men to be duped, and to walk freely and willingly into bondage. It is certainly remarkable, how many different methods men have devised to exercise tyranny over their fellows. Indeed if one reads history books in a mood of detached cynicism, one is likely to see all human history as little more than a catalogue of tyrannies - old tyrannies overthrown, to be replaced in due course by new ones, which themselves are later overthrown, and so on. It is remarkable, also, to observe how frequently new tyrannies dress themselves up in the clothes and trappings of liberty.'

'That was certainly true in the past; but modern man is more educated than his ancestors. His sensibilities are more refined, and his outlook more scientific. He cannot so easily be seduced by the hollow promises of a would-be tyrant.'

'One would like to believe it was so. Unfortunately, however, to the extent that man has indeed become more refined and scientific in his outlook, so have the nostrums peddled by would-be tyrants. It is a natural progression, you see, Watson: the more accomplished that men have become at exposing nonsense and evil, the more the purveyors of nonsense and evil must disguise its true nature. You mention the scientific outlook, and you are no doubt aware of my own efforts to place criminal detection upon a scientific footing; but there are those, arrogant in their presumption that they possess all worthwhile knowledge about mankind, who wish to direct the whole of human life according to some pretended scientific plan they have devised. The result, if such men ever succeed in gaining power, will be widespread misery and strife. For such schemes could only ever be made to work, if at all, under the iron grip of a tyrant - and such a tyrant as the world has perhaps never yet witnessed.

'These people argue that if the state controlled everything which occurred within its bounds, then the disorder which they now perceive in society could be eliminated. Half a pound of tea and a loaf of bread would be allotted to everyone equally, and all men would thus be happy. Such visionary schemes purport to be scientific, but they fail the very first test for a truly scientific proposition, in that they completely ignore most of the available data. Perhaps chief among the facts of which they take no cognisance is that men have within them a quite unquenchable thirst for liberty. This is not liberty to do this, or liberty to do that, but liberty for its own sake. Most men would rather be free with half a loaf of bread to support them, than live under someone else's command, however well-fed they were. And it is under the commands of others that men would be obliged to live under such a scheme, as I have mentioned; for the state would of necessity have to control everything in order to try to make its system work. It might at first control only a part of men's lives, and leave much of it relatively free, but depend upon it, with each crisis that arose, it would seize yet more power and control, declaring such seizure necessary in order to overcome problems. In the end, the state would control the very hour of your rising in the morning, and the hour at which you lay your head upon the pillow at night. Lord Woolmer sees this more clearly than most, and has spoken strongly against the evil inherent in such schemes. It is for this reason that those who would force men into their "new order", as they term it, have plotted against him. They have much at stake, for, of course, these people all see themselves as the scientific ones, the rational ones, the ones that will be in power and will tell everyone else what they must do. As Lord Woolmer argues so trenchantly against the abstract theories that these people espouse, so they must see their dreams of power fading away.'

'Who are these people?'

'There are many people in many countries involved in this "project" for a new order for humanity, but most of them have never properly thought the matter through, and do not realize what the end result must inevitably be. But there are a few, the prime movers of the project, who know only too well what sort of society will result from their schemes, but pursue their goal relentlessly nevertheless; for what they seek in reality is not the welfare of their fellow-men, but power for themselves: power over all men, and over the whole world. I do not myself believe that they will ever succeed, but were they ever to do so, it would be a sorry day indeed for mankind.'

'How did you discover this plot?' I asked.

'I conjectured, as I say, that the true aim of the whole business had not been to steal the papers - which were probably as unimportant as I had always believed them to be - but, rather, to discredit Lord Woolmer. As I did so, I reflected again on all aspects of the matter, as Lord Woolmer himself had described it to us, and in particular on the most singular feature of the whole affair. It no doubt struck you at the time.'

'The whole business struck me as remarkable,' I returned. 'I cannot recall that any one feature of it struck me as more so than the rest.'

'Not the singular behaviour of Viscount Hardigate with his umbrella?'

'But Viscount Hardigate did nothing with his umbrella, save tap it on the pavement!'

'That,' said Holmes, 'was the singular behaviour.'

'I do not understand.'

'On Monday evening, when Lord Woolmer accompanied Viscount Hardigate to Downing Street, it was raining. Lord Woolmer specifically mentioned the fact. He also mentioned that Viscount Hardigate had an umbrella with him. But Hardigate did not put up his umbrella, for Lord Woolmer remarked on the pompous manner in which the young man tapped it on the pavement as he walked along. Now, why was that?'

'I really have no idea. Hardigate appears to be an arrogant and self-important young man, and he was irritated at being kept waiting by Lord Woolmer. Perhaps he thought that raising his umbrella would compromise his dignity in some way.'

'It is possible, but I think it unlikely that a man of Hardigate's type would suffer his hat and coat to become sodden with rain simply to preserve his dignity. There was, I suspect, a more pressing reason why he did not put up his umbrella. He did not put it up, I believe, because he was unable to do so.'

'Whatever do you mean?'

'That if he had tried to put up his umbrella, the von Strauffhausen document would have tumbled out of it, because that is where it was hidden.'

'What!'

'Yes, Watson. Hardigate's umbrella is the key which unlocked the whole mystery for me. It was a very cunning and complex plot, of which every single facet had been worked out carefully in advance. But the one thing - the only thing - these evil schemers could not plan and control was the weather.

Unfortunately for them, it had begun to rain whilst Hardigate was waiting for Lord Woolmer to finish his dinner. He was thus placed in a difficult position when he got back out to the street. No wonder he walked on so briskly ahead of his companion! He did not wish to give Lord Woolmer any opportunity to speak to him, and perhaps suggest that he put his umbrella up! Had it not been for this chance occurrence of the rain, their plot would have been flawless, and the mystery might have remained forever unsolved!

'It would have been common knowledge that Lord Woolmer was entertaining important guests on Monday evening. Hardigate would thus know perfectly well when he called at the house that Lord Woolmer would be at the dining-table with his guests, and would not be able to come away immediately. It was a fact, I am certain, that Hardigate was relying upon. Indeed, had Lord Woolmer answered his summons at once, I suspect that Hardigate would have told him to take another five or ten minutes, and finish his meal. For what Hardigate wanted was to be left alone at the front of the house for a few minutes.

'Everyone else in the household was engaged at the rear of the house at the time, and Hardigate would easily have been able to slip quietly across the hall from the drawing-room to the study. Lord Woolmer told us, if you recall, that Viscount Hardigate and his friends had spent many an evening at his house in the past, debating political issues, and it is very likely that Hardigate had been in the study many times, and knew where the spare key to the dispatch-box was kept. It would then be a matter of a minute to unlock the box, remove the papers, roll them up inside his umbrella, lock the box up once more, and return to the drawing-room, where he could wait with no doubt increasing impatience for Lord Woolmer.'

'But Holmes!' I cried. 'This cannot be! Surely you have taken leave of your senses! The whole reason that Viscount Hardigate was sent to Lord Woolmer's house in the first place was that the von Strauffhausen papers had already been stolen, an hour or more previously. And their theft was not mere surmise or rumour, either, but hard, undeniable fact. Indeed, the papers were already upon the Prime Minister's desk before Viscount Hardigate set off to fetch Lord Woolmer, and remained there until Lord Woolmer arrived. Your theory, then, ingenious though it may be, is, unfortunately, utter and complete nonsense!'

My friend sat puffing gently at his pipe for a few moments, while I waited for him to respond. I confess that a variety of emotions coursed through my confused brain at that moment. So often in the past had I been astonished at the results my friend had achieved in the most difficult and mystifying of cases, so often had I admired that razor-sharp intellect, those quick and sure perceptions of the essential in a morass of irrelevance, that I was simply astounded now by the failure of reasoning which had led him into such a gross error.

As we sat there in silence, the sound of the door-bell came to my ears from downstairs. Holmes glanced at the clock.

'I can see that it must strike you as nonsense,' said he. 'But perhaps our visitor may be able to cast some light upon the matter. He is, unless I am much mistaken, the chief conspirator in the matter.' His tone was calm, almost careless, but I could see that there was a suppressed tension in his manner, and it was clear that the caller was not unexpected. 'Do not leave, I pray,' he said quickly, as I rose from my chair.

A moment later, Mrs Hudson entered to announce the visitor. Behind her, a tall man, in dark frock-coat and hat strode into the room. Quite who it was that I had expected, I do not know, but I confess to utter astonishment as our landlady read from the card in her hand: 'His Excellency, Gottfried von Strauffhausen.'

He was an erect, spare man, with a clean-shaven, angular jaw, and a look of fierce determination upon his features. He took the chair my companion indicated, and addressed us at once, in forthright tones.

'I received your letter upon my return to England this afternoon, Mr Holmes,' said he, in a strong Germanic accent. 'I must say that I found it both amazing and impertinent. I have answered your summons as a matter of courtesy, but I was equally inclined to put the matter immediately into the hands of the police. As it is, I should warn you that I shall be consulting my lawyers in the morning, with a view to taking action against you.' As he finished speaking, he glared at my friend, as if seeking to injure him by the power of his gaze alone.

'Come, come, your Excellency,' returned Holmes in a calm, unperturbed voice. 'We are both intelligent men: let us treat each other as such. You know that I am confident of my facts: were I not, I should not have written to you. I, for my part, know that you realize this: if you did not believe it to be so, you would not have come here tonight.'

Our visitor's features assumed a look of intense anger, and he appeared about to bluster further, but a moment later his anger passed, and when he spoke it was in a calm, measured tone:

'I am not used to being spoken to in this way, Mr Holmes. You exhibit, if I may say so, a somewhat keener intellect than I am used to finding in this country.'

'Nor can you hope to flatter me by insulting my fellow-countrymen,' interrupted Holmes.

Again the light of anger flashed up in von Strauffhausen's eyes.

'Let us waste no more time, then,' cried he. 'You claim to be in possession of information which you believe would be inconvenient for me if widely known. I find this a gross impertinence.'

'I spent several hours yesterday,' said Holmes, 'reading through the files of old newspapers and many other sources of information. My wish was to learn as much as I could about you and your companions, and what it is that you have been up to in the last year or two. I now know as much about you as anyone could ever wish to know.'

'So?' said our visitor impatiently.

'I know that you are a senior member of the International Brotherhood. You are an office-holder in the Wattenberg Association, and also in the People's Community International, and a leading light in the Charlemagne Group.'

'What of it? I make no secret of my membership of these associations. You speak of them as if they were forbidden secret societies, when they are all highly respectable bodies, who meet for discussion- '

'-and to foment political unrest.'

'Nonsense!'

'The Baltic dock-yards outrage?'

'That was not our doing.'

'Not personally, perhaps; but you deliberately encouraged it by your inflammatory pamphlets.'

'We were only pointing out to those involved where their true interests lay. The loss of life was, perhaps, regrettable. At least, some might say so. But you are English,' he added after a moment, 'and the English are said to be a nation of gardeners. You should appreciate, therefore, that waste ground must be thoroughly turned over before fresh seeds can be sown. Old weeds must be ruthlessly rooted out, so that fresh flowers may grow in their place.'

'I find your analogies despicable,' said Sherlock Holmes in a cold voice. 'You speak of human beings as if they were of no more account than chaff blowing in the wind.'

Von Strauffhausen waved his hand in a deprecating gesture. 'You disappoint me, Mr Holmes,' said he. 'Men of intelligence and education should stand together on these issues. The rabble cannot possibly understand all that is involved, and it is pointless trying to tell them. They will thank us loudly enough when our plans are realized. Until then, it is a mistake to become too involved with them or their misfortunes. But you are right, at least, to mention the wind; for there is a wind blowing, Mr Holmes. It is blowing across the length and breadth of Europe. It will blow away the old world, and usher in the new. What does your poet say? - "The old order changeth, yielding place to new". The associations you mentioned, of which I am honoured to be a member, are working to bring about that change.'

'The world does not stand still,' interrupted Holmes. 'It changes constantly, in ways which we can often scarcely perceive, save in hindsight, and certainly cannot control. It is a sufficient task for us to try to comprehend this changing world, and adapt the institutions of society to conform most harmoniously with it, without attempting to force our own sweeping changes upon it, the consequences of which cannot be known.'

'Bah!' cried von Strauffhausen. 'What a miserable lack of ambition you display, Mr Holmes! You remind me, if I may say so, of the man you mentioned in your letter to me, Lord Woolmer. He, too, is always speaking of reforming this little law, or that little law, when what is required is the changing of all laws at once, and not just in one country, but in all countries at once.'

'How your views are regarded in Germany, I would not venture to say,' remarked Holmes; 'although I know that even there they are not universally accepted, but are strongly opposed by many experienced and learned thinkers, such as, for instance, Professor Helmholtz of Konigsberg. But I know my own country, and I can tell you that you do not understand the English, if you think that they will ever accept your plans.'

'There is certainly some difficulty with the English, I grant you that,' returned von Strauffhausen. 'In my own country, ignorant old fools like Helmholtz are now very much in the minority. Our ideas are increasingly accepted by all men of culture and intelligence, and there are many men highly placed in the government who are working tirelessly to forward our aims. In England we have some support among men whose opinions are worth something - O'Shaughnessy, Fletcher Talbot and so on - but the mass of the population, with which, I am sorry to say, you appear to wish to align yourself, Mr Holmes, are backward-looking, stubborn and stupid. As is becoming the norm in all fields at the present time, Germany now leads the way. Others will follow our example, and we shall lead the world into the next glorious century!'

'And if England does not care to follow your example?'

'England will have no choice in the matter. Where Germany leads, everyone must in the end follow. It is inevitable.'

'But if England remains stubborn?'

'Then she will be crushed, like a gnat, beneath the wheel of history. No-one can resist that which is inevitable. And why is it inevitable? Because we offer the people a glorious, heroic future, free from uncertainty, and unfettered by the mistakes of the past!'

'You offer a prescription for strife and bloodshed.'

Von Strauffhausen laughed harshly. 'Of course, there will be disruption for a little while, perhaps even some suffering, as there always is in times of change. Some, perhaps, with vested interests in the old order, will foolishly attempt to resist the inevitability of the new. By so doing, they will identify themselves as enemies of mankind, just as surely as if they wore a badge proclaiming the fact. As such, they will be shown no mercy, but will be crushed out of existence. For the mass of mankind, a golden future awaits!'

'Such talk has been the common coin of aspiring tyrants and crazed visionaries throughout history,' observed Holmes. 'Those that promise a glorious future at the price of present suffering have a habit of delivering only the latter.'

Von Strauffhausen's lip curled in a sneer. 'You are a cynic, Mr Holmes, and a man of disappointingly limited imagination. You wish to cling on to the past, as a child clings to its nurse's apron, for comfort and security. But we will destroy the past, so that people will look only to the future. And what a vision they will have! No more struggle and competition between man and man, but a benign and scientific order ordained by the state, in which every man will be provided for, and each will know his place, and will be happy to play his small part in the whole! Well, well,' continued our visitor, rising to his feet; 'it has been a diverting conversation, if not a very profitable one. I cannot say that I am glad I came, and if you have nothing of any greater interest to say, I shall take my leave of you.'

'I have this to say,' returned Holmes. 'I know that you have been irked by certain speeches made by Lord Woolmer during the last year. You perceived - correctly, no doubt - that the sentiments expressed in his speeches would, if taken up generally, make it more difficult for you and your companions to convince the public of the merit of your own views.'

'The man is an old fool, who is living in the past!' cried von Strauffhausen angrily, as he sat back down again. 'Individual Liberty! Bah! Of what use is that to anyone, save to injure other people?'

'You therefore devised a complex plan to discredit Lord Woolmer, and thus, you hoped, discredit also his opinions. You persuaded your own government to let you, in your capacity as Minister for Trade, present certain proposals to the British Government, proposals which, as you knew perfectly well, neither side had much interest in. The content of this document was, however, utterly irrelevant, as its sole *raison d'être* was to vanish mysteriously whilst in the possession of Lord Woolmer, and thus, you hoped, bring about his political downfall, and banishment from public life.'

'You have no evidence for this wild claim,' our visitor interrupted in a harsh voice; but Holmes ignored his outburst, and continued in the same even tone:

'You sought a meeting with the Prime Minister, during which you mentioned your proposals, and also suggested to him, no doubt in a roundabout way, that Lord Woolmer would be the ideal man to study them. He was agreeable to this suggestion, took your document and subsequently passed it on to Lord Woolmer. All was arranged, down to the very last detail: the spy, Axel Schnelling, was notified that some confidential papers might shortly be available to purchase; but the authorities were also notified that Schnelling was expecting the papers; a dupe was found in the person of Alfred Davis, the petty criminal, to carry the papers to Schnelling, and thus be caught in possession of them; and a note was written in a deliberate imitation of Lord Woolmer's own hand in order to make his guilt appear even more certain.'

'What a charming little story,' interrupted von Strauffhausen. 'You should consider submitting it for a prize in a fairy-tale competition!'

'What no-one knew,' Holmes continued, 'was that you had prepared a second copy of the document, which was in every respect identical to the first. It was this second copy which you passed, by intermediaries, to the petty criminal Davis, and which was found in his possession when he was apprehended. Your fellow-conspirator, Viscount Hardigate, made certain that he was, on some pretext or other, in the Prime Minister's presence when the apparent loss of the document was discovered, and no doubt offered to go and bring Lord Woolmer to Downing Street. He knew that the household would be dining when he called, and that he would have a few minutes in which to cross from the drawing-room to the study and abstract the papers from the dispatch-box, probably with Lord Woolmer's own spare key, which he was aware was kept in the study. Once he had Lord Woolmer's copy of the document hidden upon his person - rolled up in his umbrella, I strongly suspect - there would be no way that anyone could ever discover that there were really two copies, and that the copy which was intercepted on its way to the spy, Axel Schnelling, was not that which had earlier been entrusted to Lord Woolmer's safekeeping.'

'I see you have a vivid imagination, after all, Mr Holmes,' interjected von Strauffhausen in a sneering tone. 'Unfortunately, your imagination has led you into the realm of fantasy. Your account of the matter is, quite frankly, incredible, and I doubt if it will command any more belief than other such monstrous fabrications. For my own part,' he added, an expression of great smugness upon his features, 'I of course know nothing of the matter. I have been out of the country, as you know. I am sorry to learn that papers entrusted to Lord Woolmer have gone missing, and have very nearly fallen into the hands of a known spy. Tut, tut! It really cannot reflect too well on the noble lord! But I suppose that even English lords may be subject to pecuniary temptation from time to time, especially, perhaps, those whose origins lie in pig-sties and cow-sheds! It must, I imagine, mark the end of Lord Woolmer's public career. What a great shame! But a man who is prepared to betray his own country for silver can hardly expect to be accorded much credibility when he preaches upon the dangers to liberty and democracy which, he alleges, others represent!'

How long this sneering, self-satisfied monologue might have continued, I do not know, but, with a shake of the head, Holmes interrupted his visitor.

'Fortunately,' said he in a confident voice, 'the matter has now been cleared up. Evidence has been found which completely exonerates Lord Woolmer from any blame.'

'What!' cried our visitor, an expression of disbelief upon his face.

'Yes. Have you not heard? The police report makes the matter clear. But, of course! How foolish of me! I was forgetting that you have been abroad, and know nothing of the matter! No doubt you will hear of it in due course! According to the police report, there is definite evidence that a window has been recently forced open at Lord Woolmer's house, and that someone has gained entry to the house that way. The inescapable conclusion, of course, is that some burglar broke into the house deliberately to steal your document. Naturally, under the circumstances, Lord Woolmer cannot be held in any way to blame for such a deliberate, planned act of theft. As for the incriminating note, which appeared to be in Lord Woolmer's own handwriting, it seems likely now that it was, after all, merely an odd coincidence.'

'This cannot be so!' cried von Strauffhausen in an angry voice.

'Apparently it is,' returned Holmes in a placid tone, beginning to refill his pipe with tobacco. 'Personally,' he continued, 'I must say that I am glad that Lord Woolmer's innocence has been established so firmly. This country needs people with such clarity of mind if we are to successfully resist the lure of alien and destructive ideologies, which promise men freedom, but give them only slavery.'

'Bah! You interfering busybody! You are responsible for this, I take it? Yes, I see that you are, you meddling devil! I have heard of you before, Mr Holmes! You make your living by poking your nose into other people's affairs! You are the very dregs of society, sir, and there will be no place for men like you in the society of the future!'

'Thank you for the compliment,' returned Holmes, putting a match to his pipe. 'I had rather be the dregs of this society, with all its faults, than the scum in the society you propose - which is, I take it, the position to which you aspire.'

'Bah!' cried von Strauffhausen again, as he sprang once more to his feet. For a moment he glared at us, a baleful expression upon his face, then, without another word, he stamped from the room and slammed the door behind him.

'What an odious, arrogant man!' I exclaimed, as I heard his heavy footsteps descend the stair, and the front door shut with a crash.

'Indeed, Watson, and a dangerous man, too!' said Holmes in a thoughtful voice. 'Were I the owner of a life assurance company, I should certainly increase the premiums of anyone who spent much time in von Strauffhausen's company!'

My friend's observation was proved accurate within six months, when, as was widely reported in the Press, a rancorous internal dispute in one of the associations of which von Strauffhausen was a member led to violence, and one of his closest associates was shot dead on a railway station in Berlin. The following year, von Strauffhausen was himself the victim of a bomb attack, which killed his coachman and left him so severely injured that he was obliged to retire from public life. As for Viscount Hardigate, readers will no doubt recall that he was stabbed to death in mysterious circumstances last year, in the small German port of Bremerhaven. It is this latter death which has freed my pen from a possible charge of libel, and enabled me to present the foregoing narrative, the first full and accurate account of the matter.

Late in the evening of our interview with Gottfried von Strauffhausen, Sherlock Holmes looked up from his desk, at which he had been writing for an hour or more.

'I have prepared a full account of the matter for Lord Woolmer,' said he, as he put down his pen, and picked up his pipe. 'What he chooses to do with the information is up to him, but he will, at least, know all that there is to know of the affair.'

'Will you make any report to the authorities on Viscount Hardigate's activities?' I asked.

My companion shook his head, as he put a match to his pipe. 'It may be that I am guilty of misprision of felony, in not doing so,' he returned; 'but I see little point in it. It would very likely not be believed, and I have no evidence with which to prove that my version of events is the true one. The net was drawn around Lord Woolmer with very great cunning, so that on the evidence as it stood, the only plausible conclusion was that he himself had passed the papers to the spy. No other explanation appeared possible. That is why it was so important that I add a little evidence of my own, in the shape of the forced window. It being impossible to prove the truth, and exonerate Lord Woolmer in that way, I was obliged to fabricate another, fictitious possibility - that someone broke into his house - and exonerate him in that way.'

'He is still determined to resign from the Government.'

'Yes; but if the plotters regard that as a triumph, I suspect it is one which will turn to ashes in their mouths, and they will find themselves hoist on their own petard. For Lord Woolmer's resignation will enable him to devote considerably more time and energy to speaking and writing upon those subjects of liberty and independence which are most dear to him, and which are so hated by his enemies. Indeed, I am confident that the coming years, so far from seeing a dimming in his eminence, will see it shining forth more brightly than ever.'

'If so, he - and the whole country - will owe you a great debt, Holmes. But I still cannot quite fathom,' I remarked after a moment, 'how you came to understand the nature of the plot in its totality, and to suspect that von Strauffhausen himself was behind it.'

'The whole business depends on a simple series of logical inferences,' returned Holmes, 'of which I feel Aristotle himself would have approved! I mentioned to you earlier how it had occurred to me, as I reflected on the *cui malo* principle, that the purpose of the plot was perhaps not really to steal the papers but to discredit Lord Woolmer. In this light, I reconsidered all that he had told us, and the curious business of Hardigate's umbrella instantly caught my attention. I conjectured what it might mean, and from that all else followed. For if Hardigate had, as I supposed, taken the papers from Lord Woolmer's dispatch-box, it followed that those found in the possession of Davis could not have been the ones which the Prime Minister had earlier handed to Lord

Woolmer. It appeared, however, that they were in every respect identical, including signatures, seals and so on. This could mean only one thing, Watson, that von Strauffhausen himself had prepared two identical copies of the document. It followed from this that the plot against Lord Woolmer was no parochial matter, but one which was international in scope. I determined then to try to confirm the hypothesis - to myself, at least - by finding some connection between Hardigate and von Strauffhausen. This, by a search of old files and records, I was soon able to do. The two men are both members of several of those organizations I mentioned earlier. This, as far as I was concerned, made my case conclusive. I realized at once, however, that I would never be able to prove the matter, and thus had to devise a different method of clearing Lord Woolmer's name, as you observed.'

'Your chain of reasoning appears very sound,' I remarked.

'Thank you, Watson,' said my friend. 'There is, however, one further link in this chain, at one end of which stands Viscount Hardigate's umbrella, and, at the other, the continuing freedom and happiness of mankind.'

'I do not follow you.'

'You recall that von Strauffhausen declared earlier that it was inevitable that his views would eventually prevail? This supposed inevitability seems quite a cornerstone of his argument. Yet his plot against Lord Woolmer rather gives the lie to it, and shows that he does not even believe it himself. For if the triumph of his tyrannical views was quite so inevitable as he claims, there would be little point in mounting such an elaborate plot to remove a man who must, in the long sweep of history, represent a very ephemeral obstacle. We have thus passed from our initial observation of Viscount Hardigate's umbrella, through the logical inferences that Hardigate therefore took Lord Woolmer's papers, that those found on Davis were therefore a duplicate set, that von Strauffhausen himself was therefore involved, that those fanatics among whom von Strauffhausen is a leading light therefore considered the plot worth mounting, to the welcome conclusion that the destruction of Liberty, and the tyranny of total state control over the lives of men is, despite all von Strauffhausen's bluster, definitely not inevitable.'

'Amazing!' I cried with a chuckle.

'Elementary,' said Sherlock Holmes.

THE SILVER BUCKLE

IT WAS IN THE LATE SUMMER OF '87 that the health of my friend, Mr Sherlock Holmes, first gave serious cause for concern. The unremitting hard work to which he invariably subjected himself allowed little time for recuperation from the everyday infirmities which are the lot of mankind, and from which even Holmes's iron constitution was not immune. So long as he remained fit, all was well, but earlier in the year he had reached a point of complete exhaustion from which he had not properly recovered. Eventually it became clear to all who knew him that unless he were removed from Baker Street, and from the constant calls upon his time which were inescapable while he remained there, he might never again fully recover his health and strength.

By chance, I had at the time been reading Boswell's account of his journey with Dr Johnson through the Highlands of Scotland to the Hebrides, and had been fascinated by the remoteness of the places they had visited. Thus inspired, I ventured to suggest to my friend that we emulate the illustrious eighteenth-century men of letters. Holmes's only response was a laconic remark that our travels should be confined to dry land. Taking this to be the nearest to enthusiasm or agreement that I was likely to get, I went ahead at once with the necessary preparations, and, four days later, the sleeping car express from Euston deposited us early in the morning upon the wind-swept platform of Inverness station. From there, after some delay, a local train took us yet further northward and westward, until we reached a small halt, standing in lonely isolation in a silent and treeless glen, where a carriage waited to take us on the last stage of our journey.

It was a strange country we passed through that afternoon, a land of reed-girt lochs, and hard, bare rocks, which thrust through the thin soil like clenched fists. For many weary hours, our road twisted this way and that between these obstacles, until at length it dropped abruptly down a steep-sided valley, beside a sparkling waterfall, and brought us at last to the west coast, and the village of Kilbuie, nestling beneath towering hills on the northern shore of Loch Echil. There was a cheery, welcoming air about the little whitewashed cottages which clustered about the harbour, and the solid, granite-built Loch Echil Hotel, but I saw as we stepped down from our carriage that Holmes's face was pale and drawn, and it was clear that the journey had shaken him badly. It troubled me greatly to see so vital a man reduced to this state, and dearly I hoped that the fine invigorating country air would act quickly to restore his shattered health.

The Loch Echil Hotel was a pleasant, well-appointed establishment, sturdily built to withstand all that a Highland winter might hurl at it, and our rooms were cosy and comfortable. I had soon unpacked, and then, leaving Holmes resting in his room, I took a stroll to familiarize myself with our new surroundings. The weather was fine, and Loch Echil lay like a looking-glass between the hills. It was nearly a mile across at this point, but narrowed considerably to the east, where it extended for perhaps a further half-mile inland. To the west, just beyond the last building of the town, it widened out into a broad bay, where the water was broken by a great many little islands and rocks. I had brought my old field-glasses with me, and spent a pleasant hour on a bench by the water's edge, watching the fishing smacks out in the bay, where the shags and cormorants clustered upon the rocks, and the gulls circled high overhead.

The islands were largely featureless, low and bare, like an oddly stationary school of hump-backed whales, but on one, which was somewhat larger than the others, there appeared to be a dark, gaunt tower, rising high above the waves and rocks about it. Intrigued by this, I mentioned it to Murdoch MacLeod, the manager of the hotel, who was in the entrance-hall when I returned.

"That is the Island of Uffa," said he, "the home of Mr MacGlevin, or *the* MacGlevin, as he prefers to be known."

"You don't mean to tell me that anyone lives out there?" I said in surprise.

He nodded his head. "He's restored the old ruined castle on the island, and has part of it for a museum of antiquities, which is open to the public, and well worth a visit. Most of your fellow-guests in the hotel went over there yesterday. He has some very interesting and valuable pieces, including the famous MacGlevin Buckle, a very fine piece of Celtic workmanship, in solid silver. His one concern in life has been to establish a permanent home for his clan, but he's certainly picked a remote spot for it! He has a fine house in Edinburgh, but it's let for most of the year, as he prefers to bide up here. Apart from an old couple, kinsfolk of his, who help him to keep the place in order, he lives in splendid isolation, laird of all he surveys - such as it is!"

"He sounds something of an eccentric!"

"Aye, you could say that," MacLeod returned in a dry tone. "You may see him about, for he comes over occasionally in his little steam-launch, *Alba*, to pick up supplies. He's a great huge fellow with a ginger beard. If you meet him, you'll not mistake him!"

I could not have imagined then just how dramatic that meeting would be.

On the first floor of the hotel, immediately over the entrance, was a broad, airy drawing-room, illuminated by a row of tall windows, which commanded a magnificent view over the harbour, the loch, and the wilder sea out to the west. When the weather was poor, and Holmes did not feel up to venturing out of doors, we would often sit by these windows as the cloud-bank rolled down the steep hills across the loch, watching the little sailing-boats, their sails puffed out by the westerly wind, making their way up the huge expanse of water towards the harbour. Often, also, I watched anglers out on the loch in the hotel's distinctive little rowing-boats, and thought how pleasant it would be to be out there myself; but although I alluded to the idea once or twice, Holmes showed little inclination for such an excursion.

Our fellow-guests in the hotel were a singularly assorted group. There was, for instance, Dr Oliphant, a balding, white-whiskered, elderly man, of a stooping, learned appearance. His voice was thin and reedy, which made him difficult to understand, but I gathered that he was something of an antiquary and archaeologist, from St Andrews, in Fife. Two sandy-haired young men I had judged to be brothers, so similar were they in appearance, and this surmise proved correct when they introduced themselves as Angus and Fergus Johnstone, up from Paisley for the fishing. A soberly-dressed and very reserved middle-aged couple, Mr and Mrs Hamish Morton, were from Glasgow, as was a very old woman, Mrs Baird Duthie, who wore widow's weeds, walked with a stick, and was almost stone deaf. It seemed unlikely that there would be much of common interest in such a group, but when the conversation of the talkative Johnstone brothers turned to angling, the quiet and withdrawn Mr Morton displayed an interest, and a discussion ensued between them on the merits of various kinds of fishing-tackle. Mrs Morton, not surprisingly, did not share in full measure her husband's interest in this subject, and I had the impression that she tolerated rather than approved of it. She herself, she informed me, had hoped to do some painting and sketching during their stay in Kilbuie, although the weather so far had limited her opportunities. This observation prompted Dr Oliphant to some remark about mankind's perennial urge to artistic creation, whereupon he, she and I engaged in a lively debate on the subject. Holmes took little part in this or any other discussion, but sat back in his chair, his eye-lids languorously half-closed. I had ceased to follow the conversation at the other side of the room, between the rival fishermen, when Mrs Morton had begun to speak of her own interests, but I watched with some amusement as each of them in turn brought in his fishing-equipment, unpacked it all upon the carpet, and argued its merits in the most serious tones.

    I had, I confess, no great knowledge of the subject, but it seemed to me that they each spoke with the authority of an expert. Odd it was, then, that the very next day, all met with calamity whilst engaged in their sport. The Johnstone brothers returned shamefacedly to the hotel about tea-time. Angus Johnstone's rod had broken, and their fishing-lines had become entangled, and in the resulting confusion, Fergus had fallen overboard, and Angus had lost his reel in the water. Mr Morton's accident had been potentially the more serious, although, in the event, he too returned to the hotel chastened but unharmed. He had been out alone, fishing among the islands in the bay, his wife having remained behind to do some drawing by the harbour, when his boat had sprung a leak. Unable to stem the inrushing water, and with nothing with which to bale out, he had rowed with all speed for the shore, but his boat had disappeared beneath him before he had reached it, and he had had to swim the remaining distance. Murdoch MacLeod was most distressed at this account, and rung his hands in his misery.

"You must have feared for your life!" he declared in a tone of great sympathy; but the other shook his head.

"I was nae worried," said he dismissively. "It was a matter of only five-and-twenty feet before my feet touched solid ground. I was more concerned about the walk home, I can tell ye! I came ashore on the south side of the bay, ye see, so I've had to walk the whole way round the loch to get back! My feet'll never be the same again!"

"And you have lost all your equipment?" inquired MacLeod.

"Aye. All sunk wi'out trace."

"We will of course compensate you for your loss- "

"We can discuss it later," said Morton, turning on his heel. "For now, all I'm interested in is a hot bath!"

"This season has been an unfortunate one for us," said MacLeod, after Morton had left the room. "At this rate, we shall soon have no-one wishing to stay here. Why, only two weeks ago, a young lady from Peebles slipped and fell down the main staircase in odd circumstances, and, just before your arrival, a Mrs Formartine from Arbroath lost a valuable pearl brooch. Now this! I felt sure that all the rowing-boats were sound. Thank goodness it was not more serious!" He shook his head as he left the room.

"What an odd and unfortunate thing!" said I.

"Indeed," said Holmes, and I seemed to read in his face that there was little point my raising again the idea of a fishing-trip.

It rained heavily that night, but the following morning dawned bright and clear, and there was much discussion at breakfast-time of plans for the day ahead. Several of the hotel-guests were to leave on the Friday, and were thus keen to make the most of their last day in Kilbuie. The Johnstone brothers, clearly undaunted by the previous day's experience, intended, once they had replaced their lost and damaged equipment, to spend their time fishing once more.

"We'll try among the islands today," remarked Angus Johnstone as they were leaving. "Whatever happens, it canna be worse than yesterday!"

To my surprise, the meek and frail-looking Dr Oliphant also announced that he would be taking a boat, his intention being to visit Stalva Island, where, he said, there were the remains of a Viking burial chamber. The Mortons hired a pony and trap and set off with a picnic hamper and Mrs Morton's sketching equipment, to visit the Falls of Druimar, a well-known beauty spot, some dozen miles inland. The weather was fine and the wind light, and Holmes and I passed a pleasant day in ambling about the town and the harbour, and along the margin of the loch.

Despite MacLeod's worries for the welfare of his guests, there were no more accidents, and they all returned in good spirits, if a little late. I observed as Holmes and I went into dinner that evening that an extra table had been laid, but no-one arrived to claim it, and I saw MacLeod glance at the clock over the mantelpiece several times, and shake his head. It was clear that he was expecting someone, but how they might arrive, unless it were by private carriage all the way from Inverness, I could not imagine, for the coach which connected with the train had long since been and gone.

This little mystery was soon solved, however. As we were taking coffee in the drawing-room after our meal, the door was opened to admit two men, introduced to us as Alexander and Donald Grice Paterson, father and son respectively, who had, they informed us, arrived in their own little yacht which they had just moored in the harbour. Alexander Grice Paterson was a small, wiry man of about fifty, dark-haired and clean-shaven, with a shrewd, crafty, almost fox-like appearance. His son, Donald, was perhaps two-and-twenty, a little taller than his father, and sported a black moustache, but with the same dark, fox-like look to him. Plates of sandwiches and cheese were brought in for them, which they devoured hungrily, and, thus restored, they began to speak in excited tones. It was clear that they had recently had a very singular experience, which they were keen to share with their fellow-guests.

The older man was a senior partner in an Edinburgh legal firm, he informed us, into which his son had recently been admitted as a junior. Their speciality was commercial law, which could sometimes be a little dry, he admitted, even for those whose vocation it was.

"It's to remedy the dryness," he remarked with a crafty twinkle in his eye, in what was clearly a much-rehearsed witticism, "that each year we spend as long as possible on the water! In short, we have a little boat, a twenty-five-footer, the *Puffin*, which we sail about hither and thither for a week or two each year.

"In the past we've been blown all over the Firth of Clyde, back and forth from the Ayrshire coast to Kintyre. This year we thought we'd venture further afield, and plotted a course up the West Coast of Argyll and beyond. We've not had the best of wind, but we've done pretty well, all things considered, and two nights ago we slipped through the Sound of Sleat and moored for the night in Loch Alsh. Since then, we've not hurried, running in and out of bays and inlets, and exploring any nook of the coast which promised interest. We expected to arrive in Kilbuie this afternoon, but the wind has been unfavourable, and we've been beating this way and that for the last few miles. At last, earlier this evening, we turned into Echil Bay - and now we come to the most singular experience of my life! We knew when we first set off that we were sailing into unknown waters, to the land of myth and magic, but we never expected that we'd be the victims of Highland magic ourselves!"

He paused and took a large mouthful of the whisky and water which stood at his elbow, glancing round as he did so, as if to judge the effect of his words, for all the world like an advocate addressing a packed court-room. His opening remarks concluded, he now came to the crux of the matter.

"We steered a course between the islands, but the wind was not so much against us now, as almost non-existent, and our progress was slow. It was just as the sun was setting behind us, and the shadows were long ahead, that we noticed what appeared to be a ruined tower, on one of the larger islands. Donald consulted the charts, and was able to inform me that the island was Uffa, and that upon it were the ruins of an ancient religious establishment. This seemed too good an opportunity to pass up, and we determined to go ashore and explore.

"We moored the *Puffin* some thirty yards from the shore, and rowed the dinghy into a little natural harbour among the great jumbled rocks at the extreme western end of the island. By the time we had our feet on dry land, the light was fading fast, but there was a well-worn path through the heather, so we were confident of soon reaching the ruins. The path meandered steeply up and down, however, and after a few minutes, we had quite lost sight of the ruins, and it became apparent that to get from the west end of Uffa to the east, where the ruins were situated, was going to take us longer than we had expected. Still, as we had by this time gone some considerable distance, we thought, like Macbeth, that it were as well to go on as go back. A mistake, perhaps, but we were not to know." He paused. "Perhaps you could tell them what happened next, Donald," he said, turning to his son.

"It was fairly dark by then," the younger man continued after a moment. "We couldn't really see very much. There seemed to be paths everywhere, and we were just wondering if we'd taken the wrong one, when we came over the brow of a small hill and saw the ruins dead ahead of us. We'd thought the sky was dark, but the ruins were darker still, and showed up as a black silhouette. To the left stood the ruined tower, tall and stark, with a huddle of lower buildings surrounding it, and to the right, some more disordered ruins; and then- " He broke off and swallowed before continuing:

"As we drew closer, picking our way carefully along the rocky path, there came all at once the sound of movement somewhere just ahead of us, and then a dark, crouching shape scuttled across the path not more than twenty feet away."

"The Black Pig!" cried Murdoch MacLeod.

"What?" cried the elder Grice Paterson in return.

"You are in superstitious country," said Dr Oliphant. "There is a belief in these parts that the appearance of the Black Pig is an omen of evil."

"There are some," said MacLeod in a low tone, "who say that the Black Pig is the Evil One himself!"

Alexander Grice Paterson snorted. "Perhaps it is fortunate for us, then," he said, "that what we saw did not remotely resemble a pig. It was more like a man, crouching down."

"Aye," said his son. "Furtive and creeping, with his robes all draggling out behind him."

"I need hardly say that we were somewhat unnerved by this apparition," the elder Grice Paterson continued. "Then, as we stood there, rooted to the spot, a faint, wavering light sprang up in a window high in the tower. I think Donald must have cried out- "

"With all respect, Pa," his son interrupted, "I believe that you were the one doing the crying out."

"Well, well. Be that as it may, next moment an oblong of bright light appeared suddenly before us, as a door was flung open at the base of the tower, and a giant of a man with a great ginger beard stepped out, carrying a lantern.

"MacGlevin," said MacLeod softly, as Grice Paterson continued:

"'Who's there?' the giant's voice boomed out."

"Why, man," cried Angus Johnstone, laughing; "it sounds more like a Grimm's fairy tale every minute!"

"No doubt," returned Alexander Grice Paterson, appearing a little annoyed at this interruption; "but it did not strike us that way at the time. We stepped forward and introduced ourselves.

"'A strange time to come paying a visit,' the giant boomed back at us. I explained our situation, that we had had no idea that the island was inhabited.

"'On our map,' said I, 'this building is marked only as a ruin.'

"'Oh, is it?' replied he. 'Then your map, Sir, is sadly in error - reprehensibly so - and I recommend that you buy yourself a new one! But, come! A MacGlevin does not turn even the meanest wretch from his door - no offence intended, Gentlemen! Pray step this way!'

"We followed him into his castle. He was most hospitable, I must say, and showed us into the clan museum that he has established there. 'I'll not light the lamps in here,' said he, 'for I ken you're in a hurry to be off, but take this lantern and have a look about, while I prepare something to warm you!' Shortly afterwards, we joined him before a blazing fire and drank his health, and five minutes later set off back to our boat, carrying the lantern he had lent us."

"Had you mentioned to him the creature you had seen earlier?" queried Holmes.

Grice Paterson shook his head. "I'd thought it best not to."

"Does he keep a dog?"

"No, and there are no sheep or other animals on the island, either."

"It's the Black Pig!" said Murdoch MacLeod again, in a tone of awe.

"One moment, if you please," said Grice Paterson. "Our story is not yet finished."

"Dear me!" cried Dr Oliphant. "Yet more adventures?"

"Indeed! You have not yet heard the strangest episode. We eventually reached the western extremity of Uffa, although it was not easy finding our way in the pitch blackness, and the lantern was little help. There, where we had secured the dinghy, was- " He paused and looked about the room.

"Well?" queried Dr Oliphant impatiently.

"Nothing."

"Nothing?"

"Not a thing. No sign whatever of our boat. Just the dark sea splashing over the black rocks. We could see the *Puffin* riding at anchor a little distance off, for we'd lit a lamp on her before we'd left, but we'd no way of reaching her. And I was as certain that the dinghy had been secured properly as I'd ever been certain of anything in my life."

"What did you do?" queried Fergus Johnstone.

"We had no choice but to trudge all the way back to MacGlevin's domain and throw ourselves on his mercy. He seemed none too pleased to see us again, but said he would row us round to the *Puffin* in his own skiff, which was moored in an inlet just below the castle. You continue, Donald."

"Just as we were rounding the western head of the island, approaching the *Puffin*, my father cried out. I looked where he pointed, and there was our little dinghy, neatly tucked in the inlet, just as we had left it. Of course, Mr MacGlevin was a wee bit upset at this, and expressed himself somewhat warmly. Even a whelk would realize, he said, that we had simply taken the wrong path and looked for our boat in the wrong place. His parting words to us as he rowed off, after setting us aboard our own dinghy, were that we should henceforth confine our inept navigational activities to the streets of Edinburgh."

"There it might have ended," continued the elder Grice Paterson: "as an embarrassing experience, but no more - although I was still convinced that the boat had not been there when we had looked for it before - but, as we were climbing from dinghy to yacht, Donald found something by his feet. Show them, my boy."

Donald Grice Paterson put his hand in his pocket, and pulled out a large, wooden-handled clasp-knife. He unfolded the blade, which was broad and strong-looking, with a curiously square end.

"It's not ours," said his father, "so how came it in the bottom of our boat?"

"May I see it?" said Holmes. He took the knife and examined it closely. "Made in Sheffield," he remarked; "which is hardly surprising information. The tip has been snapped off, which must have taken some considerable force."

The knife was passed round the room, amid much murmuring of interest, but no-one could make any useful suggestion regarding it.

"Someone has been playing tricks upon you," declared Dr Oliphant.

"Someone - or something," said Murdoch MacLeod.

"A mischievous sprite," suggested Mrs Morton.

Sherlock Holmes offered no observation of his own, and later, when I queried his silence on the matter, he shook his head and smiled.

"My dear fellow," said he, "you must have observed in the past that an unresolved mystery possesses a charm and romance which its solution can rarely aspire to. It is for this reason that - unless it is likely to involve them in a personal loss - men often prefer mystery to enlightenment. I could have suggested at least seven possible explanations, but all of them were fairly prosaic, I'm afraid, and not really what the company was seeking!"

With that he retired for the night, and there the singular adventures of the Grice Patersons might have remained, but for the surprising sequel.

We were seated at breakfast the following morning when there came the sound of raised voices from the hallway outside. Moments later, the door was flung open, and, ignoring the protests of the manager, in strode a gigantic figure, whose tangled ginger hair and beard identified him instantly as MacGlevin, closely followed by a police constable. The Laird of Uffa's eyes passed quickly over the assembled diners, until they alighted upon the luckless Grice Patersons.

"There they are!" he roared. "There are the villains! Arrest those men at once, MacPherson!"

Like everyone else, Grice Paterson had been frozen into immobility by this sudden, amazing irruption, his egg-spoon poised half-way to his lips, but now he sprang to his feet.

"How dare you!" he cried angrily. "What is the meaning of this?"

"The meaning," returned MacGlevin in an equally heated voice, "is that you have abused my hospitality. I took you in out of the dark night, and you have returned this favour by treacherously stealing that which is most dear to my clan, the MacGlevin Buckle!"

"This is nonsense," snorted Grice Paterson. "I have stolen nothing. I have never in my life taken that which was not mine. Why, I have never even seen your wretched buckle!"

MacGlevin's face assumed a dark, angry hue, and the veins on his temples stood out like whipcord.

"How dare you refer to the heirloom of my family in those insulting terms!" he roared. "You despicable villain!"

How long this aggressive exchange might have continued, it is difficult to say. Certainly, MacGlevin appeared on the verge of imposing his huge physical presence on the little Edinburgh lawyer. But Constable MacPherson placed his considerable bulk between them, and managed to calm the atmosphere a little. "Gentlemen, gentlemen," he said, "let us discuss the matter like the civilized men we are!"

The facts of the matter were soon told. The Laird of Uffa had last seen his family's heirloom during the previous afternoon, when he had been re-arranging some of the exhibits in his museum. He had not entered the museum with Mr Grice Paterson and his son, but had given them a lantern and told them to look round by themselves if they wished. They had done so for two or three minutes before rejoining him for a hot toddy. Later he had entered the museum to fetch a book, and had found the buckle gone. It had not been protected from theft in any way, but had lain, uncovered, upon a velvet cushion, atop a small stand. No-one but the Grice Patersons had entered the house all day, and nor were there any signs of a forced entry. The case against the Edinburgh men seemed, then, on circumstantial evidence at least, to be conclusive, although, having conversed with them at length the previous evening, I could not really believe either of them to be guilty of so mean a crime. For their part, they declared that they had not observed the buckle the previous evening, having taken only a cursory glance round the museum.

The impasse was broken in a surprising manner. Sherlock Holmes abruptly pushed back his chair from the breakfast-table and rose to his feet. In a very few words, he introduced himself, and although he had not then achieved the celebrity he was later to enjoy, the name was recognized instantly by several of those there.

"I followed the Maupertuis case in the papers," said the policeman with respect, but Holmes waved his hand dismissively.

"I think it would be as well to examine the scene of this crime before any arrests are contemplated," said he, in a voice of quiet authority. "It may well be that the circumstances there will decide the question of guilt or innocence once and for all, and may also suggest some other line of inquiry."

"Suggest fiddlesticks!" cried MacGlevin in contempt, but Constable MacPherson nodded his head.

"I canna arrest anybody merely on your say-so, Mr MacGlevin," said he. "This gentleman is correct. We must examine the scene. You will favour us with your assistance, Mr Holmes?"

My friend assented, and MacPherson quickly made his arrangements. Holmes and he had a brief discussion, during which my friend made several specific suggestions, the upshot being that two of the local fishermen who were special constables were to take charge of matters in Kilbuie in our absence, and the *Puffin* was to be temporarily impounded. Then MacGlevin, MacPherson, the elder Grice Paterson, Holmes and myself set off for the islands in the steam launch, *Alba*.

The black tower of MacGlevin's abode loomed above us as we approached Uffa, gaunt and solitary. Beyond it stretched the length of the bleak and featureless island, its surface a mottled dun colour. It was a strange and inhospitable place to make one's home, and perhaps the most unlikely spot in which my friend had ever investigated a crime. A hundred yards or so to the north were further, smaller islands, the sea breaking in white foam over their jagged rocks, and, perhaps two hundred yards to the south, the nearest point on the mainland, an area of tumbled rocks and tangled shrubs.

MacGlevin brought his little vessel alongside a small and rickety wooden jetty, where his servant, a short, spry elderly man with faded ginger hair, was waiting to take the rope, and we climbed ashore. A steep little pathway brought us to the front door of the building. The single tower, perhaps twenty feet square, rose high above us, its little windows set in deep embrasures. At the back of the tower was a long, low, single-storeyed wing, with a shallow-pitched roof. To the left of the tower was a wide, flat grassy area, with piles here and there of driftwood and sawn logs, and at the other side of this open space stood the jumble of lichen-blotched stones which was all that remained of the early Christian settlement.

We followed MacGlevin inside, and through to the museum, which occupied half of the single-storey wing, and which appeared as impregnable as a fortress. The walls were of stone, immensely thick, and hung all about with swords and shields, maps, paintings and tartans. High up along the left-hand wall was a row of windows, and in the sloping roof above was a series of small sky-lights, all of which had black iron bars across. The windows had all been fastened on the inside for the previous two days, the laird informed us, the skylights did not open at all, and there was no other door than the one through which we had entered, from the living-quarters of the house. Scattered about the room were several tables and cases containing exhibits, and in the middle stood a white-painted wooden pedestal, about a foot square and four feet high. Atop this was a red velvet cushion, depressed slightly in the middle. This was the usual resting-place of the MacGlevin Buckle, from which it had mysteriously disappeared.

Directing us to stand back, Holmes examined the cushion, the pedestal and the area round about with minute care, occasionally murmuring to himself. As he did so, there was a glint in his eye and an energy in his manner which it thrilled me to see. Like a weary hound who gets the scent of the chase in his nostrils, Holmes's keen, incisive nature had been kindled afresh by the task before him, and had quite thrown off the lassitude of former days. Grice Paterson caught my eye, raised his eyebrow questioningly, and seemed about to speak, but I shook my head and put my finger to my lips.

"The buckle was not fastened to the cushion in any way?" queried Holmes of MacGlevin. "No? But it appears that something was, for there is a little tear in the surface, as if something has been forcibly ripped from it." MacGlevin stepped forward to see, and declared that he had not noticed such a tear before.

Holmes was down on his hands and knees when he uttered a little cry of satisfaction as he picked something up from the floor, a couple of feet to the side of the pedestal. He continued his search for a while, without finding anything else, and presently he stood up and held out his hand. Upon the palm lay a tiny grey sphere of metal, little more than an eighth of an inch in diameter.

MacGlevin shook his head dismissively, and shrugged his shoulders. "It must have fallen from someone's pocket," he suggested. "I cannot see that it is of any significance. Why, any of my visitors might have dropped it!"

Holmes gave a little chuckle. "Really, Mr MacGlevin," said he; "if you wish your buckle to be returned to you, you would do well not to dismiss the evidence so quickly. This interesting little sphere- "

"Is a piece of lead shot of some kind," said Constable MacPherson in a thoughtful voice; "and there's little opportunity for shooting rabbits in here, Mr MacGlevin!"

Holmes laughed. "There is no more to be seen here," said he. "Let us now examine the exterior of the building."

We followed him outside, and round to the back. Where the single-storey wing joined the rear wall of the tower at a right angle, there was a soft patch of muddy ground, to which Holmes devoted his attention.

"I reap the benefits of investigating a crime in such an unfrequented spot," said he, in good spirits. "There are some wonderfully clear prints here. Your shoe size, Mr Grice Paterson?"

"Seven."

"I thought as much. And your son's will be something similar. These prints are too large to be yours, and too small to be Mr MacGlevin's. Your servant, Mr MacGlevin?"

"Wattie? A tiny fellow, as you saw, with feet to match."

"Which eliminates him also, then. It rained heavily on Wednesday night, so these prints must have been made yesterday. You did not have any visitors?"

"I never open my house to visitors on a Thursday."

"Then these are the prints of the thief."

We all pressed forward to see. A clear impression of a right foot, the toe pointing into the angle of the building, was crossed by another, slightly deeper print of the same shoe, the toe pointing away from the wall.

"He has climbed the building here," said Holmes. "The deeper print was made when he jumped back down. Might this be where you saw your ghostly figure last night, Mr Grice Paterson?"

"It could very well have been," replied the lawyer. "It crossed the path from somewhere near here towards the ruins over there."

"What figure is this?" demanded MacGlevin.

"We thought we saw something," Grice Paterson returned, "but did not mention it lest you thought us foolish."

MacGlevin snorted, but made no comment.

While they were speaking, Holmes had been examining the wall closely. Presently his hand found a projecting stone some way above his head, and he managed to haul himself up. He quickly clambered over the gutter and onto the shallow-pitched roof of the museum wing, where he moved carefully along the slates, examining each sky-light in turn.

"Oh, this is pointless!" said MacGlevin, who was becoming impatient once more. "Even if someone did climb up there, the sky-lights don't open, the panes of glass are too small for anyone to pass through, and they're all barred on the inside, anyway."

"Nevertheless," Holmes called back in an agreeable tone, "someone has recently been tampering with this one. The lead strip round the edge has been bent back, the putty chipped away, and the nails- Ah!" He had been looking behind him, down the roof to the guttering. Now he carefully reached down and plucked from the gutter a small sliver of something metallic, which he held up between his finger and thumb and examined closely. "If you would be so good as to join me," he called to MacPherson, "I should be most obliged."

The sky had been growing darker for some time, and MacGlevin, Grice Paterson and I hurried for shelter as there came a sudden downpour of rain, leaving Holmes and MacPherson in conversation upon the roof. The shower soon blew over, and twenty minutes later, after a cup of tea, we went back out to find that the clouds had parted and the sun was shining. Holmes and MacPherson were nowhere to be seen, and we were wondering what had become of them, when there came a shout from below, and we turned to see a small rowing-boat approaching the little harbour below the castle, with Holmes and MacPherson in it. The policeman was pulling sturdily on the oars, while Homes sat in the stern, placidly smoking his pipe.

"We have just had a little run-round in the boat," he explained, as they stepped ashore.

"And?" said MacGlevin.

"The case is now complete."

We returned to Kilbuie to find the hotel in tumult. Luggage of all kinds was heaped up in confusion in the entrance-hall, so that we had to shuffle sideways to get past.

Dr Oliphant ran up to us as we entered, his face a picture of agitation.

"What is the meaning of this?" he demanded of MacPherson in a shrill voice. "It is absolutely vital that I reach home this evening. I have an important lecture to deliver in Edinburgh tomorrow night, and I must have a day to prepare my notes. The coach is not here, and when I inquire why not, I am informed that it is held by order of the police!" His voice rose to a breathless cry. "This is an outrage! You have no right to detain a public coach! If it does not leave soon, we shall miss the connecting train!"

Murdoch MacLeod stepped forward, wringing his hands with anxiety.

"What is going on?" he queried in a hopeless voice. "Can you explain, Constable?"

"This is highly irregular," said Hamish Morton. "They tell us the coach cannot leave, but my wife and I must be back in

Glasgow tonight, and Mrs Baird Duthie, too, is anxious to be away. Should we make our own arrangements?"

MacPherson pulled an enormous watch out of his pocket, and consulted it for a moment.

"You'll all get where you're going," he said shortly. "If you would just step through into the dining-room for a moment- "

The hotel-servants were setting the tables for lunch, and looked up in surprise as we all filed in and arranged ourselves as best we could, here and there about the room. Old Mrs Baird Duthie was the last to shuffle in, Angus Johnstone supporting her elbow. His brother brought a chair forward for her and relieved her of her stick, and she sat down heavily. All eyes were on Sherlock Holmes, who stood patiently until everyone was settled, his hands behind his back.

"Now," said he at length. "A serious and ingenious crime has been committed. The famous MacGlevin Buckle has been stolen from the museum on the Island of Uffa. It must be returned to its rightful owner." He glanced at MacGlevin, who was standing with his arms folded by the doorway, a brooding expression on his face.

"It is, of course, most unfortunate," said Dr Oliphant; "but what is it to us?"

"The buckle is in this hotel," returned Holmes. "Constable MacPherson and his deputed officers therefore propose to search the building until they find it."

There were loud groans about the room.

"Why, man, that could take days!" said Angus Johnstone.

"Let us make a start, then," said Homes, "beginning with that." His long thin finger indicated the small leather and canvas satchel which hung from Mrs Morton's shoulder.

"But this contains only my painting and sketching things," said she, rising to her feet, the expression on her face a mixture of surprise and indignation.

"Will you open it, Madam, or shall I?" inquired MacPherson.

Reluctantly, she lowered the little bag to the floor, and began to unfasten the straps. "This is an absurd waste of time," said she, as she tipped the contents of the bag onto the carpet. I craned forward to see. There were numerous tubes of paint, several brushes and pencils tied up in a ribbon, a palette, a pad of paper, and a very dirty rag, stained with every colour of the rainbow.

"Kindly unfold that cloth," said Holmes.

"It is dirty," said she. "It is only the rag I wipe my paint-brushes on. I shall soil my gloves- "

Even as she was speaking, Holmes leaned quickly down and unfolded the screwed-up cloth. There in the middle of the multi-coloured wrapping, lay a large and ornate silver buckle. There were gasps all round the room, and, in that split second of quiet, Hamish Morton suddenly shot from his seat and bolted for the door. He had his hand on the door-knob, but MacGlevin, too, was quick, and grabbed him in a smothering embrace.

"You fool!" cried Mrs Morton to her husband, in a harsh voice. "'Let's leave Glasgow,' you said. 'Let's get away and lie low for a while'! But you just couldn't resist this, could you! And now see what you have done!"

It was startling to hear the violent tones of the woman's voice, and almost made my hair stand on end. Her husband, held tightly in the bear-like grip of the Laird of Uffa, made no response. Next instant, my blood ran cold, for with a quick, darting movement, her hand had dipped into her reticule and re-emerged gripping an evil-looking little revolver.

"Stand aside, all of you!" she said in a cold, clear voice, as she pointed the gun menacingly, from one person to another. "This pistol is loaded, and I am quite prepared to use it."

I saw Holmes catch the eye of Fergus Johnstone, then he spoke. "Mrs Morton," said he. For a fraction of a second, she turned her head, and in that instant, in a blur of movement, the gun was dashed from her hand. Fergus Johnstone, who had been standing a little to the side of her, had brought down the old lady's walking-stick on her wrist with a loud crack. Mrs Morton cried wildly with pain, and clutched her wrist, and Holmes stepped forward quickly and picked up the gun. In a minute MacPherson had whistled up his special constables and the prisoners had been taken away. Then MacGlevin stepped forward to where his precious heirloom still lay on the paint-smeared rag. With an air of reverence, he picked it up. As he did so, there came a further surprise, for there lying beneath it was an exquisite little silver clasp, set with creamy pearls.

"Mrs Formartine's brooch!" cried MacLeod, almost beside himself with joy.

Some two hours later, after lunch, we were all seated in the drawing-room of the hotel. The Mortons were safely under guard at the local police station, awaiting an escort to take them to Inverness. Dr Oliphant and Mrs Baird Duthie had long since departed, and the Loch Echil Hotel had returned to an atmosphere of normality.

"I cannot thank you enough," said Alexander Grice Paterson to Holmes. "Without your intervention, I dread to think what might have become of us."

"I regret I was a little heated," said MacGlevin in a sheepish tone, holding out his hand to the man he had accused. "I just couldna' think how anyone could've taken it but you."

"That is all right," said the other, accepting MacGlevin's hand. "Let's forgive and forget. What I'd like to know is how you got to the bottom of the matter so quickly, Mr Holmes."

"It was not difficult. I will give you a full explanation when Constable- Ah! MacPherson! We were just speaking of you."

"Please excuse the delay, Gentlemen," said the policeman briskly. "I have had a busy time of it. I wired details of the Mortons down to Glasgow, and I have their reply here. We've landed bigger fish than we realized, Mr Holmes! They're fairly certain that the man calling himself Hamish Morton is in fact Charlie Henderson, wanted in connection with the Blythswood Square burglary, earlier this year- "

" -In which the thieves got away with works of art worth thousands," interjected Holmes, "and left the owner of the house seriously injured. I recall it very well."

"And the woman, who has used so many names in her career that it's hard to keep track of her, is wanted under the name of Mary Monteith, for a long series of frauds and forgeries. Apparently she has real artistic gifts, but she's used them only in the cause of crime. She's suspected of being behind some of the most brilliant art forgeries of the last dozen years."

"Well, I never!" ejaculated Grice Paterson. "But come, Mr Holmes: Tell us how you got on to them."

"My interest was first aroused," said Holmes after a moment, "by Morton's report of his boating accident. He declared that all his fishing equipment had sunk without trace, yet when I had seen it the previous evening in this very room, I had observed, without giving it any special attention, that his rod was of the sort which is fitted with a large cork handle. It seemed unlikely that such a rod should have sunk. It might, of course, have become entangled with some other equipment, and been dragged down by it, but Morton merely said it had sunk. It seemed to me that he was lying, but I could not think why, unless he merely wished to swindle the hotel out of a few pounds by way of compensation. It was a petty matter, and I gave it little more thought.

"When we went out to Uffa, to investigate the theft, I had no pre-conceived ideas as to what had taken place there. For all I knew, the result of my examination might have been to confirm Mr Grice Paterson's guilt. You did not look a very likely pair of thieves," he remarked, turning to the Grice Patersons with a chuckle; "but I have known many criminals in my time, and a good half of them did not appear capable of the crimes they had committed; so I preserved a professional detachment on the matter, and reserved my judgement.

"My examination of the museum revealed, as you saw, a small tear in the cushion upon which Mr MacGlevin's Buckle had been lying when last he saw it, which at once suggested to me that some hook, or other sharp device, had been used to lift the buckle. This in turn suggested, of course, that the thief had not been in a position to reach it with his hand. The obvious conclusion was that a line with a hook attached had been lowered from above, through one of the sky-lights. When I found on the floor a small piece of lead shot, such as fishermen use to weight their lines, this presumption became a certainty. The weight would help the line to drop straight, and give the thief more control over it. No doubt the piece of shot we found had become detached when the hook snagged the cushion and had to be forcibly yanked free.

"The next thing then, was to examine the exterior of the building. Here I was fortunate enough to find very clear indications of where the thief had climbed the wall. The fact that I could only just reach the only usable hand-hold - and I am a good six foot in height - indicated that the thief was not a small man, as also did the size of the footprints. These indications eliminated the Grice Patersons, as far as I was concerned.

"I then examined the sky-light which lay immediately above the stand on which the buckle had been displayed, and it was obvious at once that one of the panes of glass had been removed and later replaced. The lead round the glass had clearly been bent back, and then flattened again. That would have presented no problem, and nor would it have been difficult to chip away the putty with a knife. But there were also galvanized nails bent over beneath the lead to hold the pane firmly, which would have required a greater application of force. Was this, I wondered, how the knife-blade came to be broken? This conjecture was at once confirmed, for there in the gutter below me was a little shiny triangle - the missing tip of the blade.

"It seemed clear enough, then, what had happened. The thief had been at work when you chanced upon the scene, Mr Grice Paterson, and was evidently the figure you saw cross the path in the darkness. He would then have returned to his boat, but must have taken the wrong path in the darkness, and mistakenly set off in your boat, rather than his own. You came along shortly afterwards, found your boat missing, and returned to seek Mr MacGlevin's aid. The thief, meanwhile, must have realized his mistake, and so returned your boat, in which he had dropped his knife, found his own boat, and left the island for the second time.

"So much seemed clear. But who, then, was the thief? There seemed no way of knowing. It was then that I recalled Morton's reported accident, and his claim to have lost all his fishing tackle, about which I had had some doubt at the time. Now it struck me as possible that his boat had not sunk at all, but had been deliberately hidden in the bushes by the shore on the south side of the bay, together with his fishing equipment. If that were so, he would then have been able to use it when he wished to commit this crime, without the slightest suspicion attaching to him, even if the crime were discovered before he and his accomplice had left Kilbuie. MacPherson and I therefore rowed over to the mainland, which is no great distance at that point, and soon found what we were looking for - one of this hotel's distinctive little skiffs dragged up and hidden behind some rocks, with a disordered heap of fishing tackle within it.

"The case was therefore complete, and it remained only to locate the buckle. I was quite certain that the Mortons had it, but finding it might have taken some time. However, as you may recall, they had claimed on the day the crime was committed to have gone inland so that Mrs Morton might sketch - probably they did so, earlier in the day - and had therefore had the satchel containing the art materials with them. It seemed likely, then, that the stolen buckle had been secreted in there in the first place, and, if so, it seemed to me possible that it was still there, especially as Mrs Morton was demonstrating an unusual attachment to the bag. This surmise proved correct, and the rest you know. Mr MacGlevin has his heirloom restored to him, Mrs Formartine will soon have her brooch back - that was something of an unexpected bonus, I must confess - clearly Morton had been keeping his hand in - and two dangerous criminals are safely under lock and key."

"You make it sound so obvious and straightforward, Mr Holmes!" exclaimed MacGlevin in amazement. "I'm sure that if we had spent all day examining the museum, we should not have observed the little traces which you found, nor made anything of them if we had done!"

"Aye, it's a grand job of work all right," said MacPherson with feeling. "I may get my sergeant's stripes over this arrest. I don't know how I can ever thank you, Mr Holmes," he continued, extending his hand. "Without your help, I don't know that we should ever have caught those villains!"

"It is always a pleasure to assist the forces of law and order," returned my friend with a smile. "Now, Watson," he continued, turning to me: "the fresh air on Uffa has quite invigorated me! What say you to another expedition, this time to catch something a little smaller and tastier, for our supper?"

THE BROKEN GLASS

BETWEEN THE YEARS 1882 and 1890, I had the privilege of studying the methods of Sherlock Holmes, the foremost criminal investigator of the period, and of making a record of his more interesting cases. In truth, there were very few of his cases which were *not* interesting. If a case made no appeal to his taste, if it appeared to possess none of those *outré* features which so delighted his artistic temperament, he would not infrequently decline to take it up at all. My note-books therefore contain some of the oddest, most surprising and most puzzling problems which ever beset the mind of man.

As I turn the pages over, I find there the strange case of the Honourable Reginald Langdale, a young man who fell asleep in an armchair at his club, in London's West End, and awoke to find himself in a small hotel in Wick, in the far north of Scotland. There, also, I find an account of the true identity and puzzling disappearance of the Countess of Lytton, and the full facts in the singular case of Henry Cartwright of Kensington. Cartwright, a physician, often purchased a flower for his button-hole from an elderly flower-seller outside South Kensington station, but found to his very great surprise one morning that slipped into his hand along with his change was a cryptic and disturbing note, which the flower-seller denied knowing anything about.

Any one of these cases, or countless others, would make a suitable addition to this series of tales in which I have sought to depict the remarkable and varied career of my friend, Sherlock Holmes. In this instance, however, I am inclined to select for my text the memorable and surprising Blackwell Lane Mystery, in which, perhaps more than in any other case, absurdity rubbed shoulders with tragedy, and apparent disorder and chaos concealed a cold and ruthless calculation.

It was a dull and chilly day towards the end of October '87. All day long, from dawn to dusk, the clouds had been low and heavy, and as I looked from our sitting-room window, just before seven o'clock, I saw that a fine drizzle had now begun to fall, and the cold glimmer of the street-lamps was reflected back from puddles of rain in the street.

"You will no doubt be glad you have not been called out upon such a dismal evening," I remarked to my companion, as I turned away from the window with a shiver.

Holmes looked up from where he was sitting at his chemical bench, examining the contents of a flask into which he had just tipped a few drops of some violet-coloured liquid. "On the contrary," said he in a brisk tone, as he gave the flask a shake, "I should be very glad if I *were* to be called out, Watson. It has been a dull and boring day – not the first I have had to endure recently – and needs something a little more stimulating than this mundane chemical experiment to redeem it. After all, if something seizes our interest, then the weather becomes as nothing, a trifle we are scarcely even aware of – as I'm sure you would agree."

My features must have betrayed a less than whole-hearted endorsement of this proposition, for my friend abruptly burst out laughing, in that strange, silent way which was so characteristic of him.

"Well, well," said he at length, when he had recovered himself; "we shall see. Or perhaps we shan't," he added with a wry smile, as he glanced at the clock. "I doubt that we shall have any callers now."

In this speculation, however, my friend was mistaken. Our supper had been cleared away, and we had settled to a quiet evening of, in my case, reading, and, in Holmes's case, further chemical experiments, when there came the sound of a cab pulling up outside, followed almost at once by the jangling of the doorbell. Holmes had paused in what he was doing, and now remained perfectly still, his head cocked slightly on one side, like an old hound listening for a rustle in the undergrowth.

"They are coming upstairs, Watson," said he in a sharp whisper. "But the cab has not been dismissed. Evidently it is retained for a further journey. I think we shall be required after all!" He put down the test-tube he had been holding, and sprang to his feet. As a knock came at the door, he pulled it open instantly. "Yes?" said he in an eager tone.

To my surprise, a smart young police constable stood behind the maid, towering over her. "I have been instructed to ask if you will accompany me back to Clerkenwell, sir," said the policeman.

"Instructed?" queried Holmes. "Instructed by whom?"

"By Detective-Inspector Jones, sir. He told me to tell you that it is something in your line."

"Oh? What is it, then?"

The policeman hesitated, and glanced at the maid, who was still standing beside him. "It is not yet clear, sir. It may be murder."

"Very well," said Holmes, rubbing his hands together enthusiastically. "I shall come. That will be all, Mary," he said, addressing the maid. "Kindly tell Mrs Hudson I am going out. Ask her not to put the bolt on the door, and I shall let myself in when I return. Will you come with us, Watson?" he continued, turning to me.

I did not answer at once. I felt tired. Our sitting-room was warm and cosy, and it would undoubtedly be cold and wet outside. On the other hand, I could see from his expression that Holmes wished me to accompany him, and I knew that if I did not go, and the case turned out to be an interesting one, I should regret it. "Yes, of course," I replied.

"Good man!" said Holmes. "Your hat and coat, then, and let us be off!"

In the cab, Holmes asked the constable what it was that had occurred.

"I'm not certain, sir," the other replied. "Someone has died. There's a doctor there who thinks he might have been poisoned, although whether deliberately or accidentally, no-one seems sure."

"Whereabouts is it, precisely?"

"Blackwell Lane, sir."

"Ah! A narrow street of large warehouses, as I recall."

"Yes, sir, that's correct; but there seems to be a club there, which is where the incident occurred."

"A club? Blackwell Lane seems an odd location for a club."

"Yes, sir. It's in the basement of a furniture warehouse."

"What sort of club is it? A gambling club, perhaps?"

"No, sir. Leastways, I don't think so. The gentlemen are all very shabby-looking, like a collection of tramps and beggars, but they're very well-spoken – like vicars, sir, or solicitors."

"How very curious!" said Holmes with a frown.

"Yes, sir, it *is* a bit odd, I must say. I've never seen anything like it!"

As our cab turned into Blackwell Lane, the rain was falling steadily, and the pavements glistened wet under the street-lamps. The street itself was as Holmes had described it, an unbroken row of towering warehouses hemming it in on either side, like the walls of some deep, dark canyon. Half-way along on the right, an open doorway threw a bar of bright light across the pavement, and beside the doorway stood a uniformed policeman.

Through this doorway we were conducted by our guide, and down a wide stone staircase to a lower level. There, in the dusty stair-well, three or four plain wooden doors faced us. So far, what we had seen of the building was as one might have expected, a bare, somewhat dirty, plain and unadorned commercial building. As our guide then pushed open one of the doors, however, we were met by a most surprising sight, for beyond the door was a large room decorated in the most amazingly opulent fashion. Above our heads hung a huge, dazzlingly-bright chandelier, and all around us, reflecting this light, were walls of beautiful polished wood, hung with all manner of exotic and colourful tapestries and curtains. About the room were a large number of small oblong tables, on the top of which numerous glasses of all shapes and sizes were scattered, as if a meeting had taken place there which had been hurriedly abandoned. At one end of the room, on a larger table, were wine bottles, whisky bottles and the like, and in the centre of the room stood our old friend Inspector Athelney Jones, in conversation with a small, bald-headed man in a dirty-looking jacket and ragged trousers. They turned as we entered.

"Ah! Mr Holmes!" said Jones. "And Dr Watson! I'm very glad you were able to come, gentlemen. It's a bad business, I'm afraid!"

"I'm sure we are very glad to be here," returned Holmes. "What is this place, Jones?"

The policeman snorted. "They call themselves the 'Amateur Mendicant Society'," he replied. "Mr Quantick here is chairman of the society. I'll get him to explain it all to you in a moment."

"Must I?" asked the small man in a querulous tone.

"Is there some reason you don't wish to?" demanded Jones, his voice suffused with suspicion and menace.

"No, not at all, Inspector," said the other quickly. "It's just that I've explained everything at least twice already."

"Well you should be getting better at it, then," said the unsympathetic policeman. "But, first, please guide us to the room where the deceased is lying. It's like a rabbit-warren down here," he added for our benefit, and then, as Quantick pulled open a door at the other side of the room, "brace yourselves, gentlemen!"

I had been conscious of a distant, muffled hum of conversation from somewhere, as we had been speaking to Jones and Quantick, but now, as the door was opened, this hum became a roar. The room before us – similar in size to the one we had just passed through – was full of men, a few sitting, but most standing, and all dressed in the same sort of ragged garments as Mr Quantick. The room was evidently used as a dining-room, for there were several neat rows of tables, each covered with a white cloth and laid for a meal.

Abruptly, as we entered, the room fell completely silent, and all eyes turned in our direction. Quantick nodded silently to the crowd, and then someone called out "Can we leave now?"

"No, you can't," returned Inspector Jones quickly. "I'll let you know when you can go. We are investigating a very serious business here. We'll take statements from you all in a moment."

With that, we made our way through the crowd, which parted like the Red Sea to let us through. Mr Quantick then led us through a door on the other side of the room, which gave onto a plain and unadorned corridor. "This is the way to the kitchens, and various store-rooms," said he.

Twenty yards along the corridor our guide pushed open a door on the left and we found ourselves in a small, plain room. On the floor a blanket had been spread out, and on the blanket lay the body of a man, clad in ragged clothing. A professional-looking gentleman was kneeling beside the body, making notes in a pocket-book. He looked up as we entered.

"This is the police-surgeon, Dr Archer," said Jones. "When the incident occurred, Mr Quantick here sent for the nearest doctor, a man called Plummer, who came in about five minutes. He pronounced this poor devil dead, but thought the circumstances were suspicious, so he sent for us, and waited until we arrived. He's gone now."

"What struck him as suspicious?" asked Holmes.

Dr Archer rose to his feet. "When Dr Plummer first got here," he said, "he was told that one of the members had had a heart seizure, or something of the sort. But when he examined the body, he thought that the symptoms did not really match that diagnosis, but suggested, rather, some type of poisoning."

"Cyanide?" said Holmes.

"Yes. How did you know?" asked the doctor in surprise.

"There are several indications," said Holmes, "the most obvious perhaps being the red flush on the cheeks. May I?" He bent down and put his nose close to the dead man's mouth. "Yes," he said as he stood up once more: "there is the unmistakable bitter-almond smell of Prussic acid, in other words, hydrogen cyanide."

"Are you an expert?" queried the doctor with a raise of his eyebrow.

"On poisons I am. You may have come across a small pamphlet of mine listing the most obvious and significant symptoms of forty-three different poisons, in the form of a practical field-guide for non-experts. Have the members of the society been informed of these suspicions?" he continued, turning to Inspector Jones.

The policeman shook his head. "Mr Quantick here knows all about it, but we have kept it from the others so far."

Holmes nodded. "Now, Mr Quantick, if you could tell me precisely what occurred here earlier, I should be obliged."

"Well, sir," said Quantick, who appeared impressed by Holmes's authoritative manner, "I must tell you first very briefly about our association, the Amateur Mendicant Society. Our members are all from the most respectable levels of society. We meet here at least once a month – sometimes more often – when we dine together, and one of our number presents a paper for discussion.

"Four times a year, however, we have a special meeting. Today is the day of our Michaelmas meeting, which is one of the four. On these days, each of our members must abandon for the day his usual respectable clothing, and dress in the rags of the most disreputable-looking beggar. He must then spend the day begging in the streets, before attending the quarterly meeting here. At the meeting, each member must show what he has managed to accrue during the day. The man who has gained the most is then acclaimed as the society's honorary president for the next quarter-year."

"Forgive me for mentioning it," interrupted Jones in a sarcastic tone, "but surely it would be simple for anyone to fill his pockets with coppers before leaving home in the morning, and later claim he had gained them all in the course of the day?"

"In theory, that might, I suppose, be possible," said Quantick in a tone of distaste, "and the statutes of the society recognize the possibility, however remote it may be, by providing the most severe penalties for anyone engaging in such deceitful behaviour. In short, anyone whose conduct has fallen to such a level renders himself liable to immediate expulsion from the society with no possibility of appeal. But we have never had to invoke that clause in the constitution. Our members are all men of the very greatest integrity and honour, to whom such a course of action would probably never even occur. Indeed, I would go so far as to say—"

"What happened this evening?" asked Holmes, interrupting the other's flow, "and who is the dead man?"

"His name," replied Quantick, "is George Wyndham. To begin with, his identity was established from some papers which were in his pocket. Although I know him well, as I do most of the members, I had not recognized him in his begging disguise. Some of our members are exceedingly creative with paint and other materials for changing their appearance, I must say.

"Anyway, the members began arriving here about half past six. They were all having a glass of something, and talking, very loudly and boisterously, in the reception room you saw back there, when there came a sudden sharp cry, as of pain or distress, which cut through the hubbub, and the rest of the room fell silent. I hurried forward and found one of our members lying on his back on the floor."

"Was he still alive then?" asked Holmes.

"Yes, but he was breathing very rapidly, in a hoarse, shallow sort of way. I thought he must have had a seizure. I loosened his collar and sent Thompson – the head waiter, who was in charge of the drinks table – to fetch a doctor straight away. The doctor was only a few minutes in coming, but by the time he arrived Wyndham was already dead."

Holmes nodded. "We had best speak now to those who were near him when he had his attack."

We returned to the main dining-room, and, again, the crowd fell completely silent as we entered. Quantick introduced Sherlock Holmes, who then addressed the assembly.

"The deceased gentleman was George Wyndham," said Holmes. "Will those who were speaking to him, or were standing close by him when he had his seizure, please step forward," at which four or five men pushed their way to the front of the crowd. "Was the deceased speaking or listening just before he cried out?" Holmes asked them.

"A bit of both," replied one man, who identified himself as Hodgetts. "We were all exchanging anecdotes of our day in the streets. It was a lively and humorous conversation. The deceased gentleman had, as far as I recall, spent most of his day down Cheapside way."

"That's right," agreed one of the other men, who identified himself as Howe. "He seemed in good spirits. There didn't seem anything wrong with him."

"Did any of you know at the time who he was?" asked Holmes, at which most of them shook their heads.

"We were all pretty much anonymous," said one man. "Even now I couldn't tell you who many of these – my fellow-members – are, despite the fact that I know a number of them personally." This remark was met with a murmur of agreement from the assembled throng.

"I knew who he was," said Howe. "I recognized his voice when he spoke, and then saw who it was, but I couldn't have recognized him from a distance. He was telling me that this might be his last mendicants' meeting. He said he was sorry, because he would miss it, but he might not be able to attend in future."

"Did he say why?"

"Something about moving out of London. I gathered that he owned a rural property in Surrey - near Woking, I believe – and was considering moving out there."

"I see," said Holmes. "Can any of you recall if Mr Wyndham had a glass in his hand at the time of his seizure?"

"Yes, he did," responded Hodgetts. "He had one in his right hand. It was a small tumbler – he was drinking whisky. I remember at some point he smacked his lips and said 'Ah! Good old plain whisky! I don't know why anyone ever adds anything to it!'"

"Had he finished the whisky?" asked Holmes.

"No," said Hodgetts. "He'd only had a couple of sips. But he'd only had it in his hand a moment or two, so that's not surprising."

"Had he only just arrived, then?" asked Holmes.

"No, he'd been here a while. But that wasn't his first drink."

"How are you so sure?" asked Holmes.

"Because I happened to notice while we were talking, without really thinking about it, that he had a practically empty glass in his hand at some point, and then later had a glass in his hand which wasn't so empty. Whether he went up and got a refill for himself, or someone got one for him, I really couldn't say, as I was talking to other people, too, and moving around a bit."

"Very well," said Holmes; "pray proceed with your account."

"As Mr Wyndham cried out," Hodgetts continued, "he stuck his right arm out towards me in a stiff sort of manner, so I took the glass from his hand."

"What did you do with it?"

"I put it on a table that was just behind where I was standing. I put my own glass down there, too, and tried to help Mr Wyndham. He was shaking, and appeared to be unsteady, as if he might collapse to the floor at any moment – which, in fact, he did, before anyone could prevent it."

Holmes turned to Quantick, who was standing next to him. "Do you know how many members are present this evening?" he asked.

"Not exactly. I'm not sure yet who is here and who isn't."

"Would anyone know the precise number?"

"Thompson should. He was standing by the door when members started arriving."

Thompson, the head waiter, stepped forward. He was the only man in the room not dressed in rags and tatters.

"Did you mark off the members in a register as they arrived?" Holmes asked him.

"Not exactly, sir."

"What, then?"

"Each of the members has a specially engraved metal disc, bearing the initials of the society and a membership number, which they are to show at the door to gain admittance to the meeting."

"Did everyone who entered show you such a disc?"

"Most of them, sir."

"I have told Thompson not to be too strict in his execution of the regulations, if some of the members have not brought their membership discs with them," Quantick interjected. "Sometimes discs get lost, or simply forgotten. We would not wish to deny a member entrance just because of such a minor infraction of the rules."

"So some people did not show such a disc?" Holmes asked Thompson.

"That is correct, sir. One or two members had forgotten theirs, and then, at about ten minutes to seven, the rain started falling heavily. There was quite a crowd in the street at the time, trying to get in. I didn't think I could leave them all out in the street in such wretched weather, so I opened the door wide, and the whole crowd pushed their way in. Whether they all had their membership discs with them or not, I really couldn't say."

"Quite right, too," said Quantick with emphasis.

"What is all this?" demanded a tall man at the front of the crowd. "What does it matter who had a disc and who didn't? Poor old Wyndham – if that's who it is – has had a heart seizure. Why are the police here at all, asking all these questions?"

"The police always attend sudden, unexplained deaths," said Inspector Jones in a portentous tone. "Do you have some particular reason for not wishing the police involved?"

"No, no; of course not," said the tall man, clearly somewhat abashed by the policeman's manner. "I just don't see the point of all these questions."

"Nor me," said one of the other men. "I don't imagine anyone would wish to go ahead with the supper after what has happened, so we might as well get off home now."

"Patience, gentlemen," said Holmes in a mollifying tone. "The questions are nearly over, for the moment at least. But first, we wish to know how many members are here, and as no-one made a record of it when you arrived, we shall have to count you all now."

There was much grumbling at this proposal, but at length, after several false starts, as the members milled around like a flock of reluctant and disobliging sheep, it was established that, including Mr Quantick, twenty-six members were present.

"Including Wyndham, then," said Holmes, "that makes twenty-seven. Is that the number you were expecting this evening, Mr Quantick?"

"Yes," said the chairman. "That is the full complement of our membership at the moment."

"Now," said Holmes, addressing the crowd once more: "did you all have a glass of something when you arrived here?"

This question was met with a general affirmative murmur, but as the men were all speaking at once, it was difficult to be certain what anyone had said. Holmes frowned. "Let me put it another way: did any of you *not* have a glass of something?"

At this, the room was perfectly silent. "Very well," said Holmes. "So you all had a drink. And all the glasses were left in the other room – or did anyone carry his glass through to this room?" This question, too, was met with silence. "Very good," said Holmes. He asked Mr Hodgetts, the man who had taken the glass from Wyndham's hand, to accompany him, then, signalling to me that I should do likewise, he led the way through to the reception room. As we left the dining-room, I heard Jones telling the crowd that he would have to take the name and address of everyone there, a suggestion which elicited groans, protests and complaints. "Because," I heard him say, in a loud, irritable voice, "you are all witnesses, and all witnesses must be recorded."

As we passed into the reception room, Holmes closed the door behind us to shut out the noise of the crowd. "Now, Mr Hodgetts," said he, if you would indicate where you and Mr Wyndham were standing when you took the glass from his hand and he fell to the floor, I should be most obliged."

"It was just here," replied Hodgetts, positioning himself by an oblong table which stood against the wall to the right of the doors to the dining-room. "I had my back to the table, and Wyndham was facing me, along with two or three other men. When I took his glass, I turned and put it down here, and put my own glass next to it. See, they are still here, the two of them together."

"You are certain those are the two glasses in question?"

"Yes, I'm sure they are."

"Very well. You may return to your colleagues now, Mr Hodgetts. I am grateful for your assistance. And now," continued Holmes, as the door closed, "let us see if either of these glasses bears the scent of bitter almonds. Hum! That one doesn't! And nor does that one! Would you mind examining them, Watson, to see what you think?"

I did as he requested, holding each glass in turn close to my nose, but neither of them bore that deadly scent.

"Hum!" said Holmes, rubbing his chin in a thoughtful way. "Perhaps someone has swapped the glasses round. We shall have to examine them all, then. But first, let us count them!"

This we did, independently, then compared our totals. "I make it twenty-eight," I remarked.

"So do I," said Holmes. "That is interesting! Let us examine them all, then! Try to be methodical, Watson, so that you don't miss any." I started from one end of the room, Holmes from the other, and for several minutes we moved round the room in silence, examining each glass in turn. At length, we had examined every glass we could see. I had found none bearing any scent other than one might expect – wine, whisky, sherry and so on – and I could tell from his features, without needing to ask him, that Holmes, too, had drawn a blank.

"Hum!" said my companion. "Twenty-seven members and twenty-eight glasses, and none bearing the deadly scent of Prussic acid! Let us at least see if we can account for the extra glass!" He opened the door to the dining-room, called loudly for silence, and then asked the assembled throng if any of them had used two glasses. This query was met at first with silence, then one man put his hand up to attract attention and called out.

"I had two separate drinks," he said, "but took them both in the same glass."

"So did I," called another man, followed by several others.

Holmes turned to the head waiter, Thompson, and asked him if he himself had taken a glass of anything.

"Certainly not, sir," came the prompt reply, a note of indignation in his voice.

"Can you recall, then," asked Holmes, "if any of the gentlemen brought a used glass back to you and asked for a fresh one?"

"I can, sir, and none of them did."

"Very well," said Holmes. "Carry on giving your names and addresses to Inspector Jones and his men!"

With that he closed the door again and looked round the reception room once more. "We appear to have met with a check," said he. "But, wait a moment!" he cried all at once, as much to himself as to me. He strode purposefully across the room to the large table from which, as was evident from the large number of bottles atop it, Thompson had been dispensing the drinks to the club members. Then, bending down, he pulled out a couple of large cardboard boxes from underneath the table. "Here are some spare glasses," he remarked, "and here are some unopened bottles of various types of liquor. Hum! The glasses all appear to be clean and unused." Then he pulled out from under a smaller table, to the side of the large table, another cardboard box. "More glasses," said he. "All clean. Anyone who wished to could have helped himself to a fresh glass from here." Then he pulled out a sort of large wicker waste-paper basket. "What have we here?" he murmured, as he began to remove the contents of the basket one by one. One or two wine-bottles came first, then some smaller bottles, and then he paused. "Come and look at this, Watson!" he cried.

I joined him where he was crouching down by the waste-paper basket. "See!" he cried, as he dipped his hand to the bottom of the basket, and slowly and carefully lifted it up again. In his grasp was a large, jagged chunk of a broken glass. Carefully, he held this dangerous-looking lump of glass to his nose. From the expression on his face, I could tell that he had at last found what he was looking for. Then he placed the piece of glass on the floor and invited me to examine it.

Carefully, I raised it to my nose. There could be no doubt: the scent of Prussic acid was unmistakable.

"I think, Watson," said my friend, "that we are permitted at this juncture to say 'Eureka'!"

"Indeed," I returned. "This glass was undoubtedly the one that conveyed the poison to Wyndham's lips!"

Holmes nodded. "There is the scent, also, of something else – bitters, I think – there is an opened bottle of bitters on the drinks table – which was probably added in an attempt to disguise the presence of the cyanide. But it seems likely that Wyndham still didn't care for it overmuch, which I think explains his remark to Hodgetts about the 'good old plain whisky' of his second drink."

"Yes, I'm sure you must be right," I agreed. "But now we have twenty-seven members and twenty-*nine* glasses! The matter becomes more confusing all the time!"

"It is certainly not entirely clear yet," said Holmes, "but we have made definite progress. Now we must ensure that we make further progress. Come!"

We returned to the dining-room. Inspector Jones and the two constables were just finishing taking the names and addresses of everyone there.

A stout man with a dirt-smeared face, whose hair was sticking up in odd clumps, approached the inspector. "I must go now," said he in an imperious tone.

"In a moment," returned Jones, without looking up from his notebook.

"Do you know who I am?" the man demanded. "I am head of one of the oldest private banks in the City."

"I congratulate you," said Jones. "But it doesn't make any difference who you are, the formalities must still be observed. I'm sure if it was you lying dead in that room along the corridor you'd be hoping that people would show you a little respect!"

"But why keep us here?" said another man. "We haven't done anything wrong."

"Oh no?" said Jones in a sarcastic tone. "Are there any lawyers among you?" he added, looking over the crowd. One or two men answered back that they were solicitors. "Well, then," said Jones, "you should know that under the Vagrancy Act of 1824, it is an offence to beg on the streets. If I wished to, I could have you all clapped in the cells for the night in the next five minutes!"

This announcement quietened the crowd a little, but after a moment, a small man at the front protested. "But we don't keep any of the money we collect for ourselves," he said. "We donate it all to various charitable causes."

"Oh *do* you?" said Jones. "That makes no difference to the fact that you got it by begging. And am I to understand that you don't need the money yourselves?"

"No, of course not."

"In that case I could have you all clapped in the cells on a charge of fraud and imposture. Now, just be quiet for a moment. Mr Quantick wishes to say something to you."

"But first," interrupted Holmes, "I wish to ask you a question."

"What?" came the general clamour; "more questions?"

"Did any of you break a glass?" asked Holmes, ignoring the uproar. The response was complete silence. "So, no-one broke a glass? No? Very well. Did any of you see or hear anyone else break a glass?" Again, the response was silence, then one man put his hand up and spoke:

"I thought I heard the sound of breaking glass earlier on," he said. "It was just behind me. But when I turned, I couldn't see anything, and as someone was speaking to me at the time, I didn't give it another thought."

"Where were you standing?" asked Holmes.

"Near Thompson's drinks table, with my back to it."

"Did you recognize any of those standing behind you?"

"No, not at all."

"You did not hear a glass break?" Holmes asked Thompson, at which the head waiter shook his head.

"And now," said Quantick, "if you would come forward one by one, identify yourselves and tell me how much you collected during the day, I can tick you off my list, and you can leave your takings in a general pile on this table here. Then," he continued, turning slightly towards Inspector Jones as he spoke, "I can arrange to have it taken to the charitable institute we chose for this month."

Athelney Jones left the amateur mendicants to their business, and drew Holmes to one side. "What is all this about a broken glass, Mr Holmes, and how does it relate to what has happened here this evening?"

"We have found what you might term the murder weapon," replied Holmes. "Come and see!"

The policeman followed us into the reception room, where Holmes recounted our examination of all the glasses, and the discovery of the broken glass.

"I should keep these tainted fragments of glass safe," said Holmes. "Apart from the condition of the dead man himself, they constitute the only evidence we have that Wyndham's death was not a purely natural one."

"Yes, certainly. I had, of course, intended to examine the glasses when I had finished with that crowd in the other room. What do you think we should do now?"

"There is little more we can do here," replied Holmes after a moment's thought. "I suppose you are thinking of notifying Wyndham's household of his death?"

"Yes, precisely. It's something I've got to do, of course, but it's the part of my job that I like the least, as you can imagine, being the bearer of bad news. Anyway, I've got his address from Quantick. It's not far from here, as it happens, in Bertram Street, just off the Gray's Inn Road. I was thinking of walking round there now, when we have finished with those people in there."

"Then I shall come with you, if I may, and see if we can learn anything."

"Certainly. I am a little reluctant to leave Quantick at large, but I have his address if I need to lay hands on him again."

"You harbour some suspicions of Quantick, then?"

"He is my number one suspect, if that is what you mean."

"On what grounds?"

"On the grounds that he has been the chairman of the society for years, and must know all of them pretty well. I don't believe for one moment that he could not recognize them this evening. On the grounds, also, that his manner all evening has seemed to me suspicious. I don't yet have sufficient evidence to arrest him, but as soon as I do have, I'll have the darbies on him and have him in the cells before he knows what's hit him!"

Outside, the rain was now falling steadily, and the streets were deserted. Jones had left two of the uniformed policemen behind, to finish dealing with the members of the club and supervise the removal of the body, and brought one of them, Constable Burton, with us.

"I must say," I remarked to Jones, as I turned my coat-collar up against the icy rain, "that Quantick doesn't look very guilty of anything to me. What about the head waiter, Thompson? It seems to me that no-one would have been in a better position than he was to have added something unpleasant to one of the glasses of liquor he was doling out. And no-one would have been in a better position than Thompson to put the tainted glass in the waste-paper basket and deliberately break it."

"That's true, Dr Watson," the policeman replied. "All in all, I shouldn't be surprised if we find, when we get to the bottom of the matter, that Quantick and Thompson were acting in concert, together. What do you think, Mr Holmes?"

Holmes shook his head. "It seems to me too early to reach any firm conclusions," he replied after a moment.

"Come, come, Mr Holmes," said Jones. "You must at least have a theory. You are usually such a great one for theories! You have seen the evidence. Does it suggest nothing to you?"

"There are indeed some suggestive points," returned Holmes, "but most of them are open to more than one interpretation. I would rather restrain my urge to theorize for a little while longer. Incidentally, Jones, with regard to your theory, what do you suppose Quantick's motive might be?"

"That, we don't yet know," Jones conceded, "but considering that it now seems more than likely that he and Thompson are in league in the matter, it must be something to do with their precious society. Perhaps Quantick has been pocketing for himself the society's takings from their begging activities, rather than passing it on to the charities he referred to, and Wyndham had threatened to expose him. Whatever it is, we'll get to the bottom of it eventually, you mark my words!"

A brisk walk of a little under ten minutes brought us to Bertram Street. On either side of the street were unbroken terraces of neat, attractive old houses, set back a few feet, behind low walls and railings. Beside the front-door of some of them, bushy shrubs had been planted, including outside number 54, which was the house we sought. Holmes paused for a moment before this bush, which was a good eight feet tall, and seemed very taken with it.

"This is a very fine specimen," said he in a tone of admiration. "It is, I believe, a cherry laurel."

"It is always pleasant to see a little greenery in these otherwise plain brick streets," I remarked, somewhat surprised at my companion's enthusiasm.

Jones had to knock twice before there came any sound from within the house, but, at length, the door was opened to us by a pleasant-faced young man, clad in a smoking jacket.

"Pray excuse the delay," he began with a smile. "The servants have been given the evening off, and I'm the only one in. It's been so quiet that I'm afraid I fell asleep in my chair. What can I do for you, gentlemen? If you were hoping to see Mr Wyndham, I'm afraid he's out at his club, although he should be back later."

"Might I inquire to whom I am speaking?" asked Jones in a sombre voice.

"My name is Ventnor," returned the young man, a frown of puzzlement on his features. "I'm a second cousin of old Wyndham's, and I'm staying with him for a few days. I can take a message for him if you wish."

Jones produced his card. "I'm a police officer," said he, "and I'm afraid I have some bad news for you."

"Oh?" said the young man, his mouth falling open in surprise. "You'd better come in then."

He opened the door wider, and Jones, Holmes and I filed through, into the hall, Constable Burton being instructed to wait outside. Ventnor pushed open a door, and we followed him into a warm and well-lit sitting-room, where a fire blazed in the grate.

Upon the walls, in addition to a number of paintings, were several glass display-cases of butterflies and moths.

"Now," said Ventnor, "what exactly has happened? Wait a moment," he added quickly: "where is your colleague?"

I looked round. I had thought that Holmes was standing behind me, but he was nowhere to be seen. Ventnor returned to the hall, and Jones and I peered out of the sitting-room doorway, to see what was happening. Holmes was crouching down with his hands on the floor and his face just a few inches above it, as if looking for something on the carpet.

"What are you doing?" asked Ventnor in a puzzled tone.

"I do beg your pardon," said Holmes, looking up and blinking. "My eyes must be playing tricks upon me. They're not very good today! I thought I saw one of my companions drop something onto the floor, but I must have been mistaken." He rose to his feet, shaking his head, and we all returned to the sitting-room.

"Now," said Ventnor, addressing Jones: "please tell me. What is the bad news you have brought for us?"

"Your cousin, Mr Wyndham, has met with an accident."

"An accident?" repeated Ventnor. "Good grief!" he cried, seating himself on the arm of a chair. "Is he all right?"

"I'm afraid not," said Jones. "I'm afraid he is dead."

"What!" cried Ventnor, rising sharply to his feet again. "Surely not! What on earth has happened to him?"

"He appears to have had a seizure of some kind," replied Jones, "possibly a heart seizure. Do you know if he had a weak heart?"

"No," replied Ventnor, shaking his head. "Not at all. But I understand that those sorts of conditions do not always manifest themselves very clearly. Where did it happen?"

"At his club, the Amateur Mendicant Society."

"Oh, how terrible!" said Ventnor. "He always enjoyed going to their meetings so much! It was, I think, his biggest pleasure in life."

"Was he also a lepidopterist?" inquired Holmes abruptly, bending forward and peering very closely at a case of butterflies on the wall, as if his eyesight were very poor.

"Yes he was," said Ventnor with a frown of surprise, "as you can see."

"I mean," persisted Holmes, his eyes just an inch or two from the glass case, "did he catch all these specimens himself, or did he purchase them somewhere?"

"He caught them all himself. He used to go off on expeditions to heaths and places like that." Ventnor turned to Inspector Jones with a pleading expression on his features. "Who is this man?" he inquired, indicating Holmes. "He doesn't seem much like a police officer to me. Why is he asking me all these ridiculous and irrelevant questions about butterflies when my cousin has just died?"

Jones cast a brief, nonplussed glance in my direction. "This is Mr Holmes," he said after a moment. "No, he is not a regular police officer, but he is an expert in cases such as this one, and is assisting me in the present investigation."

"Why do you refer to it as a 'case'?" asked Ventnor, "and an 'investigation'? I understood you to say that Mr Wyndham had died of heart failure – surely a medical man would be of more use than another policeman?"

"My other assistant, Dr Watson, *is* a medical man," responded Jones, indicating me.

"We understand," interjected Holmes, "from what we heard from one of the other club members, that Mr Wyndham was considering moving out of London. Can you shed any light on that?"

"I don't think so. No, wait! That might be a reference to an old cottage he'd inherited from someone, somewhere near Woking, I think. But I can't believe he was seriously considering moving out there. From the only reference I heard him make to it, I got the distinct impression that he intended to sell it and pocket the proceeds – which wouldn't amount to very much, so he said." Ventnor turned to Jones. "Do you wish me to come with you and formally identify the body?" he asked.

"First of all," said Holmes, before the policeman could respond, "we should like to inspect Mr Wyndham's wardrobe."

"His wardrobe?" repeated Ventnor. "What on earth for?"

"I speak metaphorically, of course," said Holmes. "My colleague, Dr Watson, wishes to assess Mr Wyndham's clothing from a medical perspective."

"I don't understand," protested Ventnor. "You have already told me that Wyndham almost certainly died of a heart seizure."

"That is true," said Holmes, "but heart seizures are, almost always. brought on ultimately by something else, such as, to take a simple example, tight clothing. A tight collar, for instance, constricts the blood vessels in the neck, putting stress and strain upon them, which in turn puts stress and strain upon the heart. Dr Watson must put all that sort of thing in his report."

I had listened to this outpouring of nonsense with increasing stupefaction. I had not the faintest idea what Holmes's purpose might be in making such absurd statements, but I guessed that, whatever it was, he would wish me to go along with it. I therefore did my best to adopt a serious and earnest expression. Athelney Jones glanced my way and caught my eye, and I could see from his features that he was as much in the dark as I was.

"Oh, very well," said Ventnor in an impatient tone. "Come this way."

We followed him from the sitting-room and up a narrow flight of stairs to a landing, where three or four doors faced us. Before Ventnor could indicate which of these was the door of Wyndham's bedroom or dressing-room, Holmes lumbered forward in a clumsy, uncharacteristic manner, his back bent as before and his head thrust forward as if his eyesight were poor, and seized hold of one of the door-handles and pushed the door open.

"That's not the right door," said Ventnor in a sharp tone. "That's my room." He interposed himself between Holmes and the doorway, and pulled the door firmly shut again. "This is the way," he continued, opening one of the other doors and inviting us to enter, "although it seems a complete waste of time to me, I must say."

"We followed him into the room. "Now," said he, addressing me, "what is it you wish to look at?"

"I'll start with the shirts and collars," I replied, in as natural a manner as I could muster.

Ventnor pulled open one or two of the drawers in a large tallboy. "There you are," said he. "Help yourself." He turned to me as he spoke, and I saw his expression abruptly change, from one of boredom to one of alarm. "Where has that other idiot gone?" he cried, as he pushed past me.

I turned quickly to find that Holmes had disappeared again. Barely a second later, I heard a cry of anger and a great crash, as if a piece of furniture had been knocked over. Jones and I hurried from the room. There was no-one on the landing, but the door of Ventnor's room was ajar.

As we reached the doorway, we heard Ventnor cry out.

"You impudent scoundrel! How dare you force your way into my room!"

"How dare you murder your cousin!" came Holmes's swift reply.

"You lying hound!" cried Ventnor, as he flung himself at Holmes and seized him by the throat.

Jones and I dashed forward and pulled Ventnor away. "What in the name of Heaven is going on here?" demanded Jones, who kept a tight hold on the young man.

"This idiot you have brought with you has accused me of murdering Mr Wyndham," said Ventnor in a loud voice.

"So I have," said Holmes, "because it is true." He bent down and picked up a bundle of clothes from behind a chest of drawers and flung it onto the bed. I saw at once that it was a ragged, grubby-looking outfit. "This was the costume of a beggar you wore this evening at the Amateur Mendicants' Club," continued Holmes, "when, as you had carefully planned, you murdered George Wyndham in cold blood!"

"It's a lie!" cried Ventnor, "a complete and unmitigated lie! Yes, I wore that outfit earlier in the day for a lark, when I was out with Wyndham on his begging round. But I am not a member of his club – and didn't have a booking, anyway – so when he went on to the meeting, I came home. I never set foot in his precious club! I was back here between half past four and five, and never left the house again."

"You're lying," said Holmes. "These clothes are soaking wet. But it didn't start raining until well after six o'clock. You couldn't possibly have got so wet if you had returned when you claim you did!"

"Perhaps I got the time wrong," said Ventnor. "I don't know precisely what the time was. I wasn't wearing a watch."

"You lie every time you open your mouth," said Holmes. "Let us see! Ah!" He had picked up the ragged jacket, and, turning it upside down, had tipped out the contents of the pockets onto the bed. Among a few small objects – coins, a box of matches and so on – was a small glass phial. This, Holmes picked up, and, removing the rubber stopper, he held it up to his nose. The smell was evidently a strong one, for I saw Holmes recoil slightly as he sniffed it. "Here, Watson, have a smell of this – but be careful: it's had a very concentrated distillation in it!"

I took the phial and sniffed it. The smell of hydrogen cyanide was penetrating and unmistakable. I then held it up to Jones's nose, and he recoiled from it, as Holmes had done. "That settles the matter," said the policeman. "If you would be so good as to get Constable Burton up here, Dr Watson, I'll get the darbies on this villain!"

The evening was far advanced when there came the jangling of the door-bell. I hurried downstairs to open the door, for I knew that the landlady and the servants would have been long abed. It was, as I had expected, Inspector Athelney Jones, who had said he would call round to discuss the case with us when he had completed all the necessary formalities connected with Ventnor's arrest.

"Yes, I will have a glass of something, Dr Watson," said he, as he seated himself beside our blazing fire. "It is a chilly night now, although somewhat less chilly than it might have been had we not solved the Wyndham case! You certainly had a stroke of luck in finding Ventnor's begging disguise, Mr Holmes!"

"Luck doesn't come into it," retorted Holmes, clearly nettled by the policeman's remark. "I found it because I was looking for it!"

"Oh, yes, of course, I realise that!" said Jones quickly. "I'm certainly glad that you and Dr Watson came along to Wyndham's house with me – don't think I'm not! The case had seemed nothing but chaos when we were at the mendicants' club, but then seemed to clarify itself when we got to Wyndham's house. But what was the point of all that talk about the butterflies and moths? Were you just filling in time until you could think of a way to search for his begging outfit? Or were you trying to trick Ventnor into giving himself away in some way?"

"Not at all. I'll tell you how I saw the case from the beginning, and then you can follow my train of thought."

"Certainly, certainly," said Jones. "I should like nothing better!"

"First of all," began Holmes after a moment, "when we reached the premises of the Amateur Mendicant Society we heard that one of the members had had some kind of fatal seizure. We were then told, in confidence, that the medical men were not entirely satisfied that the death was a natural one, and that the deceased might have ingested some poisonous substance. This we were quickly able to confirm for ourselves, and positively identify the poisonous substance as Prussic acid, that is, hydrogen cyanide.

"Now, hydrogen cyanide is, as you're no doubt aware, relatively quick in its effects, and as no-one at the club had yet had anything to eat, but all, it seemed, had had one or two glasses of liquor of one sort or another, it seemed practically certain that the poison had been in Wyndham's drink. No-one else had been affected, however, so the poison could not have been in one of the bottles, but must have been added to Wyndham's glass. Finding that glass took a little time, until we looked in the waste-paper basket, where it had presumably been dropped in and deliberately broken by having a wine bottle dropped on top of it. Whether this was to prevent anyone else accidentally using the tainted glass or to try to remove it from any future investigation, we cannot say; from the murderer's point of view, it no doubt seemed to serve both purposes.

"Having found the glass that Wyndham must have drunk from, we were at once faced with another puzzle, for although twenty-seven members of the society were present, including the deceased, twenty-nine glasses had been used, including the broken one. As it was clear that the glass in the waste-paper basket was the one from which Wyndham had imbibed the poison, then the glass in his hand when he had his seizure was one of the two extra glasses. But whence came the other one? It was possible, of course, that someone was lying, or had simply forgotten that he had used two glasses, but that seemed so unlikely as to be scarcely worth considering. What seemed more likely was that someone had been present earlier but had already left. This person I took to be the murderer. Clearly, he had left after Wyndham had drunk from the poisoned glass – because he had been present long enough to put that glass in the waste-paper basket – but probably before Wyndham had had his seizure – because he would not wish to draw suspicion to himself by being seen to slip away just as Wyndham was crying out, nor immediately afterwards. But a little earlier, with all the members milling about the room, and the conversation no doubt very loud, it would have been relatively easy for someone to slip out of the room and up the stair to the street – there was no-one on the door at that time, if you recall, Thompson being occupied at the drinks table.

"If, then, as I believed, the extra glass had belonged to the murderer, who was no longer there, that raised a further question as to his identity. According to Quantick's list, every member had turned up for the meeting, and all of them were still present. Who, then was the murderer, the man who had left early? Clearly, he was not a member, yet he must have been dressed in the same sort of ragged garments as everyone else, or his appearance there would have caused comment. But if he was not a member, who, then, was he?

"As I considered what must have happened with Wyndham's drinks, the matter became clearer to me. The only way, it seemed to me, that the poison could have been added to Wyndham's first glass was if someone else had fetched it from the bar for him. Obviously, Wyndham would not have added it himself, and as all the men would have been standing up, talking and laughing, no doubt each holding his glass in his hand, I doubted that anyone else could have then done so. Furthermore, despite your speculations, Watson, I could not imagine that Thompson, who was no doubt thronged by thirsty members at his bar, would have been able to do it unobserved, either. But someone who was fetching a drink both for himself and for Wyndham could have turned away from the bar carrying the two glasses, paused momentarily at that small side-table, and, with his back turned to everyone else – who would probably have all been concentrating upon getting to the front of the queue – added the cyanide to Wyndham's drink, into which he had already added a large dash of bitters while at the bar.

"Similarly, the only way that Wyndham's first glass could have been hidden and deliberately smashed was if someone else had taken that glass away and brought Wyndham his second drink in a fresh glass. But no-one but the murderer would have had any reason to do that, so clearly this was the same person in both cases, that is to say, the murderer. As this person was not a member of the society, but had twice fetched a drink for Wyndham, the overwhelming likelihood was that he was some crony of Wyndham's who had accompanied him in his begging activities during the day, and gone with him to the club."

"That seems reasonable enough," I remarked, and Jones grunted his agreement.

"When we set off for Wyndham's house, then," Holmes continued, "my principal aim was simply to try to learn something there which might shed light on the matter, perhaps including the name of some acquaintance of Wyndham's who might have accompanied him today. I was not really expecting to encounter such a person at Wyndham's house, or find that he was currently staying there. When we reached Bertram Street, however, I was at once struck by the shrub which had been planted by the front door."

"The laurel?" Jones repeated in a dismissive tone. "What on earth is striking about a laurel? Why, it must be one of the most common plants in London!"

"Common plant it may be," returned Holmes, "but it is also one of the best and easiest sources of cyanide. Collectors of butterflies and other insects have often used crushed laurel leaves in their glass 'killing jars', as the fumes released when the leaves decay kill the specimen quickly without damaging it. For keener or more frequently active lepidopterists, it is not too difficult to prepare a concentrated solution of cyanide from the crushed leaves, a few drops of which on a pad of cotton wool in the bottom of a glass jar will serve the same purpose more conveniently. In the laurel bush, therefore, I saw simply a ready source of cyanide. It was no more than that, but, still, it struck me as an odd coincidence, and raised the possibility that Wyndham's death might have been caused by poison from his own house.

"When we entered the house, I succeeded by a simple ruse in feeling the carpets, both on the stair and in the hall, and was able to confirm to my own satisfaction that both were damp, and that someone had therefore entered the house that evening, after the rain had begun to fall, and had gone upstairs. This gave the lie to Ventnor's account of his 'quiet evening', in which he implied that nobody had been in or out of the house since the servants had left in the afternoon. When we entered the drawing-room, the first thing I saw were the cases of butterflies and moths on the wall. A simple question to Ventnor established that Wyndham had caught his own specimens, which probably meant that there was indeed cyanide in the house. I had therefore established in my own mind, first, that Ventnor was almost certainly lying about not having been out that evening and, second, that he almost certainly had access to some sort of distillation of cyanide. I was therefore convinced that Ventnor was the mysterious extra person who had been at the amateur mendicants' club, where he had poisoned Wyndham's drink, taken the first glass away and smashed it, and brought the second glass before quickly leaving. All that remained, to make the case conclusive, was to find the clothes which Ventnor must have been wearing earlier in the evening, which, as you saw, I managed to do while he was distracted by Dr Watson's trawl through Wyndham's shirts and collars."

"You make it all sound so straightforward and obvious," I said with a chuckle, "which is not how it seemed to me at the time."

"Nor to me," admitted Athelney Jones with a rueful expression. "I am certainly very glad you agreed to join me this evening, Mr Holmes. We might not have got to the bottom of the business so quickly without your help! I wonder," he added after a moment, "why Ventnor plotted to murder his cousin in such a public way. You might have expected him to choose a dark, deserted alley-way somewhere, rather than a brightly-lit club, packed with people!"

Holmes shook his head. "Dark alley-ways bring their own problems for the murderer," he said. "First of all, deaths in such circumstances will always be regarded as suspicious, and then there is the problem of how to lure your victim there in the first place, the likelihood of encountering a constable on his beat, and the fact that in the absence of any other suspects, attention will inevitably be turned in your direction. To murder someone in what you describe as a 'brightly-lit club', however, avoids all these problems. Ventnor probably hoped that, if he was lucky, no-one would even realise that a murder had occurred, and would believe that Wyndham's seizure was the result of his having been out walking the cold streets all day and having then consumed several glasses of whisky in rapid succession. He would know, also, that if the true cause of death *were* discovered, then the circumstances would instantly provide nearly thirty ready suspects to occupy the attention of the authorities, and confuse their analysis of the matter. He must have been confident that he himself would escape suspicion, for, after all, Ventnor's presence at the club was known to no-one except Wyndham himself. All in all, hideous and diabolical as it was, I think Ventnor's scheme was also highly ingenious and cunning – as clever as any murder plot I have ever encountered."

"Perhaps you are right," Jones conceded. "But what do you imagine Ventnor's motive to have been?"

"We can't yet say," replied Holmes, as he reached for his pipe and tobacco, "but I shouldn't be at all surprised if it has something to do with that property which Wyndham had recently inherited in Surrey."

Holmes's speculation on this last point proved accurate. Official investigations, which Inspector Jones later relayed to us, revealed that what Ventnor had described to us as simply "an old cottage" proved to be a substantial house and estate, worth a considerable sum of money. Subsequent investigations further revealed, first, that although only Wyndham's second cousin, Ventnor was nevertheless his closest relative and thus stood to inherit whatever Wyndham might leave, and, second, that Ventnor himself had recently been living far beyond his means, and had contracted very large debts. The true character behind the smiling face which he presented to the world was perhaps best revealed by the fact that instead of trying to find an honest way out of his financial difficulties, his answer to it all had been the cold, calculated and cruel plot to murder his cousin and thus inherit all his possessions, including, of course, the property in Surrey. His plot was certainly a devilishly clever one, and I think it no exaggeration to say that it might very well have succeeded, had it not been for the perceptive intervention of my good friend, the inestimable Sherlock Holmes.

Milton Keynes UK
Ingram Content Group UK Ltd.
UKHW010703220524
443011UK00010B/155/J